A BED OF ROSES

A

BY THE SAME AUTHOR

Fireman Flower

Three

The Body

South

The Face of Innocence

The Passionate North

A BED OF  ROSES

BY WILLIAM SANSOM

HARCOURT, BRACE AND COMPANY

NEW YORK

COPYRIGHT, 1954, BY WILLIAM SANSOM

*All rights reserved, including
the right to reproduce this book
or portions thereof in any form.*

first American edition

Library of Congress Catalog Card Number: 54-6386

PRINTED IN THE UNITED STATES OF AMERICA

A BED OF ROSES

*L*OUISE was locked up in her big bedroom closet. She was angry and frightened as a child.

"Guy!" she cried, "Guy! *Guy!*"

But no sound came from outside. She held her breath, listening, terrified to hear the click of the bedroom door. Such a click, the very lightest, would mean he had left the room, abandoned her shut up all alone. But she felt he was still there. Yet—had he left the room quietly, gone softly down the stairs and away?

She cried out again, sobbing over and over his name Guy, Guy, Guy, banging his name with her two clenched fists on the tough wood door. But all that sound simply seemed to come back at her in the muffled dark, it might never have reached into the quiet room outside.

So dark inside. Where no furs had hung for years it smelled of fur. Clothes touched her with the touch of hanging bats, lightly the handless arms caressed her. She shuddered away, pressed herself forward against the wood door. Only the little keyhole gave a pin of light—she crouched down to it; but a key had been left half-turned, it was too small to see through. The dead dark all round echoed absolute and still, it might have been endless space inside her head.

It seemed to be getting hotter, she grew frightened for breath. She stopped again and listened, her ear to the little keyhole. He was just outside! He was standing just on the other side of the door, out in the light, listening to her, she

7

could hear him breathing, he must be leaning forward with his head an inch away. Despite everything, she got great comfort from his nearness, her panic subsided, her breathing lowered. But then suddenly he disappeared. He had been her own breath.

She stayed subsided, panic gone, strengthless. Big slow tears slipped down her cheeks like water in the dark from nowhere—tears of shame for being an adult woman of twenty-seven years locked like a child in a closet. Locked in wearing a dress whose everyday feel she knew so very well, yet feeling in it like a small child afraid of the dark. Her years were stripped away, desperately now she mourned them.

For some minutes she stayed still and quiet, teeth biting silently into the skin of her forefinger.

But then the darkness began to press again, she felt her breath pumping up, the little protective handkerchief screwed into the palm of her hand hardened as panic again rose.

Then from very close like a sound amplified in her ear Guy's big voice came:

"So at last we're cooling off a bit."

She was shocked how close it was. He had after all been bent listening: the bruises on her arm suddenly made themselves felt again.

"Guy, *please* let me out. Guy, it's so dark, you know how you hate it, Guy, it's *dark*."

"But it's you in there, Louise, I don't see how it concerns me. Except that I feel some little girls must learn their lesson."

"Darling, it wasn't my fault—I tried to ring you."

"It's not the first time."

"But how can I help it if you're out? You're so often out, Guy. And Uncle Robert turned up without a word. It was urgent."

The voice outside mocked a sigh, then went on with pleased pained patience:

8

"So her guardian chooses to arrive in London suddenly and little Louise thinks it fit to cast all else aside and fly to him. All appointments broken—I, for instance, can be left waiting in that so charming restaurant for two hours. Money is plainly of more importance than manners, my Louise."

"You know it wasn't money, Guy. Aunt Carrie had this stroke and—"

"It never occurred to you to telephone the restaurant?"

"I tell you I couldn't, darling. I was in there with Uncle Robert, he'd have heard and you know how he disapproves, he'd have started all over again. . . ."

"Why didn't you telephone the restaurant before he came?"

"Oh Guy—I never thought. Honestly, I was so bothered—"

Again a tired too amiable sigh from outside:

"And if you remember, that was the second time this week."

"Guy, we've been into that—you know I couldn't help it again. You're always out. I don't complain if you're out all the time, I try not to, Guy—"

"And how exactly do I know you're really seeing your blasted uncle and the other one—who was it?—yes, the amazingly coincidental dental—I'm sorry for that—surgeon?"

"I was in agony—"

"Ah!"

"I couldn't *help* it—Guy, for God's sake let me out. . . ."

She broke down then—and as her sobbing began again Guy's voice hardened:

"I don't like being stood up. You're going to stay there until you learn it."

"Guy!"

"I'm going out now. I'll take your key. I'll come back later. Perhaps in this way we'll make sure you're on time for tonight."

"*Guy!*" she screamed.

9

"Good-by."

The door slammed and then she heard his feet heavy on the stairs, down and disappearing. In terror she listened for the front door. Nothing. But then—could she have heard it at all?

But she thought: "He will go out. He's capable of anything." And sank down on the floor of the darkness and wept. The clothes hung above her now, and sometimes brushed her face. It smelled every minute thicker of hot fur.

The bedroom door opened again and Guy's voice entered brightly: "Saved by an April shower."

Her heart rose, he had been joking all the time! She could hardly believe it—this had seemed to be one of his moods.

"Oh Guy, you did frighten me. Darling you old beast!"

But the voice snapped back: "I mean, *I* was saved. Good excuse not to spend a dull afternoon talking old bloody Bergman into a job. Not trudging about in the rain for anyone."

She said nothing. Her whole body seemed to drop inside with hopelessness.

"But," he continued, "we've still got to teach your little girl's guts a lesson. Little girls must grow up and learn manners. For instance—what?—for instance . . . yes, the first thing a big girl must learn is to put away her little girl's toys. For instance—here I see on the mantelpiece a particularly nauseous collection of baby's dollies. With appalling names, as I remember: Tabitha, Mr. Toots, Somebody the Chinaman, Wonky Donkey, Callingham, and all the others. Really, Louise, you should be ashamed."

And on the voice smirked from the bedroom that now sounded so large and wide and light a room. On went the singsong catalogue of a row of small china and glass figures that she had kept from her childhood's nursery.

"Fix them well in mind, Lulu dear, you won't be seeing them again."

For those few figures she kept no baby adoration but an amused adult-sentiment. It was not her habit to impose them on others. But one night, at a misjudged moment, she had disclosed them to Guy. He had been amused, bored, finally irritated: but he had not forgotten.

"You've seen them for the last time, Louise."

Her tearfulness went, she began to get angry. But trapped in the darkness against the closet door this new strength became pitched not at Guy but at her own powerlessness, her actual indignity there in a closet. She clicked her tongue with impatience more than rage.

"Listen, Louise, I'm picking them all up—one, two, three, four, five—can you hear?"

Something indeed was clinking, tinkling like china and glass.

"Here they are, Louise, Tabitha, Toots, Wonky, and the rest. I think we'll start with this abominable Wonky. Listen hard, Louise."

There was a sharp snap, then a musical shattering as some small glass thing might have been thrown into the fireplace.

"Leg number one."

Another snap. Another and another.

"Now for Wonky's frangible sweet tail—"

A bigger smashing of glass.

"For God's sake, Guy, stop playing the fool. And let me out—it's ridiculous."

"Ridiculous?"

Louise knew he was playing some kind of a trick. With what? A pencil, a broken saucer or something. She was quite certain he would never really break up those irreplaceable things she so loved. Now she crouched biting her finger again with impatience, yet trying to be patient until this "incorrigible boy" should get tired of his game. She began, even in the absurd position that had made her a few minutes before feel so small and hopelessly a little girl—she began to feel much older than he. But it was good he was near, the dark held less terror.

However, Guy was not yet tired of his game. His voice

continued the catalogue of torture—one by one he announced the broken limbs of each toy, each time with a well-devised snap. He was as perversely studious, as delicately ordered as a small boy pulling the wings and the legs from a living fly.

However impatient, or now patient, she was, Louise could not help hearing the well-known names of her toys—and their backgrounds became in the dark clearly pictured. Wonky Donkey brought back a time when her father was still alive, and with his image the two most ordinarily evocative smells of cut grass from the lawn and pipe-tobacco smoke; and early summer sunlight: Wonky she had presented to her father one morning, there had been much fun, and somehow the gardener had come in—through French windows?—from the lawn. Tabitha, no cat but a bewildered china leopard, recalled nothing quite so happy: dark trees seen through long London windows at teatime, with a scurry somewhere of silk dresses being got ready for an evening that would not include her—Tabitha meant being left out, though looking back she felt the consolations of winter warmth, of kettle, brass fender, nanny, and fire. Mr. Toots oddly produced the Nelson Column and a donkey somewhere on some beach. Callingham was a dachshund, his name a perpetual mystery: he was cheap, but his sad eyes played fairground music on a hot summer's afternoon. The Chinaman, a pontifical figure of false jade, was a later acquisition; it was quite plain by then there had been no more mother and father—Uncle Robert stepped in here and the Chinaman was accompanied by an air of hard, almost grown-up, loneliness. But there was also a Miss Smythe who must have been much earlier—the name had come from a time when she had lisped the word "mice"; and those two small white mice with their pink eyes blotched on carelessly, so that one looked plain walleyed and the other a drunken albino, indeed brought the floor to her mind, and people's legs, and the folds of the dark delicious tablecloth, crumbs on the carpet.

Guy's voice rose suddenly in a temper: "Oh hell to it!"

12

There came a bigger crash of brittle breaking as though he had thrown up the game. And, indeed, then the key turned in the lock and he swung open the door to reveal sudden light and himself breathing hard but with a long downward smile drawing unpleasantness from his face.

She stood for a moment dazed, then stepped out.

All those toys were lying smashed in the fireplace.

She put a hand to her forehead and glanced at the mantelpiece. Empty where the toys had been. Then down again to the glazed pink tiles of the fireplace and to the glassy pulp piled there—from which now with sudden sorrow she made out distinctly the limbs of those she knew so well. Sorrow, pity, disgust.

Guy was saying: ". . . a clean sweep and good riddance. About time such nonsense was cleared up. . . ."

He was licking into each word salivary emphasis—but Louise just said: "All right, all right, Guy," and walked over to the April window. She felt tired and aimless. Over and over again she thought: "Disgusting . . . how disgusting. . . ."

Water sloshed about washing a car in the mews beneath, a lathe somewhere whined. The world, simply enough, went on. Just then the sun came out and fired the wet window-drops into mercury and the smell of April air steamed up moist and fresh from the one rogue sycamore leaning near the window, from two tubbed lilacs beneath. Once, unbelieving, she glanced down at the fireplace to her side: a shaft of sudden sunlight glittered the broken glass into pale happy life.

Guy had stopped speaking and thrown himself, hands in pockets, down backward on the bed, where he lay dangling his feet away from the crushed counterpane. He was a good-looking, hard-looking man. Pale eyes, dark lashes, colorless hair, strong bones, and a stony skin. His exact lack of color gave him an added strength. He looked made of something like concrete, his tough grayish skin had no shine to it, it made a rough surface like pale cement. One might have thought—with the shadows edged in a frown, a deep cleft in

13

the chin, heavy lines of decision setting round his jaw—that he had powdered himself: and the shadow of a rough growth of shaven beard gritted him further. His eyes—gray-brown, sometimes it seemed even yellow—shifted their pale light deceptively; or suddenly fixed it straight with an owl's glare. He had a mouth full of trustless small teeth, they grew inward and this gave them a vicious and predatory appearance: yet altogether his mouth made a charming crescent when he smiled. He was an actor by profession.

Now his trick was done he was not at all nervous: yet he acted a nervous whistle through his teeth to mark the time, the silence, and his presence. But after a few minutes he grew impatient.

"Now perhaps we'll have decent time to get dressed for once. Come on, Lou."

She turned from the window.

"I'm not going out with you, Guy."

"What?"

"I'm finished, Guy."

"Oh? For how long?"

"This time for always. That filthy, disgusting trick . . . I don't want to have anything more to do with you."

"Oh balls, darling."

"You might as well go. Right away."

Guy turned over toward her and propped his head up on one arm the better to consider this. She still stood with her back to him, a little round-shouldered now, arms limp as if defeated to either side. He laughed. He was really amused. He must have felt that he had bitten deep. However—time was getting on, one could not hang about indefinitely, there was the evening ahead.

"Really Lulu—you can't make such a fuss about a few toys!"

He laughed again, then sighed:

"A period for hurt pride. In fact—for sulking. A few tears, a tender word from me, reconciliation, embrace. That

14

should take at the very least half an hour. I think I'll go and make myself a cup of tea."

He bounced himself up into a sitting position.

"You won't," Louise said. She stood with her back to him, she was unsure yet of her face. She showed thus backward at him a bare arm. The sunlight made plain, four round red blushes that would soon bruise purple, marks of a half-hour before, when in a cool temper he had gripped her toward that closet.

"Perhaps for a start you'll take a look at these." She prodded the arm backward.

He saw his chance. Sympathy for that kind of physical hurt, easy to give, would short-circuit the whole matter. He became instantly apologetic.

"Darling," he said, getting up and going to her, "I never realized. I didn't mean anything like that . . . it's your skin, so . . ."

"Shut up!"

Now she turned and showed him her face. It was neither angry nor defeated, it was calmly measured with distaste. He might have been a sum wrongly added. He stopped talking, surprised. Her voice spoke levelly, and at a distance from him.

"You can understand a bruise. You're used to bruises. Anything else is perhaps too subtle for you to understand. I don't care about a bruise, I don't care at all. I care about all the rest. I care about your vicious, premeditated bullying. That is, I don't care any more—I'm finished. . . ."

"But Louise . . ."

"You can be sweet enough from time to time, I know all that. . . . In between, you're rotten. One always hopes it'll be different—even after that Silva business, even after the spectacles, even after—oh, I can't count—"

But it was not because of any difficulty with numbers that she could not count, it was because the images called up by those few episodes mentioned struck still so forcibly they

15

blotted all the rest—a considerable list—out of mind. Maurice da Silva had been a film director, Guy had wanted a part from him and had more or less lent Louise as a bribe: he had arranged dinner for the three in his flat, then phoned later that he was detained in the country for the night and asked Louise to "fulfill the honors." As for the spectacles, one night at a party Guy had given one of the guests—a very shortsighted girl who wore spectacles—far too much to drink. This girl had then taken it into her mind to fling herself at Guy. She flung too hard and too long. Guy was exasperated, and rightly—but his solution was unforgivable, he had leaned forward and snapped the bridge of those tortoise-shell glasses, and the girl was left wavering and crying—drunk and without her glasses blind.

"You know very well I meant nothing serious with Maurice Silva," Guy said. He gave a little kick at an electric cord disordered on the floor. "I've said I'm sorry."

"And you'll continue to say you're sorry. But no more to me." She paused. Then more softly: "To think of you snapping those things one by one with your fingers—your *fingers* —God, I'd be disgusted to be touched by them again. . . ."

She trailed off: "Anyway, we needn't argue. Good-by."

Guy took a deep breath and blew it heavily like a labored sigh out through his nose. He knew quite well that Louise was unmanageable at the moment. He was bored by what seemed a useless bother, a quarrel which would take more time to put right than usual: and blamed himself for not somehow managing the affair better. So he tried:

"Now look here Louise, I know how you feel, I didn't know you really liked those things so much, it's difficult for a man to know—"

"Please will you *go!*"

He shrugged his shoulders and turned away. Then, though he believed the situation would heal in a couple of days, he could not resist playing up to her fancy. Bitterly as if burdened by the future, he said:

16

"I must say you've chosen a nice time for this. On the eve of our trip."

She repeated wearily:

"Trip?" And then, realizing: "Oh—trip."

"Berths booked . . . all that and four days to go. A nice muddle."

As though this were a minor matter of office routine, she answered without even looking at him:

"I won't be going." Her hand was already picking up the telephone receiver: "I'll cancel mine. What was the number . . . ?"

She was dialing it; but Guy crossed over and put his hand down blocking the call. She looked up surprised, as at a stranger intruding.

"If you want it this way," he said, "let's do the thing properly. They're your friends, I don't want to go trekking around Spain with the Prescotts. It'd be ridiculous. No, I'll cancel instead."

He had a matchstick between his teeth. It was a habit of his, this chewing a matchstick. It brought his teeth together, forced his jaw forward a little, as though he were chewing not the match but the problem, or eating it.

"*You'd* do that?" She looked up at him puzzled.

"Of course."

"That's strangely good-natured . . ."

"There's a job going. I didn't tell you. Enough to carry me through into the summer. . . ."

Louise still held the receiver carelessly on her lap. The little machine buzzed angrily to itself. Out of habit she found herself asking:

"A job? You never told me. Who with?"

"Cornish romance, lonely house on a cliff. . . . Betty Andrews and David play the—"

He stopped, cursing himself. Those two names were of an actress and actor favored much by the director Da Silva. Now he saw her eyes grow indifferent again.

17

She replaced the receiver carefully.

"Well—if that's really the case, so much the better for both of us."

"Yes."

A pause. Neither moved.

"Then," Louise said, "there's no more to be said."

He thought hard: there seemed to be nothing further.

Suddenly he became angry, turned and quickly left the room. But was careful not to slam the door: to walk quietly down the stairs and close the front door behind him with exactly enough noise to reach, with finality, the room upstairs.

For some seconds after that sound reached her, Louise sat without moving. Then listlessly, but with a sort of resolution, she began to walk about the room—closing the closet door, straightening the coverlet on the bed.

Through the window the early April sun shone brightly. Outside all over the city spring warmed each stone and brick with an air once more of new life rising, trees spread the essence of their rising sap, the scent of blossom surprised the gasoline air with sudden fragrance—and both old and young, to the measure of their pleasure or bitterness in each personal memory, praised or cursed this advent of new life, feeling it to be either the birth of a new year or the death of all hope forever.

Louise stood in the center of that room now unsure of what to do next. There seemed to be nothing. There was; but her resolution was failing and resentment rising, muscles of resolve slackened and others came into play, and behind her eyelids the hot wetness began to swell. With a last impatience she strode over to the mirror and looked to see what face was there. This she had wished to do at the instant the front door had closed.

The face showed no trace whatever of feeling. There were tear marks from the closet—but otherwise it had straightened

18

itself into her ordinary, well-known face, and held simply the no-expression that normally she set toward a mirror.

Seeing the ordinary mirrored face, from habit she began to pout her lips. But they did not pout, the lips in the mirror tried, then wavered: and at last she broke down and wept long and bitterly.

CHAPTER II

"So THAT's the worst of it over!" Prescott said, smiling down to his wife.

"I'm not so sure."

"All safely stowed beneath, steward identified, purser located? . . . Oh—you mean the unpacking?"

"I mean an hour from now, dear. When we trip so gaily into the lounge. All those new people! Diplomats bound for Egypt, financiers for points further east, great men and their huge women—"

"Nonsense. They're every bit as nervous as you."

"Exactly. *Everyone* terrified, sniff-sniff-sniff, battle formation—"

"Well, we'll form a phalanx—phalanx of three, eh Louise?"

"I'm afraid we'll have to," Louise smiled.

The ship was due to sail quite shortly now. They stood against the white rail of the promenade deck and watched the end of embarkment. All was orderly. People in stumbling groups or singly straggling were herded by a polite uniformed staff who gave forth genial unhurried strength: some passengers gave thanks for the safety of such bluff double-breasted arms, but others felt immediately inferior. From down on the quay the ship, whose ends they could not see,

19

looked like no ship but a giant white skyscraper with long balconies and modernistic round windows. Could such a square and heavy house be seaworthy? A large gray Rolls-Royce sailed from a crane above their heads, no toy but a weight of heavy steel: and those who thought it might possibly fall made a momentary U in the queue.

But once up the gangway matters were different. White coats greeted them, it became quite like a ship, and what with the luggage going in different directions and the steep stairs, hurry asserted itself with the slight panic of pitching camp.

"I put the labels on *myself!*"

"The cabin's roomier than a flat, and the lovely beds—how bouncy!"

"No we shan't see Mildred when we pass Bournemouth—it'll be too dark."

"And a blue one, *blue*, steward, with a little dent on one corner"—this last cried consistently by a luggage-lorn lady running up one corridor and down another after a steward running along already with someone else's cases.

Prescott and Madeleine his wife and Louise turned away from those cries in the corridor behind and walked along toward the relative quiet of the bows. Prescott had managed matters well, he usually did, he was an efficient man and an ex-major of the army. He had driven his wife down, met Louise from her long red boat train, and led them without a hitch through a formidable crowd bound for new life in Australia. Now he walked a little ahead, limping always from his old wound, dressed carefully in some rather old-fashioned way befitting an ex-officer, a vintner, and a gentleman. He was on his way to revisit sherry-vine estates and his family warehouse in Jerez.

"I'm so sorry about Guy," whispered his wife, fallen behind with Louise.

Louise had made herself cheerful: "Oh well, he just couldn't make it, that's all—you know Guy. Though no one can blame him this time, he's had such a good job offered."

"Still—it's a shame."

"Mm. It is."

"Shame be damned," said Madeleine in her mind, "it's the one clear God-sent chance to cut her away from him."

But she quickly changed the subject, saying: "You should see who's next door to Father down in his cabin—prettiest little thing you've ever seen." And she shouted ahead: "Father, *isn't* she?"

"Who?"

"Your blond next door, isn't she splendid?"

"Good-looker all right. Her name's Molly."

"Father! Already!"

Louise tried to join in: "Better keep your eyes open, Mad . . ."

"But her father," said Prescott, "is next door on the other side. So there's not much chance there, I'm afraid. And I had a look at Pop in the passage—he's evidently taking the trip seriously."

"Molly's Pop?"

"Got his sea legs already."

"But the ship's not even started. Must be an old hand indeed."

"At the bottle."

"You don't mean to say he's—?"

"Stinking."

They had been looking over at the orange-painted machinery in the bows—winches, cranes, a capstan—that gave to the ladies a sense of security, for plainly with these machines the men would see them through, and to Prescott a pleasant sense of assumed seamanship (Mm, engine-driven capstan, eh?); and now they turned away in through doors to the main lounge.

"That's him!"

"Molly's Pop?"

In the great dun-colored lounge, deserted yet, sat a single

21

elderly man facing a large whisky and soda. The man stared at the glass, the glass glared bubbling back. Nothing stirred to disturb this dual contemplation. Tall white pillars held up an impassive ceiling, the piano on its dais stood draped and impartial, a waiter on early service stood dangling his silver tray at the far end as discreetly distant from his one customer as possible, but occasionally eyed him.

The glass won. Molly's father's hand reached in that immense silence slowly forward. He had just managed to raise the glass to his lips, but not touched them, when Louise and the Prescotts wandered past. Impossible not to greet each other—in a lonely bar, yes, but not in so vast and empty a space as the Great Lounge. Disturbed between cup and lip, Molly's father saw the danger, took a quick gulp, and slurred up brightly: "Good e'ening!"

"Good evening," the others said, and saw a round pale khaki face with affable eyes gray as water smiling up at them, and passed on. All took away the impression of a hare creature, or possibly a kangaroo—not because of any prominent teeth, for the gentleman's thin rubbery lips showed no particular of teeth, but rather because of two large, wary, back-flown ears.

"Looks a cheery sort of devil."

Prescott just grunted, not committing himself on the matter of any strange male.

"Did you notice—he had a stick," Madeleine went on, "he's lame poor thing."

"Poor thing be damned, it's gout," the Major said, limping with difficulty over the raised lintel of the deck door: "And damn these whatdyoucallems."

They passed out onto the deck and continued around the ship. There was much to inspect. A library, a dance floor, lifeboats, a playroom for children, much else. But five minutes later they came to a sudden small door designed in late Georgian fashion, naval Georgian. Over it was inscribed in gilded script on a white panel: "The Quarter-Deck." Inside

22

could be seen a prim Nelsonian bar. Inside this stood one lonely man leaning by a whisky and soda.

"Evenin'," he said, and his pale eyes peered at them. "Haven't we met before somewhere?"

"In the lounge," Prescott said, "just now."

"Of course. Silly. Nought out of ten. Name's Owen—how d'you do?"

"Prescott. And my wife. And this is Miss Abbott. We were just looking round. See you later on."

With exactitude, with no question of a pause, the Major turned his phalanx and withdrew. "A little crowded," he muttered.

"He isn't lame," Madeleine observed, "and his stick had a silver doggy on the handle."

Just then they all felt a kind of sliding, though nothing apparently slid. But Louise caught sight of a red clock tower gliding, erect as a moon-eyed sea serpent, past a window to port.

"There," she said, "we're off." And all listened with expert apprehension for the sound of engines. But none came—the enormous white liner simply slid off quietly down the river, pulled somewhere by tugs no bigger, it seemed, than dolphins.

They wandered toward the bows. Few things are so sad as a ship putting to sea by the evening light. Nothing—no nocturne across a lawn, no sound of a broken harp string—echoes so strongly the loneliness of dusk. Sound and strong as the ship may be, it becomes quickly dwarfed and pitiful as it offers itself to the gray, unpredictable horizon ahead. Lights, houses, rooms, and the safe streets sink behind. People watch the last house recede, there is a curious silence about the decks. The horizon widens, extends its water, grows colder. A heartless wind begins to slap the air, all around now only winds of aerial salt. So much is being left behind, no one knows what lies ahead. Deep disconsolations move the heart, feelings of adventure try to rise but the anguish is too

23

deep. And this poor anguish is written in the steamer's long white trail left on the going, going sea that will soon swallow it, a last pleading of departure, as though it had never been. And the iron prow cuts on into the night. It is a moment to go below and eat.

As Major Prescott leaned on the rail between his two ladies, he remembered in particular troopships that had left this same great port at eventide. For a moment thus sorrowful he felt the need to comfort others. He put his hand over Louise's and gently pressed it. "Nuisance about Guy, old girl. Sort of put a damper on the beginning of things—still, we'll have to make the best of things—us old crocks'll do the best we can."

Guy's image was easily evoked on the wistful air. He did not bear talking of. Louise tried: "You? You've got more life in you than . . . anyway, who's talking of being old?"

"Fifty, you know. But let's hope it's the prime of life. And for a good passage and then the old Rock and Seville—wish I was in your shoes seeing it for the first time."

"Getting a bit chilly, isn't it?" cut in Madeleine, who wanted to be smartly out of the sad air, it was making her feel creepy. "Let's go in and have a drink."

They turned away and, avoiding the bar occupied by Mr. Owen, descended to the smoking-room bar beneath.

"Bet he's there too," Louise said.

And he was. He was standing with a whisky and soda. But he was not alone.

"Hello there!" said Guy.

He came forward smiling, both hands outstretched, with one of which he took Madeleine's hand and the other Prescott's arm. He was evidently very pleased to have found them. He was exactly sure of himself, and exceedingly charming. "And Louise!" he laughed, winking at her while still holding the other two.

"Good heavens!" Prescott mumbled.

"Guy!" was all Louise said. She was so surprised that she

24

smiled. A great relief rose in her at the sight of him. But the next instant she remembered, the smile dropped, and she felt neither misery nor anger nor resentment but simply muddled. Then, while the others exchanged greetings:

"But Guy—how, why are you here? You said—"

"The job fell through. Last moment. Seemed to be no point in hanging about London with a perfectly good cabin booked so I got a car down and just made it."

"But—you canceled your berth."

"D'you know, I clean forgot to do that."

He had a way of enjoying his words, or perhaps the person they addressed, as if they were food—it was to do with an upper lip too long for his small inward teeth. Now this lip curled out more than usual, and with his voice too sure Louise saw he was lying.

"Well," she said coldly, "well, that's fine. I think I'll go down and dress."

Half an hour later she went to Madeleine's cabin.

That lady was half-dressed, hurrying around with her stockings hanging from her calves like the tops of pirate boots. As she hurried she shook her chestnut hair, cut in almost the latest fashion, as if she wanted it to brush itself by itself. Younger than her husband, slim, smart in the manner of some officers' wives, she seemed a little mischievous; when she spoke her tongue lay exposed by her lower teeth, so that her words sounded as if spoken through an obstruction such as a plum in the mouth. This was not unattractive. It gave an impression of eagerness. Now she bubbled instantly: "Late, late, late—that Owen got us in the end. He's an umbrella man—if you know what that is. Makes umbrellas. It's why he carries a stick. I had three ocean-going Martinis—"

"Madeleine, I've got to tell you about Guy. We've had a row."

"What, again?"

"No, this is a real row. We're finished."

25

"Oh?"

Madeleine still hurried around. Though this was hardly necessary, for she could scarcely touch anything, she held her hands outspread before her like a sleepwalker, her nail varnish was wet.

"Please, darling—this is serious. It's awkward too. He wasn't meant to come at all—but he played me a trick and forced it after all. And now we're closeted for days on this damn ship."

Madeleine stopped and stared, laying sacrosanct hands on the kneeling air.

"Louise! Poor darling! You don't really mean—*finished* . . . ?"

"You can cut the sob stuff. I know you don't like him. But you see—don't you see how difficult this is? What am I going to do?"

"I'm not all that fond of him—but I know you are—"

"Were."

For a moment then in silence, in the little soft and glittering cabin these two, cousins and good friends, faced each other. Then Madeleine said more softly:

"Would you like me, or Father perhaps, to have a word with him?"

"What's the use? He won't take any notice. It'll just be a miserable merry-go-around, chasing all over the ship . . ."

"You could of course stay in your—"

"I'm damned if I'll spend the trip in my cabin like a bloody film star."

"Lou!"

"I'll have to have it out with him myself." She paused: "Only I thought you'd better know."

Just then the ship's bugler played through loud-speakers everywhere the call for dinner.

"My!" Madeleine cried, "and Father hasn't been in to do me up! Hurry, hurry—look Lou, we'll talk later. . . ."

The chief steward had placed these four fellow passengers,

and Guy was the fourth, together at table. It was an awkward meal, and a long one. There were eight courses. These were known officially as "victualing." The steward referred to the third course, a plump quail roasted on a rich canapé, as a "sustenance" dish. Louise could have left early, or have asked for a meal in her cabin, but she was determined now not to alter her normal behavior. She sat and ate slowly through the enormous meal, coldly angry, awkwardly formal. The atmosphere was further complicated by Guy himself, who chose to be at his most amusing and attentive.

Whatever else invested Guy's character, he could exercise a great deal of what is called "charm" when he wished. Apart from his good looks, apart from an alert and ready-witted brain, apart from an athletic ease and the deportment of an actor, apart from much else that made him a most presentable fellow . . . his predominant attribute was an absolute lack of fear. This gave strength and surety to every gesture, every movement—a turn of the neck, a wave of arm, a glance. When he looked at you he seemed to see so much it was often difficult to remember what he said: his nerves had simply beaten yours.

Major Prescott was also sure of himself, but in a different way. Prescott's eyes, which always and unnecessarily blazed under black out-sprouting brows, never stopped moving in every direction—they seemed to be making sure all the time that matters everywhere and with everyone were in order. To watch this ceaseless lookout, and to see his beaked nose and near-satanic features, one might have taken him for an anglicized Levantine. But no. Prescott came of dark stock from the northern isles—and his watchfulness was a legacy of the parade ground and the barracks. He simply made sure of being sure of all that went on around him. Guy, on the other hand, had no need to trouble himself to be sure of things, he simply was so.

Now, at this first dinner, it was particularly toward Prescott that Guy directed his attention—in any case it was plain

Madeleine had determined to keep Louise occupied. Prescott had been told briefly in the rush before dinner what the trouble was. He was delighted, though apprehensive. This induced in him a measure of polite taciturnity—and in any case, in such a large strange room full of strangers, he was engaged in looking to right and left, his eyes blazed their ceaseless broadsides to left and right and from time to time he slewed his whole body half around in his chair to scan the tables exactly behind him. Nevertheless, Guy was able to win him around. A successful maneuver was to ask the Major the meaning of the badges of rank worn by the various ship's officers. He himself knew these exactly: but when Prescott made a slip, he did not correct him.

Purple in gold, epaulets of scarlet and green, bands of silver lace on the cuffs—one might have thought the army of some Oriental principality was under discussion. But at last, when Guy saw that most of the ice was broken, and when he himself was becoming a little bored, he mentioned particularly the white-and-gold cuffs of a senior assistant purser who had looked into the bar when they had been having a drink with the man Owen. He wanted to talk about Owen, who was sitting a couple of tables away with his notably blonde daughter Molly at his side.

"Did you know, Major," Guy said, "that he's one of the biggest umbrella men in England?"

He was careful not to say "sir," the generations were too close.

"Can't say I did," Prescott said.

"Umbrellas and walking sticks. He was very keen to talk about them too. In his cups, of course. Gave me quite a lecture on the one he was carrying—seems to be known as a Congo Crook."

"Oh?"

"With a chased Scarborough nose cap."

"Are you sure?"

28

"Absolutely. He went on about something else—Gentle-men's Long Ends and Ladies' Tips."

"Heavens! Have to give the fellow a wide berth." The Major furtively chuckled. "Trouble is he's nearly in the next berth to me."

"Ha ha."

"Matter of fact, it's Molly who's really berthed next to me. His daughter."

"Really? Is she the one on his left—the blond?"

"Mm. Damn pretty girl, too. Shame."

"You don't often see hair like that. A handsome job in-deed. . . ."

This was intended for Louise. She had been half-listening: and now also half off her guard, she turned without thinking and looked over at the Owens' table.

Molly had made the technical error of wearing evening dress for dinner on the first night out. But in the main this was no mistake. She was in white, and with her pale pink winter skin and her golden bob she sat like an early blossom among the tweeded others at her table. Why had Molly not confided in her mother what she had chosen to wear? Because it had been her secret. Molly had been twenty-one two months before—but this made little difference, it tended only to ac-celerate an already independent nature: besides, she knew her mother would suggest some alternative to whatever dress she might suggest, Mrs. Owen always liked to have her "say." In any case Molly had determined to begin the voyage with a splash, it was a considerable adventure for her and she meant to greet her fellow passengers from the top of a grand stair-way in her finest gown.

Molly had been brought up in an ordinary modern middle-class manner, emancipated on careful strings. She had been no teen-age rouée. Her tastes were the normal nice ones of a kind of middle-class metropolitan girl. She liked ice-skating, Shakespeare, and bebop: she also liked gossip with the other girls over morning coffee in the High Street of the Manchester

29

suburb where she and her parents lived. But these were the surfaces of Molly—deep currents had begun to course beneath, from an excited, fairly pure heart she was preparing to greet the world; with open arms, with the fated sleep-tread of moon-bound maidenhood, she was preparing, though she scarcely knew it, for sacrifice.

But Louise looking over did not see all of this, though she supposed some of it. She saw Molly's relative youth—which was an unknown quantity, too tempting or too naïve, whichever one pleased, and just then she was pleased to think too naïve for Guy. There were, too, her features to consider—a small snub nose, a short upper lip, broad cheekbones and a square little chin—the face, indeed, of a beautiful pug. Her blond hair caused a disquiet normal to Louise, who was brunette. But Louise was pleased to see that the dress, though becoming, was of undistinguished provincial taste. And she was amused, and glad, at Molly's error in wearing it—it was the mark of gaucherie, it must be making Molly feel a little small. In this she was utterly wrong. No one, not even her mother, had told Molly of her technical error. Indeed a kind elderly lady, above pretension, had said to her mother how pretty she looked. Moreover, a young gentleman at table, though undoubtedly plain and hissing his words from the side of his mouth in a sharp rush of guiltily small syllables, had managed to compliment her. She felt like a queen.

Pulled by the eyes fixed on her, she looked up. Of the three pairs of eyes, she selected by nature Guy's: she had her mouth full, chewing hard, but on finding this handsome face across the tables, slid the food to the back of her mouth for better composure. She swallowed and was about to look airily away when Owen at her side looked up to catch Guy's eyes, smiled over at him, nodded to Molly that this was a nice young fellow he had met in the bar—so that in a second Molly was able to smile too and Guy courteously to incline his head.

Thus while Louise looked away, also with a smile but a wry one, and while the chatter of the great dining saloon rose

30

and fell, while stewards in their white coats flashed their silver trays and their most willing attention, while steward officers in dark uniforms strode the table aisles like rolling vergers to bestow upon a table here, a table there, some modestly genial greeting, while new friends were made and others marked down for enmity in all those hearts bound for Gib, Port Said, and oceans east, while the turbines deep below bathed all this tweeded traveling throng with a great clean warmth of bright electricity, while the ship slid from the outer reaches of the river and around some foreland of the Kentish coast, thus in fact while the whole affair of the voyage gathered momentum—Guy and Molly momentarily smiled. Then nicely looked away.

Molly inside herself preened. She had found a friend—a handsome boy too. There was no flutter in her heart. In her good time she would see what he was like. But the first introduction had been made, the party had begun—and with what ease, how soon!

"Coffee in the lounge?"

All at the Prescott table rose.

Louise excused herself and went immediately to find the chief steward. Could he arrange seating at a different table for Major and Mrs. Prescott and herself? "Certainly."

"There's no time to be lost," she thought. "I must speak to him right away. He *must* see I'm serious. But am I? What did I feel about that poor little blond? . . . But that was surely quite natural? These things don't end cleanly? I don't expect not to suffer. What's important is to get free of the old kind of suffering, the other, the long enduring. What's important is to see straight. Heaven give you strength. . . ."

And when she looked in through the glass door of the lounge, and saw no Guy but the Prescotts sitting alone, she felt sudden relief. Yet she went straight in and asked where he was.

"Up in one of the bars," the Major said. "To get some cigarettes, I think he said."

"Do sit down, Lou, and tell me properly what it's all about."

Louise said firmly: "No," and turned away.

The Prescotts raised their eyebrows to each other.

"Pity," the Major sighed. "Bit of a bounder. But I can't say he isn't likable at times."

"Nonsense, he's a horror. Louise's got to think of her future."

"Yes dear, I suppose you're ri—"

Madeleine turned to her husband and said sharply:

"Louise is a *nice* girl."

She frowned a rising indignation at him for want of anyone else there.

The Major smiled to himself: but a certain male irritation made him ask:

"And what exactly *is* a *nice* girl?"

Her eyes opened wide, her tongue stopped like a cat's pouted just inside her underlip.

"Well!" she said at last. "Well, a nice girl's a . . . a . . . a . . ."

"Yes, dear?"

"Well, just a nice ordinary girl," she ended. Then added suspiciously, "I don't mean a 'naice' girl. I mean a nice— well, she's not stuck-up for one thing, and then she's not the fast type—"

"Not too slow either."

"You know what I mean. She's just a decent kind of modern—"

"Of course, dear."

"I'll dear you. But you must see it's absurd. There she is set up in a job she likes, a *sensible* job, all those old stones—"

"Archaeological research."

"Never you mind. Lou's all right. And she's got plenty of good friends, people like her. It's a pity about her mother and father, but I don't think you can make too much of this orphan stuff these days—"

"Of course not."

"She's got her nice flat. That's more than a lot have got. Near the park too. She's got the park."

"Got the *what?*"

"You know what I mean—she's comfortably settled. In fact everything in the Pygmalion garden's lovely and then she has to go and get messed up with this awful Guy. Whom you seem to think so much of—"

"Now that's too much! I only said—"

"Pity her father didn't leave her a bit more money, that's all I can say. She wouldn't have met the low tyke at all. It's these parties."

"Ah!"

"Stop ah-ing. And now they've been together—what is it? Three, four years? The one good thing is they haven't married, that's all I can say. She's still got a chance."

"I wonder why—"

"I don't suppose the sod's even asked her."

"Madeleine!"

"It's her blind spot, that's what. Her *blind spot.*"

"Oh come, for goodness' sake, you'll be giving the girl a little tin can and blue glasses soon. Louise's all right. She's got her head screwed on the right way. She's in love, that's all."

"That's all!"

"Now come, we're very fond of Lou, she's a nice girl—"

"Ah," Madeleine said.

But meanwhile Louise, not feeling like a nice girl at all, did not find Guy in the smoking-room bar, and climbed higher to that other, decorated in a maritime Georgian manner. There she saw him—but stopped. He was talking to Molly, and Molly's milk-smooth back in its white dress was shaking with laughter.

She stood for a while uncertain—then at last caught Guy's eye and signaled. Guy excused himself and came over. Louise

33

traced her finger over a map on the wall to appear absorbed, to avoid whatever look Molly might direct at her.

"Look, Guy, I've got to talk to you alone."

The short dark eyelashes round his pale eyes helped to flicker an amusement. His mouth mellowed into a waiting, al-most paternal smile.

"All right, Louise. What is it?"

"No, not now. Alone, Guy. Somewhere quiet."

He looked puzzled. Then sympathetic, soothing:

"On the upper deck. To starboard—that's to the right. A minute or two to get rid of—er—Miss—you know. . . ."

Louise climbed higher and went out into the air of the upper deck. Nothing between her and the starless dark sky. The two funnels loomed huge and disappeared into the dark-ness above like towers without end. Somewhere higher she saw a movement, light and vague, where the furious smoke poured up into the dark. The fresh salt wind slapped across against the ship's speed, lights blinked on the distant coast, in between lay an unknown grave of deep black sea; on the deck itself the erect shapes of giant ventilators stood about like faceless women in silent colloquy; somewhere above, the radar rotated its inquisitive vane; there was a sound of waves. The whole great iron bulk and its complicated machine growth impressed a sense of immense power as it drove through the water into the night; she felt awed, small and alone on the open deck, her hair disheveled in the wind.

She waited a quarter of an hour that seemed like a half-hour, and a half-hour that grew to disgust her in its length—first to weaken her will, then in disgust to strengthen it—be-fore Guy came up.

"Hullo there. Sorry. I say, you'll be cold."

"Of course I'm cold."

"Well—what is it?"

He stood squarely before her, feet astride against the lightly rolling deck. Half his face in light, half in dark, he looked the more powerful—like a man caught in a sudden searchlight. He was no longer smiling.

Louise came sharply to her point.

"The point is," she said quickly and coldly, "that you've tricked yourself aboard this ship, you've engineered ourselves together again when at last I had a chance to make a clean break."

"I had the ticket—I thought it'd be silly to wreck a good holiday on a moment's misunderstanding."

"It's not a moment's misunderstanding. I'm dead serious. I don't want to see you again. Ever. Since we're on this ship for the next three days, I obviously shall. I just want to appeal to anything of a man that's left in you to keep away, *keep away* from me."

"Oh God . . . you girls!"

"Will you?"

"You want me in fact to mess up these next few—what shall we say, working days?—with an artificial stiffness and then kiss and make up on our Sabbath, our day of rest?"

"I mean nothing of the sort."

"Oh, Ludov—ee—ca!" . . .

Before she knew he had got her in his arms. He pulled back her head and bit his lips down. She tried to wrench her head to one side, to give him the cold bone of a cheek—but his hand that held her head fastened round her hair and dragged so that it brought tears to her eyes and closed them with pain, and again his lips searching found hers that still she tried to keep tight-pressed but which now his strong tongue forced slowly apart. With eyes open she would have kept close to the impersonal sky, but now they closed themselves and in the dark she smelled clearer his familiar smell, he was breathing hard with effort and the exact nature of this too she remembered well, all intimate the nature of his body, and the texture of his, and his only, touch . . . so that all these senses known and once loved came to confuse and seduce her beyond the pain of anger and the drag of hair—and, as

35

though now all trouble was over, she began to slip back, to yield like a sleeper in his arms and blessedly succumbing to forget. And this she seemed to do—but at a last resilient moment only in pretense, so that for a second only she relaxed, and felt with this his grip loosen. With a quick twist she was out and panting back away from him.

She looked behind to see a dark corridor of escape between two great riveted deckworks. But Guy only stood there a second recovering his senses as well as his breath, breathing hard alone there in the bright arclight, a dark figure against orange-painted steel—then he laughed, and with no word turned and walked at leisure away.

She straightened herself. She stood for some minutes staring at the deck where he had stood—weakened by his touch, still cold inside with anger, but more than either of these perplexed and frustrated that she had not been able to convince him. Or—as the minutes passed—had she? She began to believe that perhaps this was so. She went down to her cabin and sat there convincing herself. She lay down on the bunk and tried to think what else she could do: wide awake, the same thoughts constantly recurred.

An hour later she could bear the cabin no longer. She needed action—any sort of physical movement. She went up the outer companionway to the upper deck again, bathing her lungs in the cold salt air, welcoming a freedom in the sound of the dark seas running below.

She walked around the deck. And then suddenly stopped. There, in the exact place by those giant ventilators where Guy had tried to kiss her, a slim figure in a white evening dress stood embraced in his arms. She turned away, thinking possibly that it might not have been he, knowing it was.

The next day was Sunday, the ship still lay in the Channel, and under a pale spring sky the sounds of divine service drifted down from the lounge to the decks below. And it drifted too into the cabin where at last, as she had need to,

Louise gave the long story of her trouble and her separation to Madeleine. Madeleine equally had a need to listen, and not without a certain pleasurable excitement, though what murmurs of consolation she made came from the heart. The tale was told in every detail, but without melodrama. Louise had been so tired the night before, tired in body and weary in spirit, that unexpectedly she had slept long and well. On waking, she had been worried that this might be some sign of insensibility: then she thought that if it was, then so much the better. In any case, she felt refreshed, and told her story in level tones, sometimes raising her voice in shocked disapproval but never for long, so that it all sounded no more than a tale between women of neighbors and daily life. Yet these were no elderly gossipers, they were young and pretty women.

Aloft in the main lounge, after the ship's loud-speakers had announced the service with a record of church bells, a full complement of passengers had assembled. There were as many young people as elderly, an amount of young people that normally one would not have thought to attend a church service, but that now stood and sang with vigor and even without books the hymns that the flag-draped harmonium played. All these might regularly have been churchgoers: but this service had no feeling of a service in a granite church on land, there were none of the musty smells of hymnal and pew —this service, with the ship coursing down the Channel, with light clouds seen flying high through the windows, with hearts facing the winds of salt adventure and perhaps a new life in far-off lands, this was a song of enterprise and free spirit: and its choral harmony, about which there was something of the crusader and the flag, rose from full throats to invigorate the spring air, the passing waves.

Such sounds, as they drifted distantly down into the cabin, gave a background of militant purpose to Louise's tale—and unconsciously strengthened in Madeleine a resolution to stand by her cousin in her trouble. Neither knew what Guy's next move would be, but both felt more capable of averting it. And then, to give further resonance to the moment and as if in symbol of the Sunday smell of roasting meat, the sounds of divine service were followed by a whiff of morning bouillon and the tinkle of cups as the steward on the deck above served this from his trolley. The two young women rose refreshed yet still thoughtful of an immanence of sorrow, arranged themselves, and went aloft for their elevenses.

Guy was not seen until luncheon, and then only at a distance of several tables. The Prescotts and Louise had been placed at the Owen table—perhaps the steward had noticed them all talking together the night before. This was fortunate, the ordinary pleasantries with these new acquaintances took their minds off other things. Mr. Owen showed few signs of trouble after the previous night's drinking—he was evidently used to it. He listened affably to Major Prescott's description of Seville, and only once did his wide-awake ears seem to droop and his mild kangaroo inquiry turn fierce—when Prescott mentioned the canvas canopies which in summer the Sevillians draw from housetop to housetop across the narrower streets. Mr. Owen, manufacturer, thought that parasols should be quite good enough for anyone, yes, of any creed or race you liked. This led him to explain how he and his large family—here he smiled coyly toward his wife and Molly—were bound for Australia to stay for a year with relations. It was to be a real sabbatical twelvemonth after forty years, man and boy, in the family umbrella business. On the way they would stay a little in Spain, Egypt, and Ceylon—changing boats at their leisure. It was to be quite a holiday—and especially a rest for Mother and a view of the world for Mollykins.

"Oh Dads, you're *not* to call me that. You promised."

"Promises, pie crusts," put in Mrs. Owen. "Eh—there's that fork again!" And to the dropped fork she snapped: "You wicked thing, I know *you*." Mrs. Owen talked as much to things as to people. At home, at housework, she would be heard telling the sink what she thought of it or rebuking a mop; or admonishing a door: "Now you stay *closed*," or asking the freshly polished silver: "Now we feel all the better for that, don't we?"

Mr. Owen himself was a little lost without his office to go to. Time was heavy on his hands: though he had determined to keep his eyes open and perhaps pick up a notion or two from the stick-and-sunshade habits in these hotter climes. Now that Major Prescott had mentioned Seville and this annual fair—that was a place they might all go to. Why not?

Meanwhile Louise could not help taking now and then a secret glance at the blonde daughter seated opposite her. Molly was radiant, fresh, and enjoying with unassumed wonder everything—and in her pale blue angora sweater dangerously exposed. This Louise noted with a certain shock—the two big breasts denied with emphasis her wishful thought that Molly was "just a young slip of a girl." But even then Louise caught herself—and saw how it was absurd to feel jealous since it was over between Guy and herself. She must control herself. And so she went out of her way to be sweet to Molly. Molly was at first cool in her young superior way—for she had remembered Louise calling Guy away from the bar—but later warmed, and warmed with a girl's excited enthusiasm, to Louise's overtures. She felt she had found a friend. Here was someone she could confide in. And, at the back of her mind, someone who could tell her all about that attractive Guy Harrowby.

While Louise had been glancing over Molly, and while across the tables Molly had sometimes met the eyes and the smile of a faraway Guy—a third interchange of glances had been taking place. The dining saloon had become more familiar at this second session: it was like one's second day at school, or in a strange office or house or hotel—a lot that had been alarming and confused had been digested on the previous night, and already they might have been sitting in that saloon for days. So that it was all the clearer to Louise that a young man at the next table had been studying her persistently throughout luncheon. His was by now not one of a hundred curious glances, but one by persistence definitely selected. Each time Louise happened to meet his eyes—mild behind spectacles—he lowered them. His attitude was recessive; so his general appearance. Quietly dressed, with a clean-jawed squarish face, he exhibited no emphatic feature, but seemed rather to have scrubbed clean each feature consciously to avoid emphasis: he was firmly good-looking but as firmly determined not to advertise it. Studious but suggesting action too; one might have thought him to be, say, a civic architect.

He was. This Louise discovered later that afternoon during lifeboat drill. At five o'clock the great sirens boomed their deep note out over an empty sea, empty corridors sprang alive with alarm bells—and at leisure the passengers drifted into cabins for their life belts and out to their stations on deck. No panic now: a little shamefaced laughter, a few muttered curses—and there they all were, in their groups, awkwardly collared with canvased cork and messing about with strings and tapes. Vintage passengers stood about, quickly prepared, bored and superior. Family parties screamed with laughter to see each other thus curiously clothed: some even pinched each other. But in fact a small miracle was at work: for these new cork collars framed each face in a kind of ruff, obliterating for a brief and blessed moment ill-chosen colors and textures of clothes, eliminating for once the inelegance of an assorted English crowd. Faces were isolated as with a uniform, they did not look so bad after all, they seemed on the whole good-looking.

A good-looking face, thus collared, with very white teeth smiling above a well-shaved chin, interrupted Louise, who was in difficulty with her tape.

"Perhaps I could help you?"

"Oh—thank you!"

"These things are a bit of a nuisance at first."

"I'm sure I'll never get used to them."

40

"Let's hope you don't have to."

And they both laughed, while he arranged the knots around her. An intimate process—she felt as if a strange man were hooking up the back of her evening dress.

"There. All over."

"It's very kind of you."

Only then did she place him as the young man who had observed her so intently at luncheon. Her first impulse was to retire, but this was impossible wedged among the cork collars: however, there was nothing predatory in his manner, he could not in any case have chosen this particular lifeboat station to follow her, it was plainly his allocation; he was simply polite and though evidently an admirer seemed nervous and talked so fast that not only words but sentences stumbled over each other.

"These drills are very necessary though. It would be awful at night if there was panic. Don't let's think of it. Everyone looks a bit funny, don't you think? I didn't see you at dinner last night—don't tell me you dropped in by helicopter or something?"

"Not exactly. The steward just changed our table."

"Aha!"

"Aha?"

He looked confused, caught out at saying too much.

"I was just thinking how quickly your party must have made new friends. And how fortunate—to do so."

Nervously then, not knowing quite what each was meaning, they laughed. To clear the air Louise asked:

"You're traveling alone, yourself?"

"Yes."

"All the way . . . ?"

"No. I leave at Gibraltar. First stop."

"So do we!"

"Oh, how funny!"

"Are you on holiday? Or . . . ?"

"Oh, I'm just pottering around between jobs. I want to see

41

some of this Moorish stuff—the architecture I mean. I'm an architect myself."

"A sort of busman's—"

"It always is, really. One can't help it."

"We're going to the Fair at Seville."

"Are you now? I've heard it's a tremendous business—Spain at its most Spanish, at least partly—"

Just then an officer arrived and shepherded them all into ranks. Women and children in front. At this, a firmly serious note, laughter and talk subsided—many must have heard in their ears a faint echo: "Nearer, My God, to Thee." There followed a lecture by the officer who walked to and fro with an easy efficient step and who wore brown leather gloves that impressed the gravity of the occasion.

It was soon over. They began to disperse. But that new young man showed no signs of going—he began to chat again, so that they were left alone still in their collars of cork. He introduced himself—Michael Carey—and told her how he had just completed a block of flats for a newly developed home-county township. Now he was half-planning a further project, half-holidaying. Was Major Prescott her father? he asked. And so on. They enjoyed all the exchange of material fact upon which new acquaintance so freely wheels before the more dangerous hills of character must be faced.

But after some minutes Louise became conscious of her life belt, and said she must leave to take it off.

The words came out before he could control them:

"But you're coming back?"

She looked at him startled. He saw this, heard how urgent he must have sounded, and stammered:

"I meant—I do hope you'll come up again and then we could—we could go on talking." He stiffened out of that and said formally: "Perhaps you'd have a drink with me? I'd be most honored."

He looked so naïve, so hopefully awkward, that Louise felt a kind of gratitude.

42

"I'd love to," she said.

"Good! Shall we meet—where, here in five minutes?"

"Ten," she said. "It'll take five to get out of this damn thing."

He smiled at the "damn," a concession of friendship. Louise turned and left. He found he had to go the same way, felt awkward, and waited until she had gone sufficiently ahead.

An hour later they were still talking, leaning on the rail and watching the gray spring sea. The weather held, there was still a sky of fading blue and small grayish clouds: but now in those wide reaches where the Channel became the Atlantic the ship was beginning to roll more heavily.

They began by discussing the immediate life of the ship— that there was to be a dance on the following night, and how good the food was though it needed the salt air to maintain an appetite, and how tonight and tomorrow the rough waters of the Bay of Biscay must be faced. But Michael Carey soon turned the conversation to ask more about herself.

She told him how her parents had died, how an uncle who had been her guardian now took the place of her "family," and how she had worked as a private secretary and now employed herself from time to time on certain researches—she had spent the last few months on spadework for a history of foreign settlement in London—though that didn't mean she was a bluestocking—and so on.

To all this Carey seemed to listen with unusual interest. Glancing up at his profile, noticing that studious yet physically active air, and reserve, and kindliness—she was reminded more of a Scandinavian than an Englishman. But, as she recounted her past life, Louise remembered again those childish emblems that had marked it and which Guy had destroyed—and the feeling of dull sorrow returned. The man at her side was looking at her curiously:

"I've never seen . . ." he began, then checked himself.

43

She only half-heard; and more from politeness than curiosity: "What? You've never seen . . . ?"

"I shouldn't say it—but, I've never seen anyone so young so sad. I mean so—remotely sad."

He meant, it was plain, that he had never seen anyone he liked so young and so sad.

She laughed—and to avoid any depressive talk: "Young? You're being kind, Mr. Carey. . . ."

"Twenty-three, twenty-four?" he said. She looked up at him and searched his face as she said: "Wrong. Twenty-six." She had neatly lopped one year off, more from habit than anything else. But she was pleased to notice his surprise.

It was the time for evening exercise. Behind them, as they leaned over the rail, passengers alone or in pairs sternly strode the long promenade deck. They walked briskly, weatherproof in their Biscay tweeds, as if for a morning walk on some inland heath. At each end of the deck, without pausing, they turned on their heels and came marching back: at these turns the journey looked most preposterous of all, especially when only a single man, marching as though in step with himself, turned about and stepped equally purposefully back. Louise and Carey turned and watched these, laughing, for a while: it was a relief after the endless flying sea, and with the roll and stagger of the ship the walkers, zigzagging, looked more comic than ever.

Then Guy appeared, walking with a strange young man. Louise turned to the sea—now, as always when she saw him, with a sickening in her stomach. So far, although as originally booked he had the next cabin to hers, she had not met him that day: he had obviously scorned to appear at lifeboat drill. For a while longer they talked, with Guy passing systematically at five-minute intervals. Fearful of a meeting, but at the same time determined not to be put out, Louise looked from time to time at his receding figure. She had no idea of his future intention: but he must have seen her, so perhaps after all he had decided to leave her alone. At that thought, perversely, her heart sank. But once she misjudged—or was it perhaps an unconscious desire?—and turned around to meet his eyes as he passed. He gave her an amused wink and despite the matchstick between his teeth managed to form his lips into a whistling shape, plainly indicating the man at her side. In spite of herself she almost smiled. The "incorrigible"! But Michael had happened to catch the wink too. He asked quickly, defensively or about to defend her:

"Friend of yours?"

For a moment she could say nothing—startled by the excuse forming on her lips and the extraordinary sense of betrayal it evoked. But then smoothly spoke the betrayal—for what, wearily she thought, did it matter? Especially to this casually met young man?

"No—that is yes. A friend of the family's."

"Oh."

He seemed to be reassured: but followed Guy's receding back with distaste.

Louise was not now so assured. She decided it was time to go down and dress. She brought the conversation to a close—they had been talking about the cities of Spain, of Andalusia—pulled her coat around her and asked:

"By the way—I never asked you—whereabouts, what town are you making for?"

He looked startled, seemed for a moment to consider, then in an even voice said:

"Seville."

She looked up at him with a laugh:

"Seville? You never mentioned it before!"

He only said:

"No. No I didn't."

As night came on they rounded the Ushant light and Finisterre. The ship heaved and shook. At dinner the saloon was half empty. All around in the darkness outside there was felt the presence of great waves: the lights of a passing tramp,

45

low-lying in the water, disappeared behind an unseen mountain of black water only to reappear suddenly high up in what should have been the dark, nearly starless sky.

One or two men—and among them Major Prescott—went out and lurched about the windy decks, scanning the night and pronouncing with that grave air of stern seamanship upon the ship's course, upon the weather. Molly's mother appeared in a dark pink plastic pixiehood, and her anxious middle-aged face went bobbing up and down the corridors, prepared for the worst but game to fight it, an aged fairy sea-swept from the woods. Mr. Owen stood up at the bar, muttering against her: the pixiehood always symbolized for him dangerous new competition for the umbrella industry, a plastic enemy of potentiality far greater even than the mackintosh, and whenever Mrs. Owen wore hers—and she insisted on wearing it—there was not only dirty weather above but below in Mr. Owen's breast as well. "Look like a lot of eff-ells to me," he grumbled. Now in the rough weather he drank more than usual, he drank against himself and as much again against the roll of the ship, which upset glass after glass as it was filled.

Louise sat in the lounge with the Prescotts. Purposely they all kept off the subject of Guy—and discussed with forced animation immediate plans for the day after tomorrow, when the ship was due at Gibraltar; it was decided that after a day or two's shopping on the Rock they would take a plane straight on to Seville. Prescott's business at Jerez could wait, but the date of the Sevillian Fair itself was a fixed one.

All this time Guy could be plainly seen through glass doors in a further smaller lounge. He was sitting with Molly: they seemed to talk from time to time, there were silences—the weather precluded them from the outer decks, Guy must have been bored, Molly frustrated. An air of frustration hung all about the ship after the first excitements of rough weather. Even if one is not physically sick, rough weather brings its mental sickness: it is like weather of high wind ashore, when

46

the wind seems to get inside the head and furs the brain—but aboard ship the more so, everything falls about, every step taken is a nuisance, noises and commotion and dislocation weary the hours of a day and night that seem endless.

Louise excused herself early and went below to her cabin. There, free of the restraint of the Prescotts' company, an abrupt spite took hold of her at the picture of Guy and Molly kept in that lounge by the weather: "Serve him damn well right, let it blow, let it pour." Then she sat down on the bunk with her head in her hands, ridding herself of such absurd aggression as if it were a headache.

The cabin shook, the white-painted steel bulwarks creaked, a toothbrush rattled every few seconds in its glass. Again and again, minute after minute, endlessly this itch of noise and movement—creaking, shaking, shivering, rattling, and echoing, and then from outside in the night suddenly the boom of a great wave striking the ship's hull. Louise's head began really to ache, she felt suddenly forlorn and hopeless, bruised physically by all this movement around her and wearied by her own resolution. Doubts began again. Was she, finally, sensible to leave Guy? Surely it was an idiocy, against all nature, to force such a parting when she still felt—and there was little doubt of it—a pull of something like love? Did not women—so she had been taught, so she had read and felt—go through anything, whatever the cost, to keep those men they loved? Then she didn't love Guy? A hairbrush came slithering off the table onto the carpet. She let it lie there. At times now she felt young and hopeful, eager for the future: but at others, for she was at a middle age, twenty-seven, a seriousness and almost an oldness calmed her. It was then possible to envisage less passionately what would be best for her: at such times she felt like a mother, with herself the child.

A rat's-foot sound scrabbled across in the bulwark above: she listened, suddenly alert, but it seemed after all to be no more than the spattering of water. Only the cabin, tight-closed

47

and bright-lit around her. She covered her eyes, and in the quieter grayness her thoughts again went back to Guy; with a feeling near to curiosity she wandered up and down the images that remained from their past life together. Back to the party where they first met—no more than a party, expectant of nothing particular except that of course one can never go to a party, or anywhere for that matter, without the risk of life being altogether changed . . . no flattery from him, an air mixed of compliment and contempt, formidable . . . and thereafter their first year. One night she had decided—and it was a definite decision made by herself to herself, she still saw the dress in the mirror in which thoughtfully that decision had been made—to give herself to him, in a kind of mixed trust of him (why?) and ambition for him (how quite?) and with it a blessed relief of abandon—but was that perhaps a time of her life, a time even of the year? . . . it was not possible to be certain. . . .

Thinking of that time she reached over for her bag and took from it a small pocket case: and from that a letter, furred at the edges, much read. The ship heaved, the wardrobe door swung suddenly open showing clothes quarreling on hangers. She read:

My darling, happiness is a small word, you've made happiness a small word. What has happened is so much greater—all life, everything has become more important, as if these few acres of London were plunged in a new element, magnified, glorified, each small thing given a larger presence—the fuchsia pot on the ledge, a bar of soap in the bathroom this morning, the sound of cups from the kitchen, all such things shine with a new and magnificent being. How can I explain? "The street has become a street!" Quite definitely. Oh my dear, how I love, love, love. . . .

Louise looked up and a pain crossed her brow. That letter had come a month after. But a year later, when by chance he saw it, he had laughed: "Not a bad effort, eh? I forget where I got it from. . . . Never known to fail."

Even then she had kept the letter.

48

Afterward—a year, two years?—the decline. Or, more accurately, the full and familiar knowledge of him, of his alternating selfishness and goodness, the moments of goodness becoming less and her struggle to enlarge to herself such moments, for something had to complement his lengthening moods of indifference and cruelty. He took less pleasure in actually hurting than in some kind of enforcement of his own presence and will: he was plainly a bully, but a subtle one. He needed to rely on a victim: not admitting it, she offered herself—to the extent even of forcing herself from time to time to flare up and fight back, a passive victim soon tires the bully.

Now, after nearly four years, she was exhausted. It was too young at twenty-seven to be weary in any absolute sense, her resilience could have carried her on for many years—but it was that exact age with its foreboding of thirty, and the logical need to settle her own future, which had also forced this decision finally now to leave him. She had left him many times before—over some series of studied insults, over some rather too public affair with another woman—but she had always come back. This time she felt differently.

And as these thoughts recurred she took that letter, perhaps the most prized souvenir of her sentiments, between her hands and firmly, slowly tore it in half. She folded the two halves together and tore it into quarters. She was looking down at it with curiosity, as if this object in her hands was something quite unknown, and folded the quarters on top of one another. She began again to tear—but it was not easy. She scarcely bothered to try any harder, and dropped the letter, scattering its pieces into the wastepaper basket.

Just then, from the passage outside, from that slippery lurching place of cabin doors and bathroom doors and small curtained pantries where stewards breezed their slamming errands and shapes of passengers fumbled with their doors— just then a sudden commotion of footsteps, a door slammed near and viciously, a woman's voice raised firmly:

49

"I heard you. I heard you. There! You won't do that again. Disturbing people's rest and quiet."

It was Mrs. Owen rebuking a swinging door. Then Louise's door suddenly opened and Mrs. Owen herself came backing in, carefully closing it. She turned and saw Louise.

"Oh!"

For a moment her eyes opened wide with shock at this intruder sitting on her bunk—before she saw her mistake.

"Oh—I'm so sorry. Oh, I am sorry Miss Abbott. It was that door, you see."

Louise smiled: "Please don't worry. One does get so mixed up—all these cabins—"

"And this dreadful storm! It's what I call a real cross for us to bear, isn't it? I don't know when the night'll be over."

"It *is* upsetting."

"And my Molly and her dad all over the ship, I don't know where they are from one minute to the next. But I'm not one to blame them on a night like this. And Dad's come down now, thank God."

"The best thing is to try hard to get some sleep."

"Yes, I'll try to get off. Though where that Molly is *I* don't know."

"Oh, she'll be—," Louise stopped herself just in time. Then with a lurch and a good night—"*if* you can call it a *good* night"—Mrs. Owen bustled busily off.

"Blast her," Louise said, again confronted with the vision of Molly and Guy. "No, I didn't mean that."

Impatient with herself, she quickly undressed and turned off the light. For some minutes, listening to all the night noises grown larger in the dark, she turned and stretched restlessly in the bunk.

She turned the light on again and sat up, stretching a hand to the wastepaper basket. There, from among the little balls of cotton smeared with lipstick and a toothpaste carton and the pips and skins of grapes, her fingers picked out the pieces

50

of Guy's letter. She put them carefully back in her bag and turned out the light.

Throughout the night she tossed and turned, sleeping a little, then waking and wondering where she was, fearful sometimes that the ship wouldn't stand such heavy seas—and all through in both her dreams and her waking moments the pictured moments of her life with Guy loomed uneasily, as if almost in accusation, through her troubled conscience.

Toward morning she fell finally asleep.

CHAPTER III

THE next day the ship sailed into sunlight. And by the afternoon, with Vigo past and the Portuguese coast to port, with strong salt sunlight stinging white skins and the Atlantic swell a deep bright royal blue, deck chairs were out and the ship transformed from tweed to silk and sportive cotton. Women who had the day before presented themselves fearfully to their fellow passengers in new traveling clothes now went through it again with shorts and rompers: men appeared stripped of their suited armor, a hairy gym team smoking savage indifference and stiff-legged as terriers, or bouncing with near-maidenly joy.

Everybody now felt that a line was crossed, that England was left behind, that the adventure was truly entered upon. There was the anticipation, too, that this evening would herald the first ship's dance. Anticipation enthused the air.

Louise had waked tired and unhappy: but later she had had a long talk with Madeleine, recapitulating in detail all her doubts and the anguish of the long, rolling night. Though finally a decision must be made by herself, there was always deeply the need to speak and share the affair with somebody else. She told Madeleine everything—except about Molly. Madeleine, of course, was not unaware of the beginnings of this new flirtation of Guy's—it had hardly been hidden—but she too ignored it: those two women were as friendly as that.

Her talk again had the effect of bolstering Louise's resolution. Madeleine knew well that Guy was a danger to her cousin's future and said all she could, carefully, against him. So that in the afternoon, when Louise saw Guy for a moment in the swimming pool, diving with grace and with infectious high spirits, taking the lead and stimulating all the others in that landlocked, locker-circled bath of blue tiles from which no sea could be seen—when she saw him she was able quite calmly to turn away and continue her walk around the decks.

But not so that evening.

After dinner, just before the dance began, the young man Michael Carey sought out Louise and took her along for a drink. People seemed prematurely gay. As they approached, sounds of singing echoed from the white doors of the Nelsonian bar. A male voice lurching and drawling, over and over, the single phrase:

"Floreat—this gallant ship-ahoy."

It was the youngster—a boy of perhaps eighteen—with whom Guy had walked the decks the day before. Guy was with him, amused by the fact that the boy was drunk, and ordering him more drinks.

Louise chose a table as far away as possible, but that was not far. The boy's voice filled the bar. "Floreat" resounded with deep drunken gravity followed by "this gallant shi-hip-ahoy" scrambled to a tune something like "Sweet Lavender." The boy's hair was ruffled over his eyes, his mouth was drooling wide, his eyes half-closed—yet he was one of those who had not yet learned to walk stiff-legged, he balanced on his toes with bent knees in a gawkish adolescent movement, so that when now he lurched it was with a strange daintiness. Guy kept calling him "old boy," patting him on the shoulder, asking for another rousing chorus, pressing more beer on him. He affected a facetious joviality. "One for the road" became "one for C deck," "now one for B deck" and so on. Others in the bar had turned their backs, but now and then looked around with disapproval.

"That's the fellow who's a friend of yours, isn't it?" Michael Carey said.

"Vaguely." But now she felt no sense of disloyalty in this second denial: she sat there simply ashamed of him.

"It's not fair on the kid. What's he want to do it for?"

"Floreat—flor-e-at . . . this S.S. ship-ahoy . . ." the boy sang.

A man standing near suddenly turned to Guy. He spoke quietly with a Yorkshire accent:

"Don't you think you'd better steady him up? Lad's had a bit too much."

Guy cocked an eye and turned quickly to the boy:

"Gentleman here says you've had too much. What about that, eh?"

The boy stopped singing and lurched forward, making his face ferocious.

"Wha's 'at?"

"Says you're drunk—this chap."

"Who's't says I'm drunk? Who's got the blasted cheek . . . ?"

The Yorkshireman said quietly: "I never said that. I said perhaps you oughtn't to take quite so much—for your own good, lad."

"Ee," said the boy, chin forward, in a mock North-Country accent. "Ee—aa cum fra' Yorkshire."

"Take it easy now, lad."

Guy said to the boy quietly: "Drunk eh? Are you going to stand for that?" And he stood back to let them face each other more easily.

"Stand for dam' all fra' bloody Yorkshire bloody pud," the boy stuttered.

The Yorkshireman noticed Guy's movement—it was a plain

53

invitation to the boy to fight—looked at him disgustedly and turned his back.

The boy started forward, stretching clumsily at the sleeve of the Yorkshireman's dinner jacket. But before he could touch him, Louise had risen and crossed over to step quickly in between—as far as anyone could see about to buy a drink. Once there she pretended to see Guy for the first time and cried brightly:

"Why, Guy! If it isn't you!"

For a second Guy was startled to see her there, and so broadly smiling. Then he saw the kind of smile it was. He raised his eyebrows very high.

"I thought," he said loudly, "that we were no longer on speaking terms."

She tossed her head back, laughing in a long arch trill. "Oh, Guy you silly *goose!* Now you're coming *right* over here with me to have a *nice* long drink."

"I happen to be having a nice long drink here."

The boy, standing there now purposeless, began to say: "I say . . ."

But Louise turned and gave him such a long conspiring smile, offering intimately all the attraction of her woman's face, that he only stammered: "Oh, I say . . . oh, I do say . . . yes . . ." and fell silent in wonder.

Meanwhile she had linked her arm in Guy's and was pulling him away from the bar. Too absurd for him to resist, too idiotic a tug-of-war—so she got him a few paces away from the bar. But then he did resist, he stopped dead and bent his head forward now sure of himself:

"Look, my Louise, you asked me to leave you alone. That I've done. Please for the love of God and my own peace of mind accord me the same pleasure, I'm trying to enjoy this little excursion."

Away from the bar, she needed to laugh no longer. "Then for heaven's sake behave yourself."

54

"I think I paid my own passage. That should entitle me to a little fun."

"Fun?" She took a breath and said in a sudden, quieter, unhappy voice: "I'm ashamed of you."

"*Floreat . . .*" came again behind them. The Yorkshire-man, at least, was forgotten.

Guy smiled broadly:

"But why should you be ashamed? What has it got to do with you any more?"

"Oh . . ." Louise turned away. What indeed had she to do with him? "I don't suppose it matters, no," she began—when a single sudden groan, a sob came from behind.

The boy was standing speechless and white, swaying, his eyes wide with surprise—as if he had been hit from behind. One hand, like a doll's hand moving independently, went up toward his mouth. But before it reached, the first glue of vomit shot out in a wide stream spattering everywhere.

Little cries of "Oh!" as trailing taffeta skirts received their share—and the boy stepped back in horror, clapping both hands to his mouth and reaching down and thus only further spreading what next came up.

Now people had moved back making a circle in which he stood like a man somehow bent doing a trick. The audience seemed not so much interested in him as in their trousers and skirts, they stood in all positions contorted down and round. Words came, some as always were there to mutter "disgusting"—but others knew and said "poor chap." From somewhere behind, a girl's voice sobbed: "And it was Mummy's wedding dress."

Guy stood back, laughing quietly.

Then that Yorkshireman came forward, put his hand around the boy's shoulder, patted it drawing the boy away toward the door: "That's all right, lad. Don't take on, it happens to the best of us."

The boy let himself be led, leaned on the Yorkshireman as on a father. Now after the first physical shock, a desperate

55

white shame shivered him and his face worked as if it wanted to cry. He looked up and wanly recognized the man holding him. His shame paled deeper as he remembered how he had mocked.

"Oh, it's you . . ." he moaned. But he leaned closer and must have felt in the darkness of this protective arm such thankfulness that even as his shame deepened it would have disappeared, sunk in that other man's harboring body.

"Take him down to his nanny for a clean nappy," a voice called above the others. Guy's. He turned back to the bar, tall and bored, washing his hands of the whole affair. But the boy never heard, they were out through the door, and a steward was already at the floor with a mop.

"This hem! It'll never come out," a hen's voice somewhere pecked. "Oh, that disgusting boy!"

"Easy now, Violet. Who was seedy all over our cabin last night?" a husband's voice said in fairness and exasperation.

"That was the ship, you know I can never help it! But this —this is just self-indulgence."

Guy's voice broke in tersely: "And wasn't it self-indulgence for you to come aboard the ship at all—knowing you'd sick up?"

"Oh!"

"And since you knew it and the boy didn't, you don't come off so well, ma'am."

"Oh!"

"I say, young fellow—that's my wife you're talking to."

"I can't congratulate you."

He turned and left the bar.

Over at their table Carey did not know what to say, and said: "I didn't know you knew him so well."

She looked so upset, her face struggling so for composure, that he murmured quickly: "Don't worry, please don't say anything. . . ." And placed his hand over hers in consolation.

She felt his hand long after it was there, and looked up

56

puzzled at his face leaning in such close sympathy toward her. Suddenly she wanted to pour out everything—and nearly did.

"He's—a nuisance," she said coolly, "he's a close friend and one tries to do one's best about it. But there—you see?"

"I'm sorry." He began, awkwardly, to withdraw his hand. She felt immediately guilty, and somehow gave the hand a light clasp. And brightly: "Let's go and dance!"

Between lounges lay an open space where now, on a dais draped with flags, a small band played. These five musicians looked discomforted. They were more used to the palm-lounge fiddle, and now they gave playful little smiles and sometimes small cries of abandon to "pep up" the naïve jerky rhythm that was all they could manage. Before them the dancers circled—men stiff in dinner jackets grown too small, and women mostly middle-aged, their hair set severely in the shingle of more formative days, their daughters gowned in safe organdy to suit the eye of nice authority.

When the band smoothed easily into a slow waltz—it was "Destiny"—they all felt easier: but then a samba played, half-emptied the floor, and both musicians and dancers set their teeth again. However, all this was to mellow as the evening wore on, soon the floor would be laughing and quite gay: and those who were now generally frowned upon—the exceptional woman in too décolleté or too chic a dress, the man too suave and unembarrassed—were to be accepted with open smiles, and finally all would go to bed confirming this indeed to have been a jolly evening.

Meanwhile the sea, by no means rough, maintained its even swell: the floor angled slowly from side to side, one moment up, the next down, so that dancers had to dance on the edges of their feet to keep vertical. One-two-three, one-two-three drawled the waltz in circular rhythm, and at every sixth beat the whole flat board of the dance floor swung monotonously over on its side. Yet this very sensation, bearing with it some

57

of the insecurity of a skating rink, itself added to the growing conviviality of the evening.

To see Owen, himself for other reasons unsteady, paddling with flapping ears and sawing left arm his good lady across such a floor!

To see Molly enter in her white dress, skin flushed from the outside deck, followed by the hard, tall shape of Guy! That dress threw forward more than ever the two full-grown breasts she bore before her: beneath her youthful face these looked like two great blossoms grown there suddenly she knew not how, blissful tumors resignedly nurtured which henceforth, jutting forward before her, were fated to carry her to destinies unknown. And just now would be crushed hard as the ship reeled them against Guy's stiff shirt.

To see Prescott glaring at the floor's edge! Feet astride, hands in pockets, rolling like a true sailor, blazing tufted eyes everywhere to approve everything in order, shipshape! And Madeleine beside him, standing quite easily without rolling, chatting to the ship's surgeon—but to these two now Louise and Michael Carey came on their way to dance.

"Hello!" Madeleine cried, her voice to Louise, her eyes on Carey, "so there you are!"

"It *does* seem so. But I don't think you know Mr. Carey?"

Madeleine glittered as she took Carey's hand. "I think I've seen you with Louise before." She took him like a determined hostess, welcoming him in two sentences and taking him to her heart in a third. And in a fourth: "But now I suppose you'd like to dance?"

Carey smiled nervously: "Well actually I'd asked—" He pointed to Louise.

"But that's what I meant," Madeleine laughed. That was indeed what she meant, and now as Carey took Louise onto the floor, she sighed.

"Oh, if only . . ."

"If only what?" her husband grunted.

"You know perfectly well. Shipboard romance. A solution. New life."

"And good-by to Guy? Nonsense, they've been together too long."

"But she's really making a go of it this time. She's through. And now if only this Carey . . . with this Carey to help it on . . . it's so much easier when you've got a second string about—"

"Oh come, Louise's a nice kind of—"

"Nice girls are women too."

Major Prescott looked away with the injured expression of a man to whom the great conception "women" had been suggested. He was not having any of *that*.

Molly stood with Guy against the rail of the upper deck. A warm southern wind fanned quietness into the moment, it fingered and fluttered her dress pale in the half-light. Guy stood by in silence, waiting for the night to work its magic.

Some way out lights appeared, and then the dark shape of a ship. It was a tanker, low-lying like a long insect with two bodies far apart, its thin middle drowned in the swell. Aboard it seamen must have watched the great liner move like a phantom palace across their same sea. They would think of the comfortable quarters aboard her, of the food and glittering silver—and envy and despise them.

Guy watched for a moment, then leaned toward her and whispered the word that meant more than all other endearment, her name:

"Molly."

Her hair moved closer to him; he put his hand underneath her arm. Yet her voice came suddenly surprised:

"Yes Guy?"

"Molly, I want to say something to you—Molly, you see Molly, you're somehow . . ."

Molly knew the rules. Her voice came clear and cynical. "I know—I'm *different*."

59

"No. That's just it. You're not at all different."

"Oh!"

"You're exactly, but *most* exactly the same."

"Well! The same as who may I ask?"

Lovely in the half-light her pretty pug-face tilted back from him, round eyes startled, creases of inquiry ridging her forehead. Guy leaned closer, he made a rough honeyed voice:

"You're the same. You've got hair"—he touched it lightly —"and eyes"—his fingertips blessed them—"and a nose, ears, cheeks, a mouth, neck . . ." over each part he paused his finger, and his own eyes frowned in the half-light not looking into hers but peering at these parts of her, so that she was mystified, and then uneasy to know if they looked as they should.

"You've got all those same things—that's just it—but now at this moment Molly you alone here on this deck are all the hair, eyes, mouth of all women in all the world, you're everybody rolled into one, you alone Molly are every girl in the world and that makes you the one, the only one . . ."

"You're—crazy. . . ." But her voice was trembling, at a loss, already lost.

His voice grew stronger: "You alone . . . Molly . . . you . . . your . . ."

His eyes stopped at her bosom, his voice cut itself short, he pretended torment, in pain he raised his eyes to look straight with lost sincerity into hers.

"Molly," he said low, and took her in his arms. Slowly, longingly they kissed. Her hands that had begun to resist him palms flat on his chest snaked out fingers to grip lapels, then wound themselves up and around his neck. He pressed forward, and once on her high heels bent back she staggered. Then suddenly he let her go, grasping only her hand on which she swung back.

"Molly, Molly . . . !" as if he could bear it no longer. "For God's sake—it's too much—let's go and dance."

"Oh Guy!" But she was being pulled away.

60

And then breathlessly, "Guy—my face!"

He hardly paused while with one hand she dabbed her face. He was not going to give her time to think.

Down on the dance floor the air had grown more lively. Young couples no longer looked upon the rolling parquet as an affliction bravely to be ignored, but now used it openly as a slide, crying from time to time "whoops." Older gentlemen laughingly introduced fancy side steps, threw their partners away and banged them back with all the abandon of upper middle age, and their partners pranced and slid and roared with laughter. Even the bandsmen mopped their brows.

Outside, beyond the pink-faced women and red-faced men, beyond the dinner jackets and the bobbing organdy, lay the dark sea and somewhere off in the night, unseen, the last of the Portuguese coast, along which the great liner, a leviathan unconscious of this inquiline dance on its back, relentlessly thudded its course.

Louise and Carey were dancing together. He had not for a moment tried to hide his wish to monopolize her. They had danced several times: once or twice she had thought it better to interrupt such an obvious sequence—and indeed had experienced a secret pleasure, not too easily admitted, in keeping this Michael Carey waiting. Once she had had to surrender herself to the arms of Mr. Owen—already known as Owen the Umbrella—who was well away and effected a clear passage through the other couples by means, a little exhausting, of sawing upward and downward that extended left arm of his.

And she had waltzed with Prescott, who pirouetted nervously on his toes and continually glanced over his shoulder, over both shoulders, to steer his fragile charge bumpless through the circling throng. In this he had blundered only once: he had asked her, most nonchalantly, about Carey. Louise had told him who, roughly, Carey was—and added that he too was due for Seville. The Major had just been able to swallow a whistle of approbation. It was then they had bumped.

But now Louise and Carey were dancing again, and when the music stopped he suggested a stroll out in the night's fresh air. They climbed high up to that same top deck where there was no canopy and only the wide dark sky above. Here and there lights illuminated the statuary of great funnels and cowled ventilators—but the deck stretched wide on either side, broad here across the whole upper ship, and looked with its quoits-marking like a deserted playground. In all that space in the empty night wind they were alone.

But: "Ghosts!" Michael said.

She glanced quickly along to where he was looking. In the shadows by the rail, between boat davits, a pale figure swayed lightly with what seemed to be its dark shadow. And further on another, and then another. The shadows of the ventilators became alive with people, the deserted deck was after all busy with a strange night life of darkness-loving moths, moon-deck romancers.

"We should have gotten a ticket," Michael laughed, awkwardly.

Careful to pretend to notice no one, they strolled toward the bows of the ship.

She took his arm—then instantly regretted it. His own had tautened at her touch: she remembered how much the casually given can mean to those longing to receive. A face appeared from childhood, the high white face of a strange lady wearing a feathered hat, the feathers lapped around her chin. How she had longed for a kiss from that face! And what joy when —casually at tea one day—it was given! And then with Guy . . . but she blotted him out.

"That was a deep sigh."

Michael's head, dark in the half-light, was bent down a little. She was shocked: Heavens, here am I sympathizing with him and ending by pitying myself. . . . And without

62

thinking, simply to get back to him from her wandering self, she drew his arm a little tighter.

The front end of the deck, above the bows, took the full impact of the wind. The moth-life of lovers ended, and they were alone. The wind blew mostly from the ship's passage, it was an impact of air. Above, in now a discernible starlight, black clouds hung dead-still on the sky, long-winged like a hovering of giant birds of prey. Yet down below on that midget ship they stood in what seemed a gale of wind.

"Spanish clouds," Michael said loud against the wind. "They're always there. None of your Italian serenities. God, how I'm longing to show you—"

"To show *me?*"

"I was forgetting myself. I meant, 'How I'd love to show it all to you.'"

"That's very sweet of you," she shouted. "But you haven't told me—what are your plans, where are you going?"

They clung to the rail, the scudding dark air tore at their hair and their clothes. For a moment he said nothing, seemed only to be studying the black line of the mast as lightly it swung against the sky: and strangely the mast looked steady, it was the sky and stars that seemed to reel.

"You're staying on the Rock some days?"

She mouthed the words at him: "I think four."

He paused, then shouted back: "So am I!"

Another silence. Music blew up suddenly from below as a door opened, then shut. He shouted again:

"When are you going to Seville, before or after Jerez?"

"Straight from Gibraltar."

"So'm I!"

She laughed. "W-ell, it does seem we're going to be together a bit."

"Yes," he shouted—and turned his attention casually enough to the sky again. He seemed not at all perturbed. Matters were simply comfortably settled—that was enough.

They were quite alone. But he made no move to put his

63

arm around her, or do anything else that might in the circumstances have been expected. He seemed simply satisfied to be by her side.

"But wouldn't I be a somewhat—what did you say?—sad companion?" she mouthed through the wind, through hair that blew across her face.

"You?"

"You said—the other day—how sad I looked. You mightn't like—"

He turned and looking straight down at her yelled: "I like you better than anyone I've ever met in my life."

She had raised her hand a few inches in a gesture of refusal—and now it hung there without purpose like a small paw. Instinctively she had thought of Guy. But now there was, of course, no Guy. There was no particular reason why she should not now allow this man, should he wish it, to take her in his arms. No reason against it. But a reason *for* it? His words still echoed in her ears, she peered up at him suddenly curious. He had made his declaration, he had become somebody to be reckoned with. There he was.

But he made no move: and she looking up at him felt simply disconcerted. This was new. Here was a man, his dark dinner suit outlined against the paler sky, his shirt white in some filtering light from a porthole above, his face gravely adoring and his hair alive in the wind. Why should she not kiss this man? She felt suddenly, and simply, and deeply, curious. She took a step forward—extending into an arm that puppy's paw of indecision.

But then stopped. It was impossible. He stood there so gravely courteous, so quietly containing his devotion.

She reached forward for his hand:

"Let's go and dance."

On the way down, piloting her confusion to the safety of the dance floor, she wondered suddenly: "Was it the wind? Would he otherwise have stammered those words? Or were they not difficult—but in that case why didn't he sound presumptuous, as another man might do?" It then occurred to her: "Perhaps, after all, my own false feelings were doubly deceiving—perhaps I really did want to kiss him."

The dance ended, last drinks were drunk, and the passengers drifted tired to bed.

Down in her cabin Louise undressed. It was warm. Warm air came in through the open porthole, the sound of the ship's wake echoed below like surf. Remaining naked, she reached for a cigarette. Then drew back her hand—it was better not, better to sleep with clear lungs. That left her hair to brush: and her face to clean. She sat down at the dressing table—then glanced over at the door. It was safely locked.

It was natural that the image of this new Michael Carey kept returning. What became unnatural was the image itself—his very ease made her uneasy, whatever lay between them in the future seemed to him so easily settled, as though for his part he had years to wait.

She brushed her hair hard so that it stood out all around her face in a wild way. Looking at herself in the mirror, looking at the long dark blue eyes, at pale skin beginning to freckle in the new sun, at blue-black hair, she said aloud: "Damned colleen." Then repeated it in a brogue, while her mind saw other faces that privately sometimes she would have preferred. A green-eyed, slant-eyed phthisic auburn—blue veins on the breast, a dress frilled with the lilac of dead romance?

But would one really exchange one's face for another? Louise considered this carefully. She studied again, as every day of her life, that well-known face of her own—always a kind of mystery, an unsolved problem, something not settled satisfactorily. Eyebrows—feathered, and as somebody had once said like moth wings, arching at the ends, but one arch higher than the other. Could that be right? The mole, well-placed. But a little too large? One could never be sure. And then that mouth, smiling to one side—it looked sly, and yet she felt not at all sly. This mouth, unhappily, she deplored. If only it would balance. She bared her teeth in the mirror, trying to smile levelly. It felt hopeless, she looked like a grinning actress. Yet this mouth, with its sly but in some way appealingly hurt look, was what a great many people most liked about her. She pouted at it. Yet—would one finally exchange it? The answer was obviously no. Pleasant to change for a bit, but to lose one's face, one's identity—no. She began brushing her hair straight, her mouth smiled at the successful conclusion of this little argument. "I'm—feeling—rather—pleased—with—myself—tonight," she muttered to the brush strokes. "And that wasn't on the program at all."

Then there came voices out in the corridor. A girl giggling, a man chuckling out some sort of joke. She held the brush, listening. The door of the cabin next door clicked open. Guy's cabin, Guy's voice. Molly's.

She caught one phrase: "I had them put it on ice. . . ."

Then like a secret the door clicked shut.

Louise stayed stock-still, the brush still poised above her head. But the ship was made of heavy steel, no sound whatever came through the partition. A sense of dreadful compartment, of being in a steel box packed against another steel box, inhumanly cocooned, came over her. Ice meant champagne. And the closed door? She realized her nakedness with sudden shock and went to the door for a dressing gown.

She stood not knowing what to do. Or even where to look. Her eyes kept glancing at that dividing wall: the cabin was small, the dividing wall became huge and the others shrank to nothing. She went over to the bed, above which the porthole lay open. For a breath of air? But perhaps to listen—the sea wind might throw back something from next door? She caught at herself: "Nothing to do with me—*nothing*." But then: "Next door . . . how *could* he . . ." She felt suddenly hurt, small, lost—and into the bargain an eavesdropper, clumsily a trespasser.

She looked around her. Taps, rivets, pipes, mirrors, paneling, curtains stared back at her, growing in presence. All the room pressed closer. But there was simply nothing to do. She got up and began walking to and fro—absurd in such a small space. "My God, she's only a kid. She's probably half-drunk already. She doesn't know her own mind—my heaven, I'll help the little bitch . . ." and she was already patting her hair straight in the mirror, planning to go next door, pretend conviviality, pretend heaven knew what—before suddenly she felt hopeless, sat slowly down with her hands at her face knowing quite well the ambivalence of her motives.

She was left then with nothing to do but imagine what might be going on next door.

She tried to fool herself that Guy would look different, that he would be playing some special role that would alter the mannerisms she knew so well. But as she thought of them these old images asserted themselves, she saw again small things about him she had loved—curiously soft hair at his temples, lines not of laughter but of amused criticism creasing at the corners of his eyes, the uncompromising furrow of a single deep frown centering his forehead: and she knew that just as these engraved signs would remain unchanged, would in fact be moving down now on that blond face, just so his methods of love would be those she knew so well. He would not change.

She felt at this like breaking in and tearing out the blond roots of that other woman's hair: and yet—Molly could not quite be taken seriously as a woman: if her youth was dangerous, it was nevertheless youth—and whether because of this, or because of some kind of perverted vanity in herself, it was not easy to sustain a serious jealousy. But she felt bitterer than ever against Guy.

After a further few minutes—indecisive, impossible—she swore at the wall and despite feeling ridiculous and resenting this situation forced upon her, dressed and went up to the lounges. But those last minutes did much to cement her final decision to send Guy away.

She wanted a drink. In the bar Michael Carey was talking with a group of men, the only stragglers left. He detached himself and came over to her. There were some dice on the counter. Together, sleepily sleepless and not saying much, they played on late into the night.

CHAPTER IV

ON THE following evening the ship put into Gibraltar harbor.

It had been a confusing day of late rising after the dance, of packing and inquiry, of all the uncertainties that the certainty of destination provokes. A long approach—throughout the afternoon a high wind had blown as the liner coasted the low green Andalusian hills, past Tarifa littered on its hillside like dirty newspaper, until the improbable bulk of the great Rock rose into view. But now in harbor it was calm again, all was over, the great ship had come to anchor with the dying day.

The tender drew off. The liner's huge hull made a wall of impossible height—could such a monster have housed such intimate cabins?—but then slowly resumed its shape as over the mauving water the dark little boat with its lonely-looking passengers chugged away toward the quay.

"It's quite a wrench," Carey said, looking back.

Louise nodded. "She looks so lovely—and lonely. I expect it's the evening."

"Almost too much of a symbol—big escape engine, all those old boys each with ten years off his life, each leaving ten years behind, all delighted to be playing 'ships' again—"

"Just now they're sitting down to a most adult eight-course dinner. Which we've missed."

68

"Hungry?"

"Not really, I'm too relieved," Louise said.

"Relieved? I'd have thought any parting was a sad affair." He drifted on: "I suppose it's just a simple egotism—one leaves that famous part of oneself."

She laughed a little too dryly: "Anyone can have my part of *that* little liner."

"Thank you."

"Oh no, Michael—you know what I mean."

But how could he? Absurd. She stuttered: "At least—"

He said quietly: "Yes, I do know what you mean."

"You—?"

"And I'm so sorry." He put his hand on hers—it was the first gesture of touch since they had danced.

Just then the tender swung around beside the jetty—the little stone lighthouse rocketed past as they slewed sideways at speed—and coils of rope began to fall like pancakes on the deck. The commotion—what end did one get out at?—distracted: but through it Louise kept wondering "How on earth did he know?" And then saw that the Prescotts must have told him.

She imagined the fatherly talk the Major must have given. She took her hand sharply away. But immediately felt sorry, and pretended she needed it to fumble in the pocket of her coat. Fumbling, she noticed that Guy was standing well apart at the other end of the boat. He was with the Owens. Even in that dying light she fancied that Molly looked white and strained. She checked herself impatiently. Equally absurd to be annoyed with the Prescotts for their good intentions—it was nice of them, it was mean to refuse such well-meant help.

They were moving forward. Guy's party was off first. She would let him get well ahead. The relief of that land, that gray stone jetty just now a few yards ahead! There lay the real break with London and the last weary year. Already the strange smells of this new mainland, the scent of tropical trees and of dry dust and earth, weighed solidly on the air.

But on the jetty the first person she saw was a man in the uniform of a London policeman.

He was at her elbow, his dark domed helmet outlined against the southern sky, his tall bulk like a shadow come to take her. From a girl—when "policeman" and "bogey-man" had threatened—that helmet had blushed her with a certain fear. Even now if she smiled at a child in the street, she felt a policeman might think her a baby-snatcher; if admiring the architecture of a first-floor window, she became a burglar's accomplice; if waiting for someone by a London shop window, she became a whore. So that now as the shadow of the policeman moved over her she had to press her face down into the collar of her coat, hiding even among friends. But it was worse than simply a passing flight of guilt. A moment before she had exalted in the symbol of firm land, final break with London and Guy—yet instantly there appeared this figure of accusation, robed in the exact image of London. . . . Superstition is an ally of guilt, she whispered fearfully: "God, I shouldn't have thought it so easy to get away. I shouldn't have thought myself so clever." She felt the irrational guilt that besets all who desert others, however good may be the reasons.

The policeman leaned over her and said pleasantly: "Will you be wanting a car, Madam? They're just over there by the shed."

But Prescott was bustling between to thank the policeman, and he and Carey carrying bags started to walk toward the rank of taxis. Louise suddenly laughed, and looked at the policeman. He had spoken with a Spanish accent, and now she noticed his lean brown face, his alive black eyes, the straight dark hair oiled at his neck. All dressed up as a London bobby. Gibraltar looked promising.

But just then—she might have known it—Guy came walking back. He caught her eye as he passed, and gave a large wink.

"By-by again!" And then raised an eyebrow: "And good hunting!"

She stared ahead pretending to ignore him. But she was seized again with suspicion and fear: this had happened just when she had laughed at that policeman.

She heard Guy's step hesitate, then stop. She tried not to move. He came back and stood in front of her.

"You don't really make much of an impression," he said, and she recognized a dangerous mocking tone, "with this kind of boorishness. I don't feel . . ." he flicked his fingers, "that much. But I don't know that I can leave you feeling you've made me feel—" another flick—"that much."

"I don't know what you mean. Please get out of my way."

"Say good-by like a sensible girl. Come on."

"Please will you—"

She tried to push to one side of him. He caught her arm, held it tight. She felt the fingers hard into her arm, and through them the force of his will grating at her.

"If you won't learn any manners, we'll have to teach you some. You wanted me to leave you alone. I have. Yet you can't even acknowledge this little concession with simple politeness. Right then—the concession is revoked. I'll be seeing you in Seville—"

"You're hurting me."

"Then behave yourself. See you at the Fair!"

He let go her arm and without another word passed on along the quay. For a moment she stood there unable to move. Slowly, as if in reflection, her hand went up to her arm he had gripped. It was an old trick of his, sometimes at her side in a theater or in a car among other people—a clasp of the arm that began almost as a gesture of love but always tightened slowly into a grip of possession. Once she had found herself pitying him, it had seemed suddenly not so much an assault as a cry for help. But of this she was never again sure. She was only sure it was an infliction not of pain, but of personality.

71

In the car she suddenly said:

"Let's not go to that big hotel. Let's stop at the first one we like the look of." And added lamely: "Let's do what we like, let's get the holiday feeling."

"But Louise, we've all booked—" Prescott started.

"I know . . . but . . ."

"Oh darling, he's leaving tomorrow—" Madeleine said, and cut short wishing she had not spoken. Boxed in by a sudden silence they all looked uneasily out of the windows. There was a slow disgust in Louise's voice:

"Who's leaving?"

Madeleine pretended lightly: "Oh . . . Owen and all that —didn't you mean you want to get away from the crowd?"

Louise could feel the glance exchanged across her as Madeleine's voice petered away.

"As a matter of fact," Prescott said suddenly, "I know of a place just about here. Rather more Spanish than the others. . . ." He leaned forward to tell the driver.

Louise felt the cloying nod of nurses humoring her. She burst out: "No!"

But the car had stopped. And the others were all looking at her startled. Even the chauffeur had turned. There was nothing to do but fall deeper:

"I don't know—I'm sorry, it's my head. . . ." And loathing herself she put up a hand and passed it over her brow.

Now a shower of condolence. It was the change of climate! It was too much sun too suddenly! And she was handed carefully out of the car. Only Michael Carey, who might have been supposed to fuss more than the others, seemed to hold back. He stood looking at her curiously, a little aside— though perhaps he was simply making way for her closer friends.

Inside the hotel, while the luggage was handed in and the registers made out, she stood and looked around at the blue and orange Spanish tiles, the little fountain, the potted palms

—at all these first signs of a new country—with no joy but only misgiving.

The mood had not left her by the next morning when she went for a walk along the main shopping street with Madeleine.

It was a blue Gibraltar day. The April sun set up a smell of dust and leaves and cloth in the streets: though there was still a last freshness of spring within the warmth, red geraniums and mauve wistaria and the great blue trumpets of morning-glory were spread in full bloom.

Not many flowers, though, in Main Street. This unique artery runs the length of the little town, which itself clings like a narrow sea razor to the great Rock, from Southport Gate to a bastion that new visitors may forgivably take to be named after some legendary Spanish hero—Casemates. Forgivably—for Main Street must be one of the strangest, most confusing streets in the world.

To begin with, this Spanish street annexed by the English is full of Indian bazaars. Ripe names full of the oo's of Bombay stream above shop fronts packed with colored rugs, nylon underwear, brasses, cameras, and radio sets. The rugs, featuring in turquoise and puce and ocher an Egyptian sunset or a group of giant English kittens, are likely to be made in Milan: but at their side, smoothing your eyes with lizard tongue and suède-brown skin, stands an agile, lounge-suited gentleman from Bombay. Past this gentleman, whom at first you mistake for an Andalusian, saunters at the regulation pace a real Andalusian dressed as a London policeman: it is bewildering, it is a triumph of mind over matter, how this Spaniard's resilient rapier of a body achieves the solid phlegm of a British constabular swagger. And soon this olive copper will pass no Latin letter basket but a stolid Victoria Regina mailbox, fog-loving scarlet shaded by a palm.

Between glass-covered Moorish balconies rise two houses of British Government—one a Tudor essay dreaming of

Hampton Court, and the other a fine cream Georgian lump, bastion of the Blue. From along the street a sudden blare of trumpets—a Marine band passes. An answering wail of saxophones—and an open door reveals a Spanish ladies' band, combed and shawled—there are only such ladies' bands along the half-mile Main Street, no others. And then the rest of it! Canopied gocarts, Spanish wine drays, dinky baby saloon cars; cast-iron verandas and wood balconies like pagodas; sombreroed smugglers from Ronda and gray-trousered sons of Empire; a British general striding his bright Scottish kilt past an Andalusian whore skirted on high red heels; street names in elegant iron lettering of the eighteenth century, and houses that look inside out, their tiled façades like the insides of paradisiacal lavatories: and all around the milling native Gibraltese, gibbering and gesturing as loud and lively as the Barbary apes in their rock town above. . . . Yet strangest of all, and stronger than all these individual incongruities, is the total effect, however the kaleidoscope chooses to arrange itself. Possibly this total impression results from the mood of canopy and hanging trees and wood carving, possibly it is simply the echo of a great gray navy and Madame Butterfly. For there abides over all this southern subtropical port of Gibraltar a brittle, flowery feeling of Japan.

On that particular morning Louise neither felt nor noticed any of this. Nor did Madeleine, whose voice bubbled higher and higher at the shop windows, at the sight of stockings, bags, gloves, in such inexpensive, untaxed profusion.

They walked all the way down one side of Main Street and then up the other side. Prices were asked but no purchases made—such a hoard made Madeleine wary: instead of rushing at it like a child at a plate of sudden trifle, she became like that child faced with a tableful of trifles and jellies and ices, her hands stayed outstretched and her eyes grew grave.

Louise tried through her apprehension to join in. But she

found herself studying Madeleine too closely—surely such high-pitched pleasure was assumed, was it possible that all this was put on to humor her? The voice began to ring a tinny untruth.

At length she could bear it no longer:

"Mad dear—couldn't we go somewhere and sit down for a bit?"

Madeleine's face dropped—but then smiled too much as she raised her voice even higher in sympathy. This did not help. Nor did the immediate cafés, which looked difficult for two ladies alone—so that her apologies had become desperate by the time they had found a hotel with a lounge.

But once settled in a cane chair within sight of a pile of British newspapers and smelling coffee, she subsided. She gave Louise a long look of relief. She sighed with the contentment of something attempted, something done. All would now be all right, her face indicated. She said:

"That's all over and done with. Nice and settled at last. Happy?"

Once more Louise misinterpreted her. She burst out:

"Mad, I will not have you treating me like a lousy invalid. So for God's sake stop nursing me along, I'm quite capable of looking after myself."

Madeleine's eyes and mouth stayed open wide, that tongue of hers stopped astonished on her lower teeth:

"Darling, what*ever* are you saying?"

"I know it's kind of you and you're trying to be kind but please understand—I don't need this."

"Going off your rocker, dear?"

Louise drew in a breath and gave a scornful look all around, as if this were really too much and all the empty lounge should know it. She slammed down her coffee cup on the saucer:

"Why," she cried angrily, "did you tell Michael?"

"Tell Michael?" Madeleine's eyes were wide. "Tell Mike about what?"

75

"It's Michael, not Mike. And you know very well what you told him. About me and Guy. . . ."

Madeleine's eyes from wide surprise lowered their lids as she began to nod with knowledge, getting the hang of she knew not what.

"There was absolutely no need for Michael to know anything about Guy—Michael or anyone else. Guy's over. I've told you it's finished. It's the past."

"Ah," said Madeleine, knowing now. "So that's it."

"So *that's* it," Louise mimicked back. "Michael told me on the boat last night he knew. Oh, *mournful* he was—don't you see you've made him into a damn nurse too? The first fresh person I'd met—"

"Fresh, dear?"

"Please—I'm serious."

Madeleine suddenly sat up and tapped things all around her, putting everything straight.

"I hate," she said, "to disabuse you, but I've not said a single word on the subject to Michael or anybody."

"Then who has?"

Madeleine replied in the same distant, emphatic voice: "You."

"Me?"

"Yes, you. You've had it written all over yourself for days —whenever Guy got near. A blind man would've known."

Unexpectedly Louise took this calmly. It was what she had really feared. And so her thoughts ran straight on to what else she feared:

"I'm so frightened, Mad," she said. "Guy came up to me last night—right at the last moment. Started a row—"

Madeleine listened. A mother, and wise beneath her surface frivolity, her advice was practical and immediate.

"Cut Seville out," she said. "Change your plans altogether."

"Run away? You can't mean—"

"Father and I'd fit in, you know," Madeleine went on, already planning. "Jerez is our only 'must.' We could go there instead to begin with. And then—"

"Mm?"

"It's absurd you running your head straight into trouble."

"And what about running away? That's not very pretty."

"Pride! The proudest way is to see through the weakness of pride, be serious for God's sake. And listen—Father said a funny thing the other night. He said the real trouble with Guy is not that he's a real out-and-outer, in a way you can't really despise him, it's that he's absolutely ruthless, a totalitarian, Father said. He's got courage, Father said, he's got guts—look at his war record, Father said, though I don't quite see where that comes in—but alongside all this he'll use any dirty trick, *any*, he'll do anything to get what he wants. And he'll think it right, a dirty trick with him becomes simply something free of false sentiment."

"Well?"

"It's plain as a pikestaff. You've just got to be total back."

"And call it expediency?"

"Call it what you bloody well like, my girl, but do it."

Louise stopped arguing and said simply:

"There's no question, Mad. I can't alter any plans because of him. I'd always be wondering what might have happened if I'd—what do you call it, stayed the course. I've simply got to face it. Last night I made us change our hotel. That was a lapse, I was tired and frightened. But it taught me."

"Well—you're up against a lot. The only hope," she sighed, gathering her things together, "is that Seville's big enough to hold the both of you."

"Big?"

"You think it's still a sweet little torture of winding streets? No, darling. Parks! Trams! *Thoroughfares!* It's huge!"

Louise felt a sudden disappointment—here was another ally, even this city would not leave her to face things alone.

"But," Madeleine smiled, "it's very, very beautiful."

✦

Two days later Michael Carey proposed to Louise.

Much in the meantime had happened to clear the air. In the first place, Guy had left. He had taken an early ferry into Algeciras with the Owens. In the second place, there was this air of the beginning of holiday, of new and exciting surroundings, and the company of friends. The soft warmth of a southern spring, wide spaces of sea and harbor, the circling Spanish hills, and the strangeness of its hybrid streets made Gibraltar indeed a pleasant place. What did they do? Nothing at first of precise incident. They made holiday.

The four of them met mostly at meals, at other times Louise was alone with Michael. They took a bus out to Europa Point, where the southernmost tongue of the Rock strives toward its African brother mud-caked and lion-harsh across the water. The two of them talked and lazed and laughed on the spring fields of purple and yellow ice plant, took photographs, peered below at the great drop to the sea, scanned the heights for Barbary apes and saw none at all.

Again, in the town, past the Trafalgar cemetery and through the Moorish gates, they found a bar with a map of the English fox-hunt country in Andalusia proper: Spanish village names were mixed with the marks of exiled huntsmen —names like Beauforts Copse, Mayfield Spinny, Four Mile Corner. Top-hatted gentlemen in scarlet coats galloping past cactus and agave? Possible! And what had the Andalusian riders thought?

Once they had met the Prescotts walking along Main Street —and exactly by a narrow doorway plastered with photographs of bullfighters. But these were really photographs of visiting sailors dressed as bullfighters. You could have your photo taken in *torero's* dress there and then. So all four of them did.

And what *toreros* transpired! Carey, his regular features and thoughtful eyes crowned by the slug-shaped black cap, took on a classic air, a man of parts from Toledo. The Major, his eyes as always blazing beneath their tufted eyebrows, stood swelling his golden jacket like a wild Valencian, while the ladies looked even more authentic—smooth-shaved gypsy matadors: Louise with her slight slanting smile properly contemptuous of death, Madeleine a gayer, flamboyant virtuoso from Seville. *"Olé,"* they all said.

And in that sort of way the time passed: whether it was watching a naval hockey match on the sports ground among Plymouth Hoe asphalt paths, or watching the white seaplanes landing like giant pelicans on the blue water by Algeciras, or drinking beer to the music of those portentous ladies' bands, or simply shopping and lounging and laughing and looking.

It was a lazy time—and although nothing specific was said, Louise and Michael became easily in many small ways more intimate—they walked arm-in-arm, they could sit together in tired silence without embarrassment, she could take off her shoes under the café table and he was allowed to be bored in some of the shops and to meet her later. Much of the time was spent covertly in finding out more about each other— their past lives, habits, and preferences, towns they had mutually known, and even one mutual acquaintance, whom neither much cared for but who suddenly took on a new and significant worth.

However, on the afternoon of the last day they took a walk to the tropical gardens and later climbed up the creepered steps to the terrace of the hotel above. It was empty— and there, under a ceiling of mauve wistaria, with the sea and the town spread out below them, they sat for a time in silence. Occasionally a passing sentence of English echoed from the hotel behind, a man's voice belonging to the undress uniform of that part of the Empire—gray trousers, sports jacket, new brown soft hat placed exactly straight over the eyes, a stick. Such voices, the sad wistaria drooping its mauve around, the battleships in the gulf, the very air of spring out of season filled Louise with a strangely sweet sense of exile. It was like visiting a past summer, coming from a wintry London it could never feel true weather—the warm air was dream-laden, for once those dreams of a summery past, melancholy and exquisite, seemed to come into real being. And such English voices enhanced the air—they realized all novels read of the outpost Britisher, of verandas and sundowners, of loneliness and heartsick exile—and there echoed beyond this that greater nostalgia of time, the exile of the present from the past. Already the wistaria was beginning to fall, the mauve-white petals lay dying on the wide empty terrace: spring and autumn already combined. The sun was already falling, the great gulf spread before them grew stiller in the westering light, promontories lengthened to catch the last light of day. Slowly a long gray ship began to glide out to sea. It seemed to pass so very slowly on this its evening voyage: yet suddenly it was gone. When it was gone there was nothing, nothing there on the sea at all.

Louise felt, just as slowly, the warmth of his hand on hers. It must have been there some time. She turned and saw he was smiling at her.

"You were a very long way away."

"Yes."

"Algeciras?"

"No," she smiled. Then looked around at the desolate terrace and gave a slight wakening shiver. "It's this place, I mean, I was thinking of the past."

After a moment he said: "Is it such a wrench?"

"Wrench? How?"

He said evenly: "I mean your parting with that fellow— with Guy?"

She stammered:

"But I wasn't thinking of that . . ." She paused: "Or was I? It's all so mixed up. I thought I was just thinking of—oh, summers ago, all summers gone."

"Did you know him a very long time?"

"Four years. Nearly."

"Then you've plenty of past before that—"

"Such compliments!" she said brightly.

But he persisted: "I mean that just now you'll be looking back on life as though it's only colored by this—great friend of yours. But it isn't. The real past is your earliest youth, all the truly virgin—"

"Michael!"

"—impressions of what—weather, seasons, behavior, places? All that's happened since is a repetition." He paused, and said carefully: "You must try and remember who you were before."

A light wind stirred the fallen petals, they drifted into heaps like rolls of dust.

"It's not easy to cut out just like that someone who's still there," Louise said.

"You mean you're still in—?"

"No. But in a very material sense he's still about."

"But he's not. He's gone!"

"He's only gone to Seville. He's threatened to look me up. He will."

He said easily:

"Oh—we'll surely take care of anything like *that*."

Running down Guy? She felt her face tighten with resentment. But the next second wondering at herself, let it relax. It was absurd. She did not really mind at all. And then it passed through her mind how differently she would have felt if Madeleine had spoken in the same way.

She frowned at him, searching for a proof of she did not know what. She got it. There was no mistaking the tenderness in his eyes and the small ashamed smile drawing the corners of his mouth. He made no attempt to hide this. His hand was still on hers. She saw suddenly how they were sitting—a picture of two thus on an empty, flower-hung terrace overlooking the vast loops of land and water lying like a map of whales below—and knew what surely he must be going to say. She had never exactly thought of this. Now in great confusion her mind began to move all ways at once.

81

A pause before he spoke again. But then only to say softly: "Do you love him very much?"

"No—no," she stammered loudly. "No, no I don't. I don't at all—" and stopped herself quickly, it had sounded like a schoolgirl excusing herself. Strange enthusiasm! What on earth was going on? And added gravely: "I did once. But now—well—I don't feel anything."

With his free hand he was making a pattern of twigs on the table, pushing at them too quickly. They sat there again in silence, again the great stillness around. Suddenly he brushed all those twigs impatiently aside:

"Louise . . ." he began.

She looked up at him too quickly. Her mind raced wondering how she could do this, why she didn't take her hand away, why in every way she was encouraging him to speak, why all her instincts strained to hear—when she had no idea what answer could be given. The presence of the question, it absurdly seemed, would provide that answer. But then, as fractionally he paused searching for words, her nerves took charge, the great landscape and the wide terrace seemed to close in, she searched frantically for anything at all to say that would stop him. And said, with enormous calm:

"But how did you know all this about me?"

"Eh?" He looked up puzzled, too abruptly pulled from his deeper thoughts. "Oh—that—it was hardly difficult. One's packed pretty close on a ship. You can hardly hide—"

"Heavens!"

She was looking with bolt bright horror at her watch. "Look at the time!"

"Louise . . ." he began again fiercely—but broke off, and they both suddenly saw that the sun had set and it was quite dark.

"I—I never heard the gun," Louise said, now really surprised.

"No. Nor did I."

They looked at each other startled, on the point of laugh-

82

ing at this strange coincidence: but both now aware of a deepening mystery between them.

A huddle of lights, those of Algeciras, studded the slow black tongue of distant hills, the yellow portholes of ships made an electric picnic of the silver water, the evening star shone out like steel in soft blueness framed now with black creeper. Overhead an aircraft drudged high and slow—red and green eyes of a Chinese ghost traversing the lonely sky.

"Perhaps—we'd better go?"

And all Michael said was simply: "Yes."

They walked down to their hotel now uneasy. The simple air of friendship was gone. They spoke almost formally, once or twice made staccato apologies as on a narrow pavement they touched. No more arm-in-arm. A sense of danger between them. But beneath this repression Louise felt herself beating with excitement. She was happy.

But after a big dinner, and the wine and the company of the Prescotts that went with it, the old ease slowly returned. And afterward, since this was their last night in Gibraltar, they all went along to one of the cafés to listen to the music and take a liqueur.

The café occupied a wide high room lit by bare electric globes and tiled nearly to the nicotined ceiling with green and blue Spanish tiles. With its dark wood tables set in rows like desks, with those obtrusive greenish walls and naked lights it felt at first like a vast Victorian schoolroom: but for the beer bottles; but for the bright uniforms of marines and sailors; but for the heavy raised dais, the cynosure of the room, upon which no pedant stood but a large brassy band of dark-eyed *señoritas*. As they entered, one of these, ablaze in the layered frills of her red Andalusian skirt and a fiercely turquoise shawl, blared from a golden trumpet the last long breast-breaking notes of "Come Back to Sorrento."

"Not too near the band, Father," Madeleine was saying in her best evening-out voice—but already her husband's eyes had reconnoitered the table layout and he was leading them to a table a little recessed from the others.

"Doesn't do to butt in on these fellows. Embarrasses 'em."

And indeed just then a marine corporal, sitting straight-necked like a big upright doll, said loudly, but staring carefully in another direction: "Slumming."

"See what I mean," the Major whispered.

But when they all sat down a red-faced naval rating, his cap well back on his head, gave Louise a great broad friendly toothless wink. And others there turned, mixed marines and sailors, and smiled a greeting.

"Father's always right," Madeleine murmured as they all smiled back. But Louise had seen a passing anxiety in Michael's face at that big playful wink. Then of course he was laughing with the others. Yet this was enough to bring back the new tension between them. Accordingly she became bright. The others responded—it was an exciting night, their last night in Gibraltar, the moment before the question mark of Spain. Brightness bred the juice of real laughter. They began to have a very good time indeed.

There was no dancing. The navy simply sat and drank beer: sometimes they sang. The tables were set in exact rows, and they sat purposely on only one side of these—again the sense of a carnival classroom—so that they could keep their eyes well on the dais and that seductive orchestra. Several sat without ever talking at all, simply emptying bottle after bottle of beer, never smiling, moving, or laughing, simply staring at this amazing female mirage.

And the band played on. These were no ordinary lady musicians—no spinsterhood of the fiddle, no coy pajamaed bobbers of the teatime saxophone. This band, despite its jazz, stayed Spanish. Each woman sat with dignity, straight-backed and proud-necked: each wore her black hair piled and brushed and polished into an exquisite ebony crown set with a tortoise-shell comb and a carnation by the ear: each wore the bright, sun-loving colors of an Andalusian fiesta, fringed

84

and frilled: and each face, with its bright black eyes, its white teeth, its fierce dark dignity, was brightly rouged and painted —but without harlotry, with a careful art that made the face a picture of a face. From such faces they stared and sometimes smiled back at the sailors. One expected them to get up and dance, to move as women. But they simply sat. Though to the sailors—what bright lascivious ranks! They seemed to be making love to their instruments, kissing the mouthpieces of trumpets, licking saxophones, fondling the little violin body with a side caress of the cheek, eyes away in a dream. That whole edifice was one of careful frustration. As if in comment, a notice hung beneath the dais: TO MOUNT IS FORBIDDEN.

But every twenty minutes or so a special lady appeared from the back of the café and performed an Andalusian dance on the platform. She was dressed with Spanish formality from ankle to neck: and danced a formal measure of arabesque and intricate stamping. Nevertheless she was loudly applauded. And as the beer went down, and as souvenirs—watches and ornaments that later would decorate wrists and mantelpieces up and down the length of the home country—were produced and discussed, and as the music and the female mirage jollied them, so the great green café grew less garishly bleak and in a thickening fog of tobacco smoke took on a growing gaiety. Yet a certain puritan atmosphere, sadly comic in a great warm southern seaport, persisted: and one knew, for instance, that the hours of liquor license would come to a close long before midnight. Perhaps this, or perhaps a thought of the journey on the morrow, reminded Prescott of the need for a good night's rest—or was it a nod of surreptitious tact from his wife?—and they rose to leave.

Michael rose too. But just then a tableful of sailors got to their feet—it seemed that everyone was rising—and began pushing a small petty officer toward the platform. They wanted him to sing. He was not, of course, allowed to mount the dais—but gave the name of his song to the leading *señorita* and stood waiting, chest rigid, eyes on the ceiling, among the tables. The ladies took up their instruments and drawled out the opening bars, once again, of "Come Back to Sorrento."

Louise caught at Michael's sleeve:

"Do let's listen. It's early yet. He looks sweet."

The first long high strong tenor note struck like a wire cord through the air. They looked at each other in horror, laughed silently—but now close together were glad to sit down. The Prescotts, running the gauntlet of that inimical young marine, who belched purposefully as they passed, had made off quickly. Louise still had her hand on Michael's sleeve—but now alone with him she was quick to pretend she needed it for her glass.

All that evening various of her attitudes toward Michael had been somersaulted. Toward his physical fact, for instance. It is possible to know that a man has, as Michael had, a very fine growth of pale hair molding the back of his hand, even to know this in detail. And then, a moment later, when something has overturned the emotions, to know the same thing in a different way altogether. Intimately and now dangerously—the difference between a bayonet in a museum and the sentry's steel an inch from your belly.

But now also whenever her eyes were turned toward his face, his hands, and his clothes and the body inside them— she made astonishing discoveries, delivered strange and moving judgments to herself. Like an animal sniffing she saw gray shadows, evidence of care or study, beneath his eyes; a down turn to his high-bridged nose, odd in a squarish face: a pale wart behind an ear—she considered this, almost rejected it, then was moved to a great tenderness: good shoulders, and a way of turning these and his whole chest toward you when he was talking, confiding thus everything: a light sober suit, but lapels turning up at corners—no one to press them? Such and so much more she noticed with a strange

86

new wonder: considered and approved. And suddenly she
thought: How old is he?

> "Then say not good-by,
> Come back again beloved,"

the tenor sang close-eyed, mouth wide, all power and no
feeling, a street singer with a voice of high steel: a tough
little sailor in a dark jacket, not much past a boy, exiled
now so many miles from the streets and bars of his long-
away home.

Yet the sound was terrible, it made a loveless pylon of the
ballad. Louise and Michael had been laughing quietly—now
suddenly she glanced to see exactly how he was laughing,
found thankfully he showed as well a look of sympathy that
the sailor deserved. They began to have a good time. They
ordered more anisette and both cheered loudly when "Sorrento" burst to its end and the sailor, expressionless, as if
he had just completed a routine gun drill, walked stiffly to
his table and buried his nose in a glass of ale.

The next moment a brown-skinned Gibraltese in a pink
gabardine suit was up gesticulating at the band. Again the
ladies took their instruments from their lips, words were
exchanged, and this stranger turned, pushed his hat to the
back of his head, threw his chest out, flung his arms out to
either side and waited propped like a tall gaunt postured
bird caught in some act.

But what an act!

For once again the lips of those ladies drawled, as fresh
as ever, the first notes of the introduction to that same fate-
ful song, the man opened his mouth wide, and Louise and
Michael broke down helplessly. Now the Neapolitan words
came with a softer drama:

> *"Nu prufumo accussi fino*
> *Din t'o core se ne va"*

87

And Michael suddenly found himself at a height of what was a private giggle looking into Louise's eyes and becoming fixed there. And then, freed in the ease of laughter and caught in the intimacy of her eyes, the words came freewheeling out of him:

"Oh Louise, oh dearest, I've been walking about this rock for days with my heart full of words and now it's too full and God in Heaven they have to come out in a place like this. . . . Louise!—"

He seemed to take a breath, then said it, mixed and humbly the wrong way round:

"Louise . . . may—may I marry you?"

"Will you be my wife?" he said.

"O my darling I love you," he said now quieter, awed by the sound of it.

> "*Ma nun ce lassa*
> *Nun darme stu turmiento*"

pealed around the room, around sailors and beer bottles, through the mist of smoke and high up among the Spanish tiles.

But all she said back to him was his name, and this as though it hurt her—while she searched all over his eyes, his mouth, his whole face, as though she wished to get at something that lay behind inside, like a nurse examining an illness.

But he went straight on talking, fast now, flushed on this new elation. She simply looked at him and then looked down and shook her head it seemed helplessly, listening with wonder to all he was saying, wondering at so much coming from a face so reserved, wondering and at the same time becoming swept away by it. The only words that came to her were: "Michael—dear—it's all so sudden." And then smiled at this, and he laughed too. She began crying tears of laughter into her handkerchief.

But even then he never stopped. He became almost like a salesman so sure of his wares that he holds them back. He

88

raised his hands, made a gesture with them: "Don't answer now! You don't have to say anything. Please—not now. Think about it . . . there . . . all you have to do is . . . think . . . my darling. . . ."

"*Torna a Surriento*
Famme campà"

sobbed its great yell as the song ended, the café was loud with clapping, cheers, whistles so that no other words could pass between them and all Michael could do was mouth and continue pressing her away with his hands while both of them helplessly smiled, never leaving each other's eyes.

But suddenly he did leave her—in all that noise with a silencing finger to his lips!

A great many things seemed to happen at once. The clapping had hardly died when he was up by the orchestra gesturing to the pianist, the pianist was shaking her head, then he was turning and appealing to the sailors (he couldn't be asking for another "Sorrento"?) and suddenly the nearest group of sailors laughed and one very tall sailor was pushed forward and put a foot up on the forbidden platform. Michael gave him a shove up from behind, the ladies twittered with shock, then shouted angrily as the sailor went straight to the piano and sat down and began to play. He grinned around toward Louise, Michael waved, and all the sailors around there threw back their heads and sang:

"Every little breeze
Seems to whisper Louise. . . ."

A simple trick, and obvious: but Louise loved it. She blushed, waved back. Awfully at parties this had happened before, on countless hearty occasions distinguished only by their exact lack of real heart. But Michael so plainly could not help what he was doing, he was so simply excited, and the faces all around laughed such simple affection that her heart was touched, it was a gift of beauty.

89

A man by the door had slipped out as the song began. And the manager of the café, who was already waving his hands hopelessly at the sailor on the orchestra platform, had seen this and now tried to shout up against the singing.

But the noise was so great, all in the café now bawled and thumped out the well-known old song, that no one heard him until the climax, its last long note—when three naval policemen threw open the street door and stood there.

Huge, heavily sober, tough as their truncheons, they stood like statues among the moving ease of the tables. They looked at the sailor rising drunkenly from the piano.

Michael on his way back toward Louise's table saw them and stopped. He glanced back at the sailor, looked serious, turned to the police.

Louise felt suddenly alarmed for him: but when she got over to them he was smiling again, talking as fast as ever, and apparently overjoyed to do so. The three policemen stood and looked at him silently. They had not moved, nor in fact expressed anything, since they had entered the room. They stood in their huge bodies strangely disembodied, only their eyes alive and moving.

"It was my fault," Michael was saying, and added, "Officer."

"Yes," he went on, "entirely my fault. I got him to go up there. He was the only one who could play it. 'Louise,' that is. That's my—my, that's her name. . . ."

Legs firmly apart, arms on hips, the policemen seemed not yet fully to have recognized his presence: they seemed to be listening through him. One had turned his face to another, as if hearing music a long way off.

"It was a celebration, you see," Michael went on. "Special."

"You see," he broke out happily, "we've just got engaged."

He stopped, smiling proudly and conclusively at one after another of them, a boy with a conjuring trick. But at that word "engaged," Louise felt a veil slide from around her.

Then one of the police faces moved, it was a big broad face, it lurched slowly into both a scowl and a smile at the same time, brows closed furiously but the big lips pleasantly opening.

"I take it you confirm this gentleman's statement, Miss?" came deep official Cockney.

Louise opened her mouth, but no sound came. She swallowed and then it came:

"Oh, yes, oh, yes, yes!"

And turned to Michael, and her voice rose: "Oh Michael yes, *yes*, YES!"

All three police began to smile, Michael took her by the arm and all they wanted to do was sink into each other and realize the moment. But on the point of that their first embrace they stopped, for there they were standing among so many sitting, and facing those police who, however, were already moving away.

One had reached for the door handle and looked at it in his hands, saying in mock surprise: "Why this is where we came in."

"Best wishes to all of you from all of us," another said, "I'm sure."

The third touched his cap. They took a last blind look around the now orderly room and then they were gone.

The bill, and a fumbling moment waiting for it, and then Michael's arm was around her leading her out. He looked white and amazed.

The warm soft night greeted them, the air now heavy with the scent of blossom. They walked slowly, saying nothing, pressed together.

From another café a few doors away there sounded, suddenly on a high echoing trumpet note, the coda of "Sorrento." Neither of them laughed.

CHAPTER V

HE next morning the whole party flew to Seville.

Up in the air, after first exclaiming at the patterned map below, they settled down to doing nothing.

But Louise that morning could not stop talking nor keep quite still. After a while Madeleine said:

"Never been up in a plane before, dear?"

"You know very well I have. Why?"

"Well—for instance, what's sort of up?"

Louise and Michael had agreed to make no announcement of the engagement until all were settled comfortably on land in the Sevillian hotel.

Madeleine persisted:

"The air must *really* be like champagne."

Louise looked down at a small cloud floating alone above the brown mud far below. Suddenly she could hold out no longer. Perhaps the word "champagne" did it. She swung herself full around to Madeleine and the Major and brought the word out again with a big round smile:

"Champagne—if you want to know, the air *is* like champagne. And Michael and I are engaged to be married. There!"

Michael looked at her for one moment in despair, then turned too:

"It's all fixed," he said.

"Good Lord!" Prescott said.

"Darling!" smiled Madeleine.

Then there were excited questions and congratulations: which as suddenly subsided when they realized that they were up in the air, and that this was a moment for celebration, for champagne, and how was one to get that in a two-engine ten-seater so far above the earth?

This was exasperating, and the more so for the Major, who felt it was his responsibility: they could do nothing but settle down again to a more prolonged, but now awkward discussion.

Then suddenly, pretending shock, Madeleine cried:

"And what about all our plans? You two will be going off!"

"Of course we won't! Nothing's changed—"

"Not?" Madeleine said, now really shocked and of course thinking of Guy. "You're pulling my leg."

"Michael says we should just go on as if nothing's happened—which I think is rather silly, because of course it has—and I agree with Michael."

"After all, why should it be different?" Michael put in. "We like to be with you." He added, "Even if we might lose you now and then."

"Of course," the Major said reasonably, "it's not their honeymoon is it?"

"Father!" Madeleine beseeched. And then in despair started to fire her last gun: "But don't you see how Father and I'll be hopping around the corner away from you all the time, it's us who'll have no peace, no peace at all. . . ."

"Fasten your safety belts," said a Spanish voice, official as a loud-speaker, "we're going down."

And they then descended in breath-held silence to make a safe, smooth landing on the airfield by Seville.

The hotel faced on the Plaza Neuva. From bedroom balconies one looked out onto a broad marble-paved square ringed with tall old palm trees up which red roses had been trained: other roses, red and yellow and white, shone from the darkness of beds planted at the sides: an equestrian statue lent dignity to the center: wrought-iron lamp standards stood in the shadow of palm leaves and about all the plaza there hung still an undisturbed air of the turn of the century.

They settled in quickly—the need to celebrate grew more intense at every moment—and met as soon as possible in the old-fashioned lounge downstairs.

And there stood the Owens.

"Ee—look what cat's brought in!" Owen cried, hurrying over, already at that early hour not too steady.

His wife smiled from under a pale blue peaked helmet, blue as her anxious eyes, and said unpredictably: "No sooner said than done."

"Louise!" came oversweetly from Molly. "How smashing!"

They all greeted each other, and then the engagement was announced all over again. Madeleine took the opportunity to slip away to inquire whether a Mr. Guy Harrowby was staying. No, she was told, he had canceled his room. Relieved but puzzled, she rejoined the others, who were then led out by Major Prescott, all of them, for it would have been difficult now to omit the Owens, to a place he knew of.

They walked up the plaza, now on foot for the first time feeling the strong distinct quality of Spain, not Italy and nowhere else but Spain—the hot air that could almost be grasped in the hand, the smell of sun on old plaster, the scents of flowers and oil and Havana smoke erupting, vanishing, reappearing as powerfully as bars of black shadow on the hot white pavement. Tram bells, the clatter of hoofs and guttural Spanish words invigorated the ears. And for the eyes new richnesses which at first merged into a general feeling of flowers, leaves, leather, black cloth, and brass.

They crossed into the Sierpes and turned up into the little Plaza del Salvador, where the big shellfish house was already crowded.

The Major limped hurriedly to grab a table whose occu-

94

pants had scarcely risen fully to their feet. "There," he said as they all sat down almost on the curb but still beneath the red-and-white striped awning. "At last! Now what's it to be—champagne, or Spanish style?"

"Oh Spanish!" like well-bred children they all echoed. So he clapped his hands, the waiter came hurrying, and in a minute there were bottles of manzanilla and black-eyed crayfish on the table.

Louise was at last just raising her thirsty glass to her lips when Owen, who had been quicker and had already half-emptied his, flourished it in the air and cried:

"To the happy couple!"

So she had to lower her glass while they all drank. She was just raising it again when Michael, innocently wishing to give her the first place in these proceedings, said with a long look into her eyes:

"To Louise!"

She had to lower it again. But she was double-quick then to raise it, to shout:

"And to Michael—and all of you!"

So that she took a long big sip while they sat smiling and immobilized.

Prescott refilled the glasses and they broke the heads off their crayfish and began to chatter and look around.

"You'll have to look after her, Michael," Olive Owen said. "Molly was picked up the very first moment she set foot out."

"Oh Mother no! I only said he spoke to me, he might have been only asking the time."

"You should know by the look in a gentleman's eye what they're asking at your age. Kittikins, yes, and what day it is."

She nodded severely at a tall thin horse come to a stand-still nearby and added: "Shouldn't she, Dad?"

But Owen in his third manzanilla had not heard. He was saying to the Major: "You'd think we wouldn't like it, wouldn't you? You'd say: The buggers stretch their pieces of canvas right over the tops of their streets to keep the sun

95

out and so nobody's going to need any sunshades. Right? Well, you're wrong. What it does is make an arcade. Now arcades is a godsend in rainy weather—and don't tell me you don't get a spell of the old one-two now and again. Well, if it wasn't for arcades nobody would leave their homes at all. But they've-got-to-get-from-their-homes-to-these-arcades. See? So it's umbrellas, hey presto." And he finished: "God bless arcades."

The Major was looking hopelessly into the hatpin eyes of a pale *langostino* frothed with whiskery feelers like a pink Sikh. "But they put the awnings over these narrow streets against the sun, not the rain . . ." he muttered.

"Same thing. Need parasol to get there." And he began to chant astonishingly, but what must have been a family joke: "God save ar-gracious-cades."

Around them a flurry of people ate, drank, talked, a milling of hot clothes and voices in the bright noon air. Crushed shells already made a pink carpet on the pavement. As on a stage, on the set of the narrow plaza, passed the purposeful Spanish crowd—mostly men, some capped, some in Cordovan sombreros, but all walking with a pride and dignity not seen elsewhere in Europe. The workmen in gray overalls, police uniforms of an identical gray, the poor clutching precious parcels or the poor begging—all walked with upright dignity, knowing their right. While horses and mules and cars whinnied and hooted, while lottery-sellers yelled and bootblacks shouted—and beggars whispered, yet looked you straight in the eye.

Madeleine had Louise at her side and was whispering excitedly such as: "Aren't you excited, darling!"

And Louise looked lazy, satisfied: "Yes . . . I do love him so."

Then looked suddenly frightened: "And to think I never knew it . . . no, just do look at him now. . . ."

Molly's voice sailed into the pause, petulant: ". . . and come to that, time or no tell the time, I wouldn't so much

96

mind being picked up by one of them, dark, handsome, smashing . . ."

And Madeleine, warming up well to the easy facetious party spirit of the occasion, bubbled across the table at Michael: "Hear that? Competition you have, my Mike! Where's my comb? Better take a leaf out of the local vade mecum. . . ."

She caught hold of Michael's head and began to comb his hair straight back in Spanish fashion, then ripped his tie off to show a plain collar as the Andalusians prefer—and now when amid laughter he hunched up his shoulders he did indeed look a little Spanish.

"*Olé!*" they all shouted.

Then Molly gave a little yelp and waved: "And *olé* again —there's Guy!"

"Why yes, we saw him once before, didn't we?" said Mrs. Owen, preening herself. "He's staying quite near, isn't he?"

They all turned to see Guy indeed traversing the plaza. He was still dressed carelessly in a dark serge suit from London, tie flapping free, a collar end turned up, a strand of sand-dry hair fallen over his frowning forehead: among so many dark-skinned people, the chalk white of his blue-shaven face looked more powdered than ever. He strode fixedly, on long legs whose muscle gave them a slight bandiness, or rather an arced strength, like two pliant longbows. One hand in a pocket, the arm gripping a parcel, he had the air of a man tousled with work, an active legislator hurrying to an occasion. As usual, his teeth were gripped chewing a match.

But however preoccupied his eyes may have been, he could scarcely have missed Molly's wildly waving white arm.

"Why!" And equally he said each of their names as he smiled, pleasantly, his welcome.

"So you've arrived," he then said.

They all said yes.

A pause. Major Prescott saved it: "And where are you— er—staying? Not parking with us?"

"No, Major, a bit upstage for me. However, I'm not far along the road."

Molly was making a movement with her chair—a space for a chair for Guy. She was just beginning: "Guy, won't you . . ." when Madeleine's hand came down gripping hard on her wrist under the table, an unquestionable restraint, as brightly she said:

"Now what on earth is this, Guy? Candles? A black mass some place?"

She had seen that the box under his arm was labeled, in flowery lettering, with words denoting votive candles.

"Always so sweet, Madeleine dear. No, I bought them purely for their looks."

"And they are so pretty aren't they? And how are you liking Spain? What do you think of the Spanish people?"

"Sight better than white folk."

"Guy," put in Molly, "this is a great day! We're having a little celebr—"

Madeleine carefully knocked the whole pile of crayfish shells into her lap. On Molly's new pale spring skirt the empty husks of these wet insect-fish dribbled their last salt leavings.

"Oh it *would* happen to me! Everything happens to me," she wailed. "And at a time like this . . ."

"But Guy," Madeleine went on, busily wiping her up, through apologies, "what about the children? All these lovely brown children, you must say they're sweeties."

"When they're not starving."

"But you know they're the very last to be let starve!"

Guy was standing all this time. Olive Owen was vigorously rubbing Molly's skirt: "Now *you*—I know *you*, come on you dirty skirt you." The Major and Michael had their heads together on some bullfighting matter—occasionally they glanced up at Guy politely to include him—and in all this Louise found she felt safely armored, almost equally distant from Guy. However, it was not exactly comfortable.

98

"Children," Guy was saying. "Corrupters of innocence—"

"The poor mites!" said Madeleine, keeping it going.

"Poor mites be damned. Every time a child is born, honest dealing takes a backward step. Anything to gain more for the brat. All tolerance to the wall!"

"What utter nonsense! What about the extra love a child brings?"

"Within the family circle," Guy repeated, "which becomes henceforth an armed camp."

Madeleine drew herself up now angrily, the biter bit. Her cheekbones flushed red. Guy was beginning to enjoy himself. So Prescott felt it necessary to intervene:

"Extraordinary thing," he said, "the other day a Spanish chap came up and asked Molly the time. Right there in the street."

"Oh?"

There was a pause at this.

Guy looked puzzled: "And what time *was* it?" he said. Prescott gathered himself, laughed it off, saw that a clean sweep must be made. He made shifting movements, grabbing at his stick, leaning around for the waiter.

"Time we were all off and away. Waiter!"

But Guy then said he must be going too, and adding he would see them soon again, abruptly walked off. He had paid no attention to Molly. One white hand moved out as he went, as if to follow him: she looked strained and older.

The waiter was standing over Prescott, who now said jovially, not bothering to dissimulate:

"Now we can have another. Same again? Same again." He added: "What I can't understand is what the fellow wants with those candles?"

Louise opened her mouth, she was just going to tell them, then stopped herself in time.

After a long luncheon they took a walk about the inner streets of the city.

In the main thoroughfares a busy traffic of yellow trams belled against motors and drays, and the clatter of so many horses wove a leathern strength in between. Yet a second away, by a corner's turn, the side street was narrow and shaded and quiet, an alley of white walls inked with wrought-iron balconies from which flowers and soft green creeper hung.

No more the first confused impression—facets of the city's character distinguished themselves. As the mind preferred it, a life of limousines and plate-glass shop fronts: or a sun-baked baroque backwater, tough with palms and dark-muscled men strutting, smoking, gravely laughing: or some shaded labyrinth of white side streets, cool patios, miniature plazas: or a city of broad vistas that lead to a Moorish palace, the Gothic cathedral, a huge plateresque government office, or the tree-shaded gateways of a park: or the river, Seville of the Guadalquivir, with dredgers at work in the broad silver-mud waters, sirens booming and a destroyer of the royal Spanish navy flying its red and yellow standard against wide cobbled quays: or, over the bridge in Triana, a wasteland of gypsies and packed houses of poverty.

Thus those four wandered—the Owens had gone off—watching and wondering, and exclaiming at so much that was strange: at a little girl-gypsy, ragged and dust-caked, but sparkling with life and with her lips rouged; at a knife-grinder blowing his call on the five-fluted Panpipe; at the sudden appearance, among trams, of a cow led by a man beating a drum.

More fun was made of Michael's hair, now drawn back in the Spanish fashion. Madeleine insisted on buying him, on the spot, a further bond with Spain—a black tie.

"Oh no!" Louise objected.

"But my dear they *all* wear them, they *adore* their death."

Some shadow of Guy's appearance must have still hung over her—for now this emblem of mourning took on too large a presence, she suddenly felt frightened. She became

100

immediately conscious of the predominance of that same emblem all around—black arm bands, black ties, the black clothes of older women, even the great dark sherry casks. Absurd—but her mind was troubled, she fell behind the others to speak to Michael alone.

"You know," she said quietly, "it was wrong not to tell Guy."

"Tell Guy?"

"About us, silly."

Michael looked surprised. "But didn't anyone tell him? I thought—I took it for granted."

"He ought to be told. Madeleine obviously stopped it."

They paused to watch a horseman pass, black Cordovan hat firmly down-tilted, his woman in a long frilled skirt sitting sideways behind him. Already they were riding in for the *Feria* to come.

"I suppose she didn't want any hysterics," Michael said. "Just then, celebrating and all that."

"You think there would have been?"

"In his place I'd have screamed the bloody place down."

"Michael now, seriously—he'd better be told. It's absurd Madeleine making him into a sort of ogre."

"Then let's tell him. But naturally, in due course. The important thing is not to make a fuss of it."

Louise took a breath and plunged: "Look, Michael—I've been wondering whether we're right after all about that. I mean, altogether. Perhaps we should chuck up Seville and go off somewhere into the blue." She noticed his face—and tailed off: "Or whatever color you . . ."

"You're not serious?"

"Look how awkward it was with Guy this morning."

"But it hardly affects us, does it?"

"No, darling—it's only that it's all so uncomfortable. I wanted this week to be perfect in every way."

"So it will be. I don't expect we'll be running into him all that . . ."

"Oh, but we will. You watch."

"In a city as big as this?"

"Silly, the center of the town is its area—as far as us tourists are concerned."

He stopped. They were opposite a photographer's window full of pictures of bullfighters from past *Ferias*. To these *toreros*, as much as to her, he went on gravely: "But *most* seriously, darling—I'm still sure we oughtn't to run away. If we start off by not facing the first small trouble . . . well . . ."

"Michael!"

"Oh, I know it'd be 'for the best.' . . . What is it—expedient? . . . common-sense comfort? . . ."

She looked up at him and saw with surprise a look of uneasiness on his face. His voice came easily, but his eyes were unsure.

It was instantly plain what this was. She hated herself—of course he must think she was afraid of Guy, even afraid perhaps that she could not quite trust herself. None of this could be said—so like a child she reached for his lapel and tugged it:

"Well, let's forget the whole silly business, it's trivial. We'll stay. You're quite, quite right!"

He only said, though in fact as an answer or as a statement of bond between them:

"Smell."

They had come back past the great buttresses of the gray cathedral, past the huge city hall and nearly into their own Plaza Nueva, and now suddenly a new and overwhelming presence had fanned out on the air. Evening was falling, it was the hour of the *paseo* when after the hot afternoon the crowd strolled the cooling streets: and now, as if to sanctify that hour, an enormous perfume was spreading on the air, a scent as palpable as the hot sunlight earlier, the night scent of a thousand white flowers of orange blossom.

Among the palms, the climbing roses, the carnation beds,

102

this perfumed entreaty to the night added a final beauty to the wide marble plaza, to the gracious windows of their hotel now yellow with welcoming light.

The next day was the day before the great *Feria*.

They had agreed, over that celebratory manzanilla, to go to a bullfight that afternoon. The Owens had included themselves in the party—that had been inevitable. Olive Owen had at first refused, having always believed this to be cruel sport, but father and daughter had won her over, the one contending that one must see everything while one has the chance, the other complaining that she seldom had a chance to see anything. "Oh you wicked girl," Mrs. Owen had cried, "with your dad taking you on this trip. All the way to Australia too! Kangaroos you'll be seeing! What next!" Mr. Owen had said, "Let her be, Ma," and a light squabble had subsided. Molly cared not at all for the opinions of either of them, she was only once more put in the place of an adolescent, she wished both of them were a thousand miles away and this filled her with grim, secret decision.

But before lunch Prescott took his wife and Louise and Michael alone along Mendez Nuñez to another hotel for an *apéritif*. Their own had been an international affair from the 'eighties—it was furnished above the tiled floor with padded leather sofas, mahogany writing desks, big brass cuspidors, heavily framed photographs of past royalties descending from carriages or later from upright early motor-cars.

But this was very different—here the southern romance had been left pure. Wide enclosed patios were faïenced with flashing *azulejos*, one sat in an arbor of small palms, plantains, and roses: large oil jars stood about the tiles, a coolness of pottery standing on pottery: black bulls' heads glazed reproach from the walls: a fountain played—but just inside from the mosaic patio there lay in deeper shadow a fashionable bar.

103

The tables were crowded. This was a meeting place of the high world of Seville, Lisbon, and Madrid. It was a smart crowd, nonentitous and chic. Coming in from the patio, one heard the high hum of a cocktail party—a claustrophobic sound from which it is strange that more approaching feet do not turn away. And it was like a cocktail party inside. Among glasses and biscuits and olives these elegant people moved from table to table to exchange greetings; as many were thus always standing as sitting. But it was not too bad for these English visitors—they did not have to stand, there was no host to hustle them: instead they had the two positive pleasures of drink and the passing theater of people cleaned and dressed for show. And more—the noise, in a foreign language, was pleasantly unintelligible.

"Tomorrow," said Prescott, "they'll all be up in their little huts on the Prado, you won't see a soul here. A couple of lost foreigners perhaps."

"And the Owens," his wife murmured.

"What *are* we going to do about them?" she added.

"Do about them?" the Major said, pouring more sherry from the little bottles, tolerant. "They're not so bad. And they've got a boat to catch in two or three days."

"Two or three days! D'you know what that man said to me yesterday? 'I saw a lady this morning,' he said, 'with a first-class ebony crutch.'" She paused. "Only to keep the sun off, of course."

They all giggled. But Madeleine's tongue went on pouting: "Owen the Umbrella, indeed. The old man's a drunk, Molly's a sex maniac, and Mother's nearly off her rocker keeping the party clean."

"Molly? Nonsense!"

"Well who wouldn't be at her age?"

"Madeleine!"

"I mean it's natural. In its way. Trouble with Mum is she's so busy watching she hasn't noticed a thing."

104

And Michael said, probably simply to join in: "And who's Molly got her eye on now? Who's the lucky man?"

"Oh come, Michael," Louise said quickly, "it should be pretty obvious."

Too late he remembered, "Oh of course!" There was an awkward pause. Guy might have been sitting there himself.

So Michael tried sententiously:

"The trouble with the Owens is that most of the time they behave like a perfectly ordinary middle-class family. Then, like many other eccentrics, they suddenly catch you below the belt. . . ."

But Prescott rose, once more feeling he must make a show of being the man in charge, once more having to combat Guy's presence.

"Never a truer word. Now if we don't get along, and get something else below our belts"—he twinkled mischievously at this—"we'll miss the bulls."

As they walked out of the hotel there passed against the sun-creamed white of houses opposite a posse of a dozen riders coming in from the outlying ranches. All the men sat erect in short jackets, gray or brown, their leather trousers stretched out in long stirrups; the women mostly in black rode sidesaddle, a red carnation tucked down by one ear, small round casques tilted on their brilliant black hair; the horses were magnificently curried, they trod with fine dignity the tramlines: it was a most graceful sight. And this was occurring throughout Seville. All day long riders would be riding in for the Fair, all around from the big outlying bull ranches and from cattle farms and farms of corn and sugar and olive—from all points across the baked plains and the new-green fields a momentum was gathering, it could be sensed in the air.

They lunched off baked eggs and roast kid, along with the wines and great glasses of orange juice. No one knew that above their heads, in a bedroom on the first floor, a young man who had overnight flown in from Madrid, where he had just killed two bulls, was kneeling before his dressing table and praying to the Holy Virgin. The dressing table, like others all over Spain, had been made for the moment into an altar. Candles, an effigy, and photographs stood upon it. The big cigar-smoking men, promoters and *aficionados,* who had sat watching him pull on the pink stockings and lace the tight gold-embroidered trousers, had now left him to his prayer. Earlier the young man had constantly watched the window for any changes in weather or wind, scanning the sky like a naval lieutenant. But now he was alone, on his knees, murmuring to the dressing table.

They chanced to see him later, as they were leaving the hotel for the fight. In the full gold and rose of a matador he hurried through the small crowd of porters into his waiting car. This was a dark Hispano-Suiza of enormous proportion, a huge high square-cut wagon as big and black as a hearse. The roof was packed with capes and sword cases. Inside a number of grave brown faces peered from the shadows—the assistants. The slender young man slipped in among these, the door closed, and the hearse drew swiftly off.

A stream of people on foot marched in a southerly direction toward the Guadalquivir, a crowd already elated, all arguing points of the *corrida* to come, laughing and strutting, blood already roused in anticipation of the tonic ritual as yet unplayed. The Prescott party followed, at first walking awkwardly among so much ferocious grace but finally infected by it. By the time they reached the bull ring Michael was able to fight as hard as Prescott, who was an old hand, for the small hired leather cushions.

They had good seats in the shade a few rows above the barrier and the sand. That wide circle of yellow sand stared up emptily, in its emptiness the more apprehensive of things to come. A high restless murmur and movement from the crowd accentuated this: and a band—brass and blue uniforms of the South—blared a rising *paso-doble* of military shape that filled the air with holiday, that echoed its bright brassy

106

chords out over all the glittering and expectant tiers, over newspapers and *gaseosa* sellers, over sombreros and cigar smoke and colored shawls and high mantillas and all bright dresses of the women, and up high to where the arena's roof curved against a sky of hard deep blue—but most of all downward over that wide and terrible emptiness of golden sand below.

That sand made a circle so wide and bare that you expected a giant to strut in. So that when at last the first fanfare was blown and the *alguaciles* entered they looked for a moment grotesquely small, lead figures of the nursery floor despite their horses and high-plumed hats. But the eyes grew accustomed, the illusion passed: and now the band played the grand march-in of *toreros* and horses—and all that glittering array of gold braid, color, capes, grotesque tall horses and caparisoned mules entered in its real proportion, with a brave and measured tread that seemed to fill the vast arena, provoked the air with a full flourish, asserted all the stern bravado of what ritual had to come.

Then suddenly, as the body of *toreros* retired, a greater sound than any before—the no-sound of abrupt breathless silence.

A dead, impossible moment of silence, so short that it might never have been, yet of astonishing presence and weight. . . .

A door at one end of the arena flung open and the bull crashed in, tossed, stopped dead, and stared.

The ring grew small. Its sharp black shape shook with power. All bulked shoulders and chest it stood with head raised inquiring with its curved horns this way, that. It was dazzled. It was fighting mad. Yet standing there, locomotive bulk gracefully poised on delicate hoofs like the tripping hoofs of a pony, it looked simply inquisitive, vaguely benevolent, an animal from a child's book startled but willing to join in the game.

But that bull was no bull of the buttercup fields—it was

107

bred for fighting, it was wicked and now its blood was up. And this its great defiant entrance was the zenith, as the moment of truth would later be to the matador, of its performance. Proud, defiant, blazing angry—a proved match for lions. Yet poised there in all its black wrath, tail switching like a wild snake, hoofs pawing, it looked in that great arena most of all just lonely, a lonely giant.

Like a slow vice the ritual of the fight closed around it. Gold-strutting *toreros* shouted their *"Euh! Euh!"* urging at it like a common mule. Capes of bold magenta whirled drawing it always nearer the heavy picadors on their gaunt horses. Then the first charge, the rearing horse buffeted through its armor, the first wound from the wedge-ended lance: the black bunch of muscles above the bull's great head streamed suddenly scarlet—and this curtain of fresh wet red blood blazed brighter than all other colors around the arena, all of the gold and yellow sand and blue sky and glitter: neck muscles torn, the great head hung lower.

A fanfare, the horses withdrew, a *banderillero* danced in. Close to the bull, running like an athlete he plunged his colored barbs into the black and bloody scruff of muscle: for a moment, arms extended straight above the head, long barbs poised, this man looked like a gold-armored warrior and poised for battle—before the swift plunge that left the hooks there hanging in the muscle to pull at each further move the bull might make.

And then—for time was short, in the prescribed few minutes the bull was learning all the time and soon would become too knowledgeable and dangerous—the matador's assistants withdrew leaving that one slender man alone in the ring with his weakening but ever more dangerous opponent.

The passes. Impeccable grace an inch from the slashing of horn, bravery of a religious kind, grave beauty. Yet this particular time not purely grave—for the matador fought in the Sevillian manner with an eye to the lyric, a virtuoso inventing flourishes and playing rather to the crowd. Down on a

108

knee before the bull: or calmly, but boastfully, turning his back to it. The crowd applauded, but gave no ovation: it was like the applause for a competent clown. Finally he killed the bull badly, using three swords.

The mules came jangling in and dragged out the black slack hoof-in-air carcass; the sand was raked over where blood had been and everyone sat back.

"Well—what do you think of it?" asked the Major, the old hand. He was careful to look apologetic.

They all began to speak at once, saying nothing definitely, all as yet unsure. Only Owen said nothing at all. He seemed to be disassociating himself altogether from the question, and kept glancing away up at the sky. Across the sky drifted several of the solitary, almost motionless clouds peculiar to Spain. Louise noticed his disquiet—and wondered whether those clouds had reminded him again of rain and his business of umbrellas. Men are easily distracted by concerns of their trade—engineers, farmers, umbrella-makers. Or was it that Mr. Owen simply wanted a drink?

The second bull was in the ring and the ritual began again. The peons started at it with their long capes, enticing it toward the picador seated heavy and fat on his tall thin horse— and Louise suddenly saw how, with their capes in front of them, these vaunted fighters looked a little like women with big aprons shooing at what should have been a goose: their black hats had the shape of bunned-up hair: and, heavens, now as they stood there she saw clearly how with breeches and silk stockings they looked also like footmen in livery, capes on arms like the cloaks of guests! A monstrous comparison—she clutched Michael's arm to tell him, and was still telling him, laughing, when the bull charged the horse, threw the picador, and got his horn in under the padding and into the horse's belly. Its entrails, freshly pink and blue, flowed out, and it sank to the ground.

They gasped, leaned forward, turned away in horror: then watched anxiously silent. But Owen stared fixedly at a cloud

109

high up and far away. The bull was distracted from the wounded horse and now followed the peons in the direction of the second horse waiting blindfolded across the arena. The fallen picador was up now, stamping his heavy padded boots. He looked at the horse, pulled at its bridle. The horse looked back at him with a soft, mildly surprised eye: it seemed to make no complaint, it seemed simply to have been caught unawares during some private business and could not quite understand what was now wanted. Lying there with its guts piled from its stomach, it might have been a mare disturbed with foal. But it soon knew what was wanted, three ring servants jumped the barrier and put their arms under its back and heaved. The picador heaved at the bridle, pulling its head hard. Wearily it stumbled with these helpful hands to its feet and stood. Passively, head bowed, it was led away. It walked stiffly, the splanchnic mess hanging down just off the ground and swinging to and fro. Pale-colored against all the glitter, this looked simply like something private, of the animal's own concern. It was impolite to watch.

Meanwhile the bull was charging the second horse, whose padding held firm. The *pica* descended and once more blood came pumping from the bull's back. It jetted in a good inch of thick fountain before splashing down the black hide.

"Excuse me—don't any of you please trouble—I'm going," came Owen's voice. He had dragged his eyes down from that cloud, glanced swiftly at the arena, and then kept them cast down among the seats where he was picking up his stick.

"You know," Prescott said, leaning toward him, "that was a fluke. The padding pretty near always holds."

Owen's big rubbery face looked almost apologetic, yet firm. "If it isn't the horses," he murmured, "then it's the bulls. And if it's not the bulls, then it's the men. I don't care for it. I am not a violent man."

Mrs. Owen's lips were pressed in their disapproval. "You're quite right, Dad. I'm coming with you."

"No, Mother, you stay with Molly. You might as well see

what it's all about. I'll see you back at the hotel." He shook his head and repeated, "You see, I'm simply not a violent man."

"Father was an objector during the first war," put in Mrs. Owen.

"Certainly, certainly." Major Prescott, who had not been, looked uncomfortable. Then he peered fiercely this way and that, seeing that all was right for Owen's passage along the row.

Mrs. Owen half-rose, disapproving but undecided: "Well, I don't know I'm sure . . ."

Molly was ashamed and bored by so much fuss. "Oh, do stay, Mother. Disturbing people," she said.

"Very well," said Mrs. Owen threateningly, "I will." She settled down again, arranging herself with all the complicated care of a stout middle-aged woman, and looked up just in time to see the bull sink slowly to the ground and roll over.

Photographs of bullfights look grimmer than the fight looks in the ring, the softening glitter of color is lost. A darkness seems to shadow them. And the photographers go close up— threats and tense anxieties stay set on the dark faces of the *toreros*, the heavy mass of the bull looks hairy against a gritty gray sand. But at the real ringside, however near one is, the affair is somehow minimized—the whole wide arena lies empty around, and beyond that there are the crowds and the sky to distract. There is no photograph frame to limit what action occurs. Color clothes the toughness. Even the bull's blood, a scarlet saddle on a black hide, may look unreal and beautiful. It is a spectacle, too, whose true values are artificial and can only be realized by education. It may be exciting, horrific, or beautiful without this: but it will not be true.

Much must be learned. It must be remembered that the bull weighs half a ton, and charges with the force of a steam engine: and that it is no ordinary bull, it is of a kind bred solely for fighting, and fighting is and always has been its

111

way of life. On the other side, when the *toreros* with their long capes look, as they did to Louise, whimsically like gilded fishwives in colored aprons—it must be known what risks they take: and every action of the matador himself is calculated to appear calm and elegant and the cumulative effect of this naturally tends to minimize the appearance of danger—unless the spectator can constantly remind himself of what really is happening. Quite apart from the varying risks of each pass, the original element of danger must be remembered. And each moment the bull is learning, it learns quickly the methods of its new strange enemy—with each mounting moment it becomes more dangerous.

So those six English watched as four bulls were killed and the penultimate fifth came into play. All watched with varying views, varying understanding. Major Prescott was used to it, long ago his first qualms had been assuaged by no intelligent effort of his own but simply by the habit of watching, and now he watched with a professional eye, he enjoyed it very much.

Mrs. Owen remained in principle disapproving. She had always been told to disapprove of this cruel sport, "they" had said this and "they" had said that. But in point of fact she quite enjoyed herself. She felt pleasantly flustered by the novelty of the scene, she enjoyed the company of these her new holiday acquaintances, she liked the whole "picnic" spirit of the sunny crowd, and she was of course interested in the dresses of the neighboring Spanish ladies.

Molly was simply bored. She had been excited by the first two fights, but the novelty had quickly worn off. She had had her eye on one of the matadors, but after inventing a few romantic encounters with him had used him up. In fact—she wanted action, this was her holiday and she wanted something to happen. She did not want to waste time sitting all the afternoon with her mother watching the same thing over and over again. She wanted something to happen to *her*, and she wanted Guy. She had also a lot to occupy her private

112

thoughts. Since the night of that ship's dance she could and did call herself "a woman." She thought of this tenderly, sometimes with a hard efficiency, but usually with a warmth of sentiment, a feeling mixed of wonder and despair—wonder that she had crossed a great bridge, despair that the old road was left behind. And then suddenly she would remember she was due to be unwell in less than two weeks, and a gulp of terror would grip her throat.

Madeleine Prescott was enjoying herself, she always enjoyed herself. It was an occasion: as a soldier's daughter and having spent her first married years as a soldier's wife she had grown used to blessing an occasion: it was the sweet of military life. However, at the moment she would dearly have liked one of her smart and red-lipped friends from London to chat to—Louise was not much use, too involved at present. Madeleine welcomed an occasion, but liked also to debunk it. She was one of those who stand at the side of the room in a group heady with private jokes—the naughty girls' corner. In her time, earlier, she might have been called "fast." At the moment plums kept rising to her mouth that would forever remain unspoken. As to the horses, she felt for them—she felt also a healthy impatience for idealizing without action: she knew well that the only hope for the horses was the growing popularity of *el fútbol,* which might finally kick bullfighting clean out of the ring. Every now and then Madeleine would wonder about her two children then on their way back to boarding school. Socks, she would think; socks?

Michael's mind had wandered automatically over the area, had compared it unfavorably with the eighteenth-century *maestranza* at Ronda—but that was enough of that: he was content to sit anywhere as long as Louise was at his side. He was still in a state of wonder. He was still astounded that Louise had accepted him. Now and again he would slyly study her: then would turn away, a kind of hopeless smile starting his lips, and almost shrug his shoulders. "Well," the shoulders said, "well I'm blowed." He could not help feeling like a small boy with an unhoped-for prize: yet at the same time like a most middle-aged man, now he had to think more seriously of income and houses and the other practical supports of life. So as to the wounded horse, his first feeling had been for Louise—would it have sickened her? When he saw that this was not so, that she had winced but soon looked back at the ring to watch equably another stage of the fight, he had relapsed into his own sensations: on the whole he considered that the horse would otherwise have been worked to death, and that this, objectively, was a fairly quick kind of slaughter.

Louise liked it all very much. But at that time she would have liked anything. She was in love and those in love taste a pantheist joy, the whole of life assumes an indiscriminate splendor: beauties are more beautiful, small comedies of the street more comic, tragedies more picturesque than tragic, less tragic because nothing can really shadow the time of joy. Thus it was less cold-bloodedly than too privately warm-bloodedly that she was able to pass over the episode of the wounded horse so easily. Its suffering was a long way away: all the world may love a lover, but no one is more merciless to the world. Thus she sat and reveled in the whole wide sun-lit scene. As a good-looking woman she attracted some attention from the male Spaniards sitting near—her blue eyes and delicate dark eyebrows were unusual. A fortnight before she would have been either pleased by or impatient of the long Spanish stare. But now she felt nothing. Her feelings were exactly innocent to all men but Michael: and so all men seemed innocent to her. She carried within herself a kind of sign that said SOLD.

Now the fifth bull was in the arena, and it was a big bull with long horns and a temper: what is called a brave bull. Facing it was the young matador whom they had watched leave their hotel, he who had prayed above them at luncheon. The *banderillas* were in, and the big beast stood hoofing the ground: occasionally belying its size, it gave a quiet high-pitched whinny. The young matador sauntered toward it, red *muleta* in hand. No one but those two in the whole wide glare of yellow sand.

They could have stood there, watching or ignoring each other, for a very long time. The bull had exhausted its first fury, its head was lowered by *pica* wounds, the *banderillas* hung now quiet. But this bull was not tired, it was instead dazed and growing more cunning, it was going to charge no one just now unless goaded. It was up to the matador to goad, lure, present himself for attack. He had to invite disaster, then avoid it. The danger must be of his own election: very different from the gladiator fighting for his life—he had to present voluntarily his life to death.

Now and again this young man, a gypsy from Toledo, presented his life. He stamped his foot impatiently to attract— he looked like a servant rebuking some great black dawdling child: and sometimes as he fluttered the red *muleta* he spoke to the bull—and then it seemed the words were strangely confidential, as though these two had a secret between them. And indeed they had. However, he made no great display of this: he fought recessively, gravely, classically, in the manner of his formal masters from further north. Now he developed an arrogant, thoughtful, perfect *faena*—three passes, and at such leisure, yet so close that when at last he walked away with his back to the panting bull he might have been some philosopher strolling from his books, so sad and wise he looked. And when the crowd's great ovation came, when the *olés* thundered the air and the air itself seemed to spark like hot *gaseosa*—he raised his head to the president's box and seemed not to accept the applause with a matador's pride or bravado but simply to be scanning with inward thought the sky. He was deep in the mystery.

When at last he took his sword and walked to the bull, the bull watched him closely, now waiting to see what this strange two-legged magician had left up his hated sleeve: the great head was down, the curved crescent of wide white horns, sharp and plinthed on a half-ton of muscle, moved slightly

115

from side to side, as if each horn itself were eyed and search-ing. The matador profiled, his thin silver blade raised and pointed, his neck arched forward as he peered down the glint-ing line to the place over and beyond the horns where, arcing across the dangerous points, he must bury his slender stroke of death.

The crowd stayed breathless quiet, the moment ballooned. Then, just as that matador raised himself on his toes and let his body follow across the horns to kill—the bull charged. The sword disappeared in one straight lunge into the heavy black mass—but at the exact same moment the horns tossed upward in a giant last stab, the matador was too close, it seemed he hung legs together over the bull, then the legs wid-ened as one horn took his chest and over he went to fall feet away crumpled on the sand.

The bull never looked to see what he had done. Tragically, pathetically he sank to his knees, slowly praying like a circus beast, then dripping one last cough of blood and tongue out pale against the black muzzle—toppled over and lay with legs stiff upward dead.

Both man and bull lay there for some seconds. Then the matador rose painfully to his feet and looked around. His sword was gone but his arm stayed proudly arched as if he still held it, and now his other arm raised itself to rest thoughtfully on his hip as he considered the beast there be-fore him. The transition was done, the man stood fertile with all the strength of blood and testicle he had killed. He turned and walked, now a little stiffly, a little wide-legged though always that costume suggests a bandiness, toward the barrier. His peons had run to him. He was not—his gestures said—hurt. But plainly he was bruised, shaken. Above all he had been lucky. Now he insisted on walking around the ring to take his ovation—no longer the philosopher but proud and smiling, his teeth set in his brown arrogant face like the set teeth of a leathern death's-head.

All around the crowd waved and stamped and howled and

116

drummed; threw hats, flowers, cigars, money, purses, into the ring—while Prescott translated to the others what all were arguing: *aguantando* or *recibiendo,* receiving, that he killed it receiving the bull's charge—though this indeed was by chance and a short charge. Yet it was a way of killing seldom now seen, it was a wonder. And indeed it must have been—on all the faces of that party of English, Mrs. Owen included, various excitement showed, their eyes were alive and it seemed they sat more upright and with straighter backs in the Spanish manner, something had been transferred to them either directly from the dark ritual down in the lonely arena or from the crowd itself reverberating an emotion far different from, far more profound than the enthusiasm of the ordinary audience of a sports event.

Then the fanfare sounded again, and the last bull charged in. But the shadows were lengthening, the crowd was emotionally spent; and indeed this last play, as if it drew a palpable deflation from the massed tired people, was slow and flat and mediocre. It was an anticlimax, an unfair flop.

But as soon as it was all over and the crowd began to move off the tiers, that mass excitement seemed to revive. Released physically, walking, strutting, there was now much to be talked of—they all went back in their minds to the best moments, relived them, and came swinging along the tiers and the passages as excitedly as ever, greeting friends, clapping backs, full of blood.

As with the others all jostled in that throng Louise passed under the exit arch, she not only felt that stirring of blood around her—but, in fact, saw blood. The doorway to the butchery stood wide open. Muscular men in bloodstained aprons and high rubber boots pulled at heavy chains raising heavy skinned hulks of red meat to hang: others hacked and sawed: all the walls were tapestried with a dribbling tonnage of stripped carcass from the brave dead dismembered giants: the floor was awash with blood and these butchers waded the viscose red in their big boots, while sadly, sadly islanded in

117

blood there rose with closed eyes the proud black decapitated head of one great bull—it might have been a head swimming blindly through a red lake, its body deep below the level of the floor.

Tiles, chains, blood, and that one head . . . Louise looked in with curiosity—yet she did not mind, she stood there calmly and she felt no flinch of horror. Nursing and childbirth are truer to a woman than lavender and the vapors—a woman can stay profoundly and unpitiably near to blood and torn flesh. Or perhaps that other dark air of mystery outside held the air so charged that such a butchery was neither pathetic nor horrible, simply a trivial adjunct?

They passed on and out. The forecourt of the Plaza and the quays beyond bristled with energy. A police officer of high rank sauntered his duty chewing a cigar—and there was more than fat and muscle emanant from the body beneath the tunic. A lady in full mantilla strode like burning ice to her car, within her cool brown skin and her long erect neck there burned a vehemence of eruption: and in the poorly dressed young man whom at that moment she passed, and who neither stepped back from her nor was expected to, and in whose sour black eyes a light now blazed—in this man too as in all others the muscle of contained vitality could almost physically be felt, a something Spanish and nothing else, a tough arrogance and a loving dignity baked hard in the hot air.

Way was casually made for dignitaries and their long cars pennanted with red and yellow, colors again of blood and sun: and for the rich from outlying ranches, who now stepped across to the line of horse carriages stretching as far as the eye could see. Many of these were drawn by five horses, a first chariot fan of three narrowing to two, all harnessed with brass and leathern glitter and festooned with bright-colored wreaths and tasseling. On the box sat the driver and companion, stiff-backed and short-jacketed in the ubiquitous Cordovan livery.

118

For some minutes they watched this gritty, tough, splendid scene and then they turned and left the bulls and the mud shine of the Guadalquivir to walk with the crowd back into the white streets, to the flowered elegance of the inner city and the palmy old Plaza Nueva where already that orange blossom was preparing its perfume for the nightly *paseo*.

Prescott said, "Who's for the Sanlucar?"

"What's that?"

"*Bodega*. Much favored by the bull boys."

"Anything for a drink," they said.

"I'm afraid I'll have to cry off," Mrs. Owen said. "I've simply got to go to the hotel and see how Dad is."

"Fat lot of Dad you'll find there," Molly growled. But nevertheless she followed her mother: if it was a bore to herd along with her mother, it was even worse sitting with these others out of her generation and so oddly cold, she had noticed, toward Guy. Besides, she could escape more easily from the family. And she knew Guy's hotel.

They walked on and around and in and out and finally found the big old black *bodega*. It was cool, the dark dazzled after the sun, it smelled of wood and wine. Prescott greeted the man behind the bar, shook hands with another standing close, ordered wine. They sat then and drank, surrounded by walls covered with posters of past *corridas* whose fierce colors had matured with the dust and nicotine of years into what seemed a blended wallpaper.

"I don't suppose you can really blame old Owen," Michael was saying.

Prescott shrugged. "It was unfortunate. It scarcely ever happens."

"It's pretty pathetic."

"The padding's more so."

"Yes, yes—this eternal 'decline of bullfighting' and so on. . . ."

"Well—what would you prefer, a goring and a pretty quick death or a bloodless bellyful—"

119

"Father!"

"—of torn ligaments? No blood for the audience, enduring pain for the horse. Eye service, nothing more."

"But the sawdust, the way they used to stitch 'em up . . . ?"

"Money-grubbing. Bad in the bull ring, bad in a sweatshop. Indefensible anywhere."

And then began one of those long indeterminate arguments on the interminable bullfighting subject.

The Spaniard whom Prescott had greeted came over and joined in. He apologized for his English, but spoke it well: yet as a Spaniard feeling any foreign tongue to be unserious, kept breaking back into Spanish. He was a long-faced leathery man, with strong downward grooves by his mouth and sad eyes: dressed in sober black, proudly polite. Occasionally one gold tooth flashed out like a jewel in the half-darkness— again like a flicker of the fire within.

A smell of oil fry rose from behind the bar—with each sherry came a little plate of octopus to be pecked with a toothpick. Among the vintage bullfight posters a modernist design from the 'twenties stared above their table—all sharpnesses and cubes, strangely Aztec, and with its *señoritas* incongruously Eton-cropped. Enormous thin-legged spiders had woven a dead web across it. Only the doorway was truly alive, a rectangle of bright light that made it difficult to see who entered—and thus it seemed all the more sudden when Owen's shape abruptly stood there, his rubber mouth already moving, his voice already thick with the first drinks:

"Just slipped out for a quickski while the Missus's at her ablutions—she said you might be here. How goes it?"

"Owen, this is my good friend *Señor* Echevarría. *Señor* Owen."

"Honored, I'm sure."

"*Señor* Echevarría is a Basque who prefers to bask in the sun of Jerez. He is an expert, as they say an *aficionado* of the bulls."

Owen's face fell: "Oh, the bulls," he said.

The Spaniard replied politely, thinking to interest him: "We were talking of the use of the *pica* . . ."

"*Pica?*" said Owen.

"Yes, you say—lance? The lance the horsemen use."

Owen's eyes fell: "Oh those horses . . ." he muttered. "Why can't they leave it to the toreador, at least that . . ."

"Ah!" smiled *Señor* Echevarría, holding up a finger. "Not toreador. *Torero,* you must say."

"You seem to know a lot," Owen said.

"One must know all to understand. For instance—you know what is the *muleta?*"

Owen frowned. The mention of the horses had irritated him. Suddenly he poked his face forward and shouted: "And what's a swedge?"

"Pardon—a sw . . . ?"

"And what's a muffle? That's got you. . . ."

The Spaniard laughed. "Ah—you're joking. . . ."

"No bloody fear," Owen grunted. "You expect me to know your infernal trade, I expect you to know mine. Tit for bloody tat. Simple as . . ."

Prescott broke in anxiously: "Come on, Owen—steady the Buffs!" And whispered to the Spaniard: "*Es un poco borracho.*"

Echevarría's gold tooth glittered amused. But he still faced Owen in polite attention.

"What's," thundered Owen, "what's . . . a . . . what's . . ."—he spread his hands out wide as if to invoke the greatest, the Deity—"what's a Rattan Partridge Crook, eh, what's *that?*"

Prescott's eyes were all over the place. He looked everywhere at once—yet anxiously caressed Echevarría's arm: "He makes umbrellas . . . you must excuse . . ." he whispered loudly, "umbrellas and walking sticks."

Echevarría's composure was perfect. He cocked an eyebrow and said quickly, easily: "Walking sticks? Then, sir, we have something in common."

Owen stopped and stared.

"What?" he spluttered.

The Spaniard shrugged and smiled. "What but a bull's— you call it pizzle?"

Instant reconciliation. Old rubber-mouth Owen, a kind man and weak, a heavy drinker drooling on very few drinks, instantly forgot the dead horses in reverence, he heard the Spaniard's word and clasped him by the shoulders in gratitude. "Good! *Bonza!* Bully for you—cripes, *bully,* not half-bad either, bully. . . ."

There was a general sigh of relief, Louise and Madeleine exchanged a thankful look, Michael went to the bar and ordered more wine. Then he quietly countermanded the glass meant for Owen.

In the next second Guy came in through the door.

"Hello, hello, hello! Heard you mention the old Lucar yesterday—"

"Filthy old Lucar," Owen was chanting at some pesetas in his hand. "Where's my bloody drink?"

"Evening, Lou," he said to Louise alone.

"Been to the bulls?" Prescott tried.

"I have. Martorell put up a wonderful show with his first. Christ, what a brave man."

"We were all talking about the horses—what do you think?"

Guy shrugged: "As usual, the horses. Me? I don't think. I go there, Major, as I think you do, to see the finest performance. The braver the better—God, I admire some of those fellows. But others . . ." he shrugged again, "I suppose some of them could do with a saddle and the weight of a picador to see what it felt like when Mr. *Toro* charges. . . ."

Señor Echevarría raised his dark eyes to the ceiling: "Horses, horses, horses! Always the English and the horses!" And then made, though still with a smile, the standard Spanish answer: "At least in Spain we do not ill-treat our children. Whereas . . ."

Guy interrupted sharply: "Whereas in England we provide our children with more than shrimps' heads from the gutter, we teach them to say more than 'give me a peseta' all day." Guy did not smile. He spoke as to an inferior.

The Spaniard smiled gravely: "A long question." Then brightened, "Still, I am glad to hear the *Señor* admires our Martorell—though personally I thought Medina the better—"

"I still prefer Martorell," Guy said shortly and turned away.

Echevarría's eyes, which had smiled through Owen's small importunity, darkened.

Michael, determined to treat Guy pleasantly, pointed to an empty chair between Louise and himself: "Come and sit down, Harrowby."

"Thanks," Guy smiled back. He seemed in good spirits this evening. His attitude to Echevarría had simply been an English boorishness to a bothersome foreigner. He seemed now simply to want to talk idly, pleasantly over a drink. He saw the bullfight posters from the 'twenties:

"My," he pointed to the Eton-cropped lady, "look at her!"

But just at that moment Owen's voice lurched over them, he was swinging a drink wide and high like a censer: "That's right—just go and sit between the happy couple!"

"Happy couple?"

Madeleine had been helping her husband with *Señor* Echevarría. Now she stamped around and cried: "Mr. Owen only means—"

But Dudley Owen was involved in what he would have called speechifying: "The Happy Couple," he chanted, "duly betrothed to Love, Honor, and Obey, on my left Miss Louise Whatsurname, and on my right Mr. Michael Whatsisnameforgodsake. . . ."

Guy sat up.

He looked around at them all: "What's that? Are you serious?"

Louise spoke levelly, looking not at him but at Michael: "Yes Guy. *Very* serious."

Guy swung his head around too fast toward Michael and gaped. He was for once put off his balance: "Good heavens!"

His hard powdered-looking face had gone whiter. He was shaken, but quickly regained himself.

"Well," he said.

"Well—congratulations," he added in an amused, too amused voice.

Michael's lips pressed a little closer. But he opened them to say "thank you" calmly and distinctly.

For a moment no one else said anything.

Then, in the silence, in the dark, beneath the posters, Guy began to chuckle. It began somewhere in the back of his nose, like a scraping of paper, then took deeper shape as it hit his throat, fell to his chest and began to shake him, so that he raised his head slowly as if the chuckle itself was lifting him and finally opened his mouth and let it all come out between those strong ingrowing teeth in a long, muted laugh. He shook inside with it, and then as it went on slowly raised his finger to point.

He pointed at the poster of modernist *señoritas*.

"That *is* the funniest thing, isn't it?"

Everyone knew he was not laughing at the poster—it was a deeply amused laugh, a laugh at some paradox that hardly could have happened and that never could be taken seriously.

He got up still laughing, screwing his eyes at the poster in some pretense of dissimulation—thus in fact the more insolent—and then turned abruptly to Owen.

"Molly, Mr. Owen—I really dropped in to ask—is she back at the hotel? We had a sort of arrangement to meet."

Owen had speared a fat prawn on a toothpick and was balancing it unsteadily toward his mouth. Thus suddenly addressed, he rocketed it with luck straight in, but took the

124

toothpick in as well. So now he could not speak but with the little wood spike successfully caught between teeth nodded to Guy, and toward the hotel:

"Mm. Mm. M-mm."

He had not realized what had just then transpired. Now in a haze he took Guy's arm, nodded to the others with the toothpick still in his mouth, had the presence of mind—and indeed the wish and the natural manners—to shake the Spaniard by the hand, and led Guy out through that rectangle of light. From the doorway Guy gave them all a careless salute of the hand: "See you soon!"

An awkward, astounded silence. Only Madeleine made a bloated noise under her breath: "Bloody swine."

"Well," Prescott said, "that's packed up that. Last we'll see of *that* fellow."

Madeleine's head jerked around at him and stared, her mouth dropped open in real astonishment, eyes peering to see whether the sound had been real, that this man was really her husband.

CHAPTER VI

The next day was the 18th of April, the first day of the great Sevillian Fair.

For five days and nights now the people of Seville and anyone else with the time and money to spare would live in a state of fiesta. Each morning a grand cavalcade of riders and carriages would grace the avenues of the Prado de San Sebastián, each afternoon a major bullfight would energize the Sevillian Plaza, each evening and through the night the whole city would crowd to the Prado and spill color and dance and sing among the countless fantastic tents. Not much sleep to be had during these days. Astonishing quantities of strong wine to be drunk. But riding upon digestions as leathern as their horses and drawing upon vitalities dark with sun the women and men of Seville show no sign of fatigue as the five days rise to their climax—they only regret the day it is over.

To the *Desfila,* the parade of horsemen and amazons, Louise and the rest went that opening day at noon.

It was stupendous. They had all been left a little depressed by the passage with Guy the day before. No one felt this deeply, its unpleasantness simply itched, and dulled the edge of things. But the extraordinary spectacle that now greeted them abruptly dispelled every anxiety, it was overwhelming.

Over the many acres of the San Sebastián Prado there had been set up a fantastic summer city of small open-fronted striped tents, the little houses, the *casetas.* Between these ran wide avenues decked with triumphal poles and banners, with wreaths and runners of green leaves and flags and paper lanterns: vistas reached further than the eye could see, the sudden-sprung fiesta town seemed endless: it was conceived on a huge scale, it was no Battle of Flowers for tourists, and now all these avenues and houses were filled with a moving, laughing, strutting, endazzling crowd of horses, carriages, and people in fiesta dress difficult to believe true in this half-measure century.

Every second woman wore a froth of wide flounced skirt that chased her close bodice like a loving dragon: every second man wore the short jacket, the sash, the high heels, and the broad-brimmed hat of Andalusia. They were not reviving a tradition, the tradition had never been dead. It was the time of fiesta—and the people simply made themselves beautiful as they knew how: the result was no succession of carnival shock, but instead a scene of beauty and elegance endless and joyful.

In strong sunshine, among so many flowers and streamers and flounces, white bright light seemed to froth and foam—

126

bright white everywhere caught the eye, white of skirt, of teeth, of rose, of canvas, of frilled paper everywhere blinding against the deeper bright colors and dark shapes of tents and men and shadow. Sometimes a bar tent scruffy with beer bottles, here and there a camera-bound tourist—but for once the beauty was so preponderant that these were scarcely noticed.

Each three-walled *caseta*—there would have been many hundreds of them—was open to the passing eye like an intimate stage. Each was furnished from the family home—so that one might contain elegancies from the eighteenth century, the next a grandfather clock and oleographs and horsehair, another a confection of wrought iron and guitars and bulls' heads. These rooms rose one against the other, no more than a jamb of canvas between—it might have been some orgiastic Ideal Homes Exhibition. Except that none was empty: in each sat and drank and ate members of the family who for five days now would make this their home: and who later would each play their music and dance the formal *sevillanas* throughout the night, each on their own stage, theater after theater for the public eye.

Along such astonishing avenues Louise and the others strolled and could say little else to each other but "Look!" No one had time to rest the eyes but was always pulled on. And yet all this was only a background—for it was the hour of the *Desfila*, and coursing slowly through the wide long avenues of this strange man-size doll's town passed a stronger condiment than all the rest, the parade of riders and carriages.

No more abundant and leisurely equestrian elegance remains in the world today. Round and round the mile of intersected avenues some hundreds of riders and carriages wound their walking way. Phaetons, brakes, landaus, and all others of strange and old design—all painted and varnished and brassed and polished as finely as the day they were made. Carriages of black lacquer piped with the colors

127

of a bull ranch, carriages of good-grained varnished wood, yellow carriages, and some of a dark and ducal blue, carriages with wheels scarlet-spoked and others trimmed with a flash of lemon, carriages curiously upright like coffins on wheels and carriages slung low and ranging like armchairs on the sway of deep-swinging springs. Yet none affectedly exotic, no sea shells nor carnival cars—all true carriages of the long dry Andalusian road. Drawn by brown, black, gray, dappled horses or ponies or mules, in teams of five with three leaders abreast like a fan, or by a smart-stepping pair of two; all curried and dressed and caparisoned with tasseling and flashing harness as proud as their drivers erect in livery above. And in among these carriages that passed in two thick streams this way and that along the avenues the taller life of the horsemen presided—always the man with his Cordovan hat, his blanket, his leather chaps, and short coat, often with a woman seated sideways behind him splaying out her wide frilled skirt like layers of foam over the horse's polished haunch: and the women riders too, the amazons, flower behind ear and curious round casque tilted forward over the eye, habited in braid and high white collar and for the most part riding an elegant sidesaddle.

So among flowers in sunlight this great procession passed to and fro, all exactly traditional, all on a splendid Spanish note of the gravely gay. It passed and repassed for the morning hours till time for the late luncheon; then Prescott led them to a large *caseta* owned by that same Echevarría they had met the day before, and where beneath the hot striped awning to a guttural Spanish twittering of a party of some thirty guests they were entertained—and again the abundance seemed not of these years, the generosity overwhelming—to a long, lively, indigestible meal.

At four o'clock Louise and Michael escaped. They walked out alone into the nearby park, the Maria Luisa. It was strangely silent after the jangling of cries and laughter, they walked into a green aqueous calm under tall overhanging

128

trees: as if they had dived from a crowded sun beach into some immense and shadowy rock pool.

"And all that splendor," Michael suddenly sobered was murmuring, "with hundreds half-starved across in Triana . . . how far? A few hundred yards away."

"Still . . ."

"Still?"

"I mean, if there have to be rich, that is, as things are— and they are, aren't they?" she was screwing up her eyes and stuttering, "—then it's best the money's splashed on something for everyone to see. . . ."

"Slap in their faces?"

"They love it!"

"The fed do. The fed up, no."

"I don't know—think of something similar, think of a London first night—the crowds just to watch the dresses and so on. It isn't envy, it's the dream, isn't it?"

"The moderately fed can dream. Otherwise the mind turns on the horse's full basin of oats and the empty plate for baby at home."

She looked up at him downcast. "You win. You must win."

"Yes—" he paused, "if I was given carte blanche to build the finest private palace I could imagine, what would I do?"

"Refuse," she commanded loudly.

"No, build it," he sighed. "Oh hell."

"Oh hell."

Walking on, he gestured with his free arm at the avenues of green about them. "At least this," he said, "is blameless— and very beautiful."

"Think of the cost of the fertilizers," she grunted.

He swung around on her: "You're a rotten damn bad fiancée—" and took her by the back of her neck and prodded her face about at the trees. "*This* is romance. Look at it while you can. Drink it in. Eat it up."

Then they saw he was asking her to eat up also a park ranger standing statuesque in brown and peacock uniform like an exotic tree himself and now watching the more rigid in amazement. For a moment they stared at him, then turned away in conspiring laughter and hurried on arm-in-arm down the beautiful avenue.

Indeed it was beautiful. It was a park of trees, very high trees of many kinds, tropical and temperate, palms and elms intermingled to make a great high green bower through which sometimes a high stream of sunlight fell like a white torch beam throwing into brilliance the white roses that had climbed to the very highest vaulting of green branches. So high these roses had climbed that it seemed they had been scattered in from some giant peddler above, they seemed to be climbing down rather than up. And thus again there were bright points of white everywhere, a whiteness of flowers scattering like stars up and down tranquil echoless halls of tapestried green. Birds sang far up in the heights; and sometimes the paths below turned their corners to reveal a blue Moorish garden, or a frock-coated statue blindly sleeping on its white marble chair.

Against this gracious tapestry Louise and Michael strolled arm-in-arm, more youthful than they were, exchanging the pleasantries, immanently dear but never to be repeated, of those in love. Then presently they grew serious and began to talk of what had not yet been discussed outside their minds, the future. How to live, and where.

They sat down at a table in a curious woodland café, all of whose oblong tables were set in single rows along an aisle among trees, and with seats to one side only, so that sitting side by side and all customers facing one way it felt like sitting in a wide, stationary tram that never moved upon the green forest beyond. There, to the taste of iced crushed oranges, to the occasional interruption of a beggar's brown-cupped hand, to the clapping of other commanding hands and the insistent song of birds above, they evoked in each other's eyes and on the weathered table top visions of a small flat in London, not too central but nearish, of a room with a drawing board and another with an electric cooker, of a *pied-à-terre* for the first years until a small house, home-designed, could be built against the beeches of a Buckinghamshire wood: while in front of their sylvan tram there strolled the dark-haired figures of Spain and a gold-toothed seller of balloons came to stand, his stick of colored orbs held high like a fisherman of festive moons in the priestly center of the aisle.

These moons were colored turquoise, sapphire, magenta, pink, and lemon. They shone against the sunless green, light seemed to breed inside them. And it was as these bobbed and sailed, a livid constellation of breathless fighting southern colors quickly wearying to the eye, that a situation endemic in the lives of the young in love occurred.

They were talking earnestly of the future flat and the way of life it would engender. Both, in many matters small and large, wanted to give way to the other. It was the opposite to the ordinary disagreement, it became a sort of Dutch auction of selfless argument. Louise wanted to leave the main room absolutely free for her husband's work; the husband would not hear of this, there was room for both and he could quite easily work with her there. The question of traveling occurred—Michael, she thought, should go away as and when he wanted, he must study abroad and they would not be able to afford expenses for both; he would not hear of it —there were libraries, he said. But I want to *help*, she said. And so on. Until Michael suddenly drew his hand across his brow and said wearily:

"Oh for heaven's sake, darling—you can sharpen my pencils."

She opened her eyes wide, astonished yet also seeming to feign it, shut her mouth tight then opened it:

"I beg your pardon?"

Again he had his hand to his brow. But tried to smile: "Sorry, I didn't mean—really I didn't. Must have been lunch. . . ."

131

Her eyes, still thus half-pretending surprise, were peering distantly about his face. But suddenly they alerted:

"Michael, your forehead!"

Where he had normally worn a sideways brush of hair, and because a day or two before they had played at plastering this straight back in the Spanish manner, there was now an angry new triangle of red sunburn.

"Your head—it looks awful," she said, brushing the hair back into place.

"It does ache a bit," he said. And she was busy soaking a handkerchief in iced orange juice and bathing cool the sun's flush.

So there they had had the first small row. And had made it up. And as happens at the beginning, but not later on in life, it brought them closer together; there was none of the estranged suspicion that follows a real quarrel, but instead a greater ease, a closer humanity between them.

They rose to go back to the hotel.

"And good-by to those balloons," they both said at once. And that was a shock, speaking at once—pleasant, ominous, now laughable.

Later the Prescotts came back from the bulls, tired but elated; and later still, having dined, they all returned to the *Feria* for the evening. Such a day of fresh impressions, and of overeating and of heat, might have demanded a quiet evening, but there was so strong an animation of fiesta in the air that no one felt the wish to rest, it was infectious and beyond all tiredness invigorating.

They walked up past the slumbering gray elephant of a cathedral, then around to where the enormous old tobacco factory plays its baroque opera of urns and pediments and columns, more a place of military splendor than a workhouse for Carmen, but then—as if that lady had indeed been properly invoked—ahead there blazed into being all the lights and lanterns and banners and wreaths of the fair, a

132

different land of color, a splendid erection of garish night that now flashed red, green, blue tinsel into the metal tramlines streaming toward it.

In through the great main archway draped with a hundred lemon lanterns—and then again the lines of *casetas,* now all brightly lit, each an illuminated theater, and now for the first time . . . music! Music everywhere. Each of those many *casetas* playing its own—and the discovery that this was a town of barrel organs, *caseta* after *caseta* churned its evocative metal music, a jangling lovable sound that elsewhere is dying lived again. And these played, over and over again, with the true Spanish genius for doing time and again the same thing yet enjoying it, the wistful descending music of the *seguidilla,* the formal fiesta dance. Where there was no mechanical piano an orchestra of stamping and clapping accompanied the hardly heard honey of a guitar and the lonely, loving, petulant rise and fall of a voice raised in *flamenco.* And far away to one side blared the old steam calliopes of a fun fair. Yet this vast ordination of music never seemed to clash. It was as if each little house was a separate funnel of sound, projecting only and exactly from the mouthpiece of its open front. Thus as they passed along through the crowded avenues there was always music but never too much: it seemed soaked up in the open air, drowned in so many people, and if stray strains and clappings and cries echoed out above the lanterns then they intermingled into a moving distant orchestration, like the sound of a fair heard over fields on a summer's night, of their own upper air.

As with the music, so with the dance. In every *caseta* the chairs had been cleared aside, and *seguidillas* or the wilder *gitana* dances filled the floor. Sometimes half a dozen girls in their graceful skirts stamped and rotated in unison, a minuet danced by colored snakes. Sometimes all sat on the chairs and clapped rhythm and cried their *olés* as a man with raised arms stamped his pattern of sensual wrath round a yielding, biting, swaying pillar of shawl and comb and silk that enclosed the never-seen brown body of his partner, his solo love. Sometimes the dancing paused and brass trays of manzanilla brought glasses for the lips that never seemed to cease their *olé*. Everywhere, everywhere *olé*—murmured, shouted, whispered, but never laughed. And in one tent owned by a local cycling club, a sullen young man played boogie-woogie on his whining, muddled accordion. But his adventure was drowned in the wide Andalusian sea of color and sound and grace and great energetic joy, of prawn munching and spitting and wine toasting, of stamping and clapping and singing, of furious swaggering and graceful greeting—of all this great fiesta crowd where beneath the lanterns and in the flare light nobody was drunk yet everybody drank, where nobody hurried yet all with dignity danced or strolled, where nobody was sick or fought, where the air vibrated with chained brown love yet none so much as kissed.

That infectious word, that *olé*, came helplessly to the lips of those four English, as they passed from *caseta* to *caseta*.

"*Olé!*" plopped the plum in Madeleine's lips as she watched a lean man stamp out a *zapateado*, arms raised above his head like two furious cobras, against what looked like a mild Victorian drawing room with plush-framed landscapes on the wall.

"*Olé!*" grunted Prescott as five girls swirled their white flounces—yet with his sideways eye and his ear on a black-shawled old woman carved from teak who was clapping out a rhythm in the next *caseta*, clapping correctly with three fingers of one hand into the cupped palm of the other. Quite correct, Prescott approved.

And *Olé! Olé!* those two newly engaged muttered, pulling at each other to see always something else, distracted in the colloquy of two that never rests and never really sees: but together, never quite losing each other.

However, later, quite suddenly, Louise did lose him. It was difficult to say how it happened. This was no carnival of rushing crowds, no sea of clowns to drown in. It was a sauntering affair, alive but not turbulent. Perhaps he was only a yard away, and others had momentarily strolled between, a barrier of color? Perhaps he had stopped a moment, waiting for the Prescotts to catch up? Whatever—she was suddenly alone, and so many people standing about or slowly moving or converging from group to group made it as difficult to search as in a crowd moving fast. So much color, and the strange angles of electric light and shadow, confused her further.

But it scarcely mattered. The avenues were set straight and met at clean right angles, it was not like being lost in a maze of alleys. She walked on, only vaguely searching: in the back of her mind was the reassurance that they would eventually meet—Prescott had suggested food in a distinctive place, the gypsy lines. She drifted, occasionally distracted—once by the vista of a green grass floor shining with so many crushed shellfish husks that the floor looked made of coral with the grass itself insurgent. She hesitated outside the Echevarrías' *caseta*, but did not like to intrude.

Then came a complication. Not only one but several men accosted her within a few minutes. In southern Spain a young woman seldom walks alone. If she does, she knows well that she must never let her eyes rest on a man: she knows she is there to be looked at—but she must not herself meet the watching eye, the technique of looking through and past has by tradition been perfected. But Louise's eyes, eyes of an inquisitive northerner, wandered easily everywhere. Naturally the men responded—with insistence. She began to hurry. Hurrying with no direction, searching now with lowered eyes.

Nevertheless she suddenly saw Guy and her heart instinctively jumped relief. Her lips opened to shout at this familiar beacon, "Gu . . ."—but then she remembered, caught herself, and hurried now hiding on. He had not seen her. He had been walking with Molly. That might mean the other Owens were about, she would have to avoid them too. She felt more than ever lost, it was all too complicated. She had a vision of Michael looking for her, following exactly in her tracks, blindly, forever pacing these avenues. She smiled. Then lost her temper and walked fast around the next square of streets and back down to the gypsy lines to wait.

And ran straight into Guy and Molly. It was darker here. Fogged with brazier smoke. Weaker lights. Darker forms everywhere. Many people seemed to speak to her at once.

"Why," Guy grunted, mouth full of meal cake, catching her arm. "Look who's here!"

"Hello Louise!" Molly cried, glad to be found with Guy now all hers.

"Le gusta? Señorito, Señorita," urged at her the love voice of a gypsy girl holding out smoking quoits of cake. And another tapped her arm, flashing eyes and teeth to come rather to her. She tried to grab herself away but Guy held on, his eyes peering quickly above her and around through the smoke-mist to make sure she was alone.

"Have one," he munched. "But what's up? New-boy deserted you already?"

"For God's sake, my arm . . . and *no,* they're coming directly."

Molly furrowed up her brow in line after line of mindless ecstasy: "Louise, isn't it all wonderful? It's too good to be true, that's what I say."

"You've lost 'em," Guy persisted. "I know that face."

"Please!"

"Ah, but I've been wanting a word alone with you."

"Señorita! Come!"

"Louise, they're *real* gypsies . . . look! Let her look, Guy."

"Molly, I want a word alone with Louise. Just you wait here a moment. Look at the pretty gypsies all you like."

"Oh!"

Molly even in the red brazier light seemed to go white— but she quickly recovered, pouting not to mind: "Go on then, you two. Don't be long though—I might be gone!"

Guy led Louise away muttering: "Too much to hope for. . . ." His grip on her arm was so strong, she had to go; to object would have meant a scene, among these shadowy forms of courtesy unthinkable.

Flares and brazier fires caught brightly at half a face, white teeth, the sudden full figure of a gypsy painted and jeweled and with the lick of black curl plastered by her brow. A light smoke hazed further what after the richnesses beyond was a darkly mysterious, eastern place.

"Now darling, do tell me all about it," Guy smiled down at her, eyes as easily possessive as ever, "don't tell me you're serious."

"I've told you I am. For God's sake let me go."

"But not with new-boy, you *can't* be. I know I deserve it—but really it's going a bit too far—"

"Can't you for God's sake *understand?*"

"Honestly, it's hardly fair on the chap, after all I suppose he's quite a decent—"

"Fair?"

"You might just have flirted about, had an affair even—"

"Guy, is it impossible for you to see that this—has—nothing—to—do—with—you?"

His eyes were wisely knowing:

"No rebound? No lady-play? No make-big-boy-jealous? Come off it." He hugged her again. "Come right off it—it's gone on long enough. Let's get together again."

They had come to the end of the alley. There was no further way to walk. Only a fence, and then darkness. She was tired of talking, it was impossible to go on giving the same answer. For a moment she stood there at this dark end and then quite slowly, as if it were the natural thing to do at the turning point of a walk, began to propel him back, purposely strolling. Guy let her, he was still talking.

". . . let's forget it all, we've been together a long time, we know each other so well—you know, Lou, I need you, I do need you very much. I know I've behaved badly, you're

137

damn right I have, and I'm sorry, I'm going to try and make it up. . . ."

His head was hanging over her as they walked, she knew his lips would never be closed as they spoke, always staying somehow half-open as though another voice spoke within his mouth, and his eyes like those lips would be set on her, munching at their leisure.

Beyond the ordinary words the voice was low and persuasive, she knew that tone and remembered how much at other times it had affected her . . . and suddenly some last resistance in her broke, she felt absolutely and finally tired. Too tired even to continue her pretended stroll, to get him back to the main *casetas*.

She stopped dead. "Guy," she said, looking up at him, her face suddenly blank, as if a pain held her somewhere inside, "I think I'm going to scream."

"What?"

"Let me go, quick. I'm going to . . ."

He let go her arm. He looked truly startled.

She pressed her chin into her neck—trying not to be sick, swallowing her scream?—and then looked up at him, her face white in the flare light, and with a queer weak twist to her lips said in a small voice:

"I'm sorry, Guy."

For a moment a real kindness softened his eyes:

"That's all right."

She swallowed, look around dazed. Clouds of frying fat rose blue against the dark green and red dress and the dark skin of a gold-bangled gypsy. No longer Spanish, now Hindu. Vaguely she saw—but without surprise—that the seller of colored balloons was there too. They bobbed and shone against the dark.

"I mean, you know, about screaming," she said. "Silly."

"I know."

"But the other . . ." she gestured a kind of shrug of the hand, ". . . that's fixed. I'm in love with him."

138

She turned and started to walk away.

Guy's hand went out to her arm, but paused. He looked simply puzzled. For the first time he must have realized that she was in earnest.

"But Lou . . ." his voice sounded, for him, appealing, nearly lost.

He hurried after her and began to speak quickly, urgently regaining himself:

"Darling, what am I going to do? How am I going to—"

A cry ahead. Michael's face welcoming, Madeleine waving, Prescott limping behind.

Michael hurried up and took her hand: "Where've you been? We wondered whatever had happened! What's—"

Then he saw Guy and stopped. "Oh. . . ."

Louise made a kind of half-sigh half-sob: "Michael, oh Michael . . ."

He laughed down at her: "Here, it's not as bad as that!" Then he frowned, looked up abruptly at Guy: "Or is it?"

Molly piped in: "Guy and I were just having these doughnut things and Louise found us, she'd been looking *everywhere* for you, and—"

Louise regained herself: "That's right, Michael. I'm sorry to be so silly. I just felt lost."

"Well, everything's fine then. We can move on," Prescott said, edging them away.

Guy stood curiously alone in all that crowd. "Yes," he said in a singsong voice, "everything's fine now you've got new-boy again."

No one answered. *Flamenco* from a near *caseta* seemed to swell up wailing all around them.

Then Prescott grunted: "Control yourself, Harrowby."

"Siding with new-boy against old friends, Major? What kind of a thing is that?"

"Oh Guy, be quiet," Louise said. And pulling Michael's arm: "Come on. Let's go."

Guy began to chuckle. To no one in particular, more to

139

himself as an inward thought, he said aloud, chanting and chuckling: "Louise Carey, Lu-lu Carey, Lindy Lou Carey—lovely."

"Oh come on," Louise said. "For God's sake."

Michael stood still. "No. Wait."

He freed his arm and walked up to Guy.

"Old Mother Louisa bloody Carey," Guy still chuckled. "Well—well."

Michael said levelly: "Listen, Harrowby. First, you're going to leave Louise alone. Absolutely and from now on. Secondly, you're going to keep that mouth shut. Understand?"

Guy smiled at him, a loving hungry smile.

"Mister Louise Carey," he said, nodding the words now openly as at a rhyme.

"Shut up!"

No voices had been raised.

No one passing noticed anything unusual in these two talking in a foreign language, one of them amiably smiling. The *flamenco* was crying high, the clapping seemed to quicken, the balloons bobbed turquoise and pink and lemon and sinful magenta against the sky, the gypsies in their smoke stood around like Hindu myths, gray circles beneath dark eyes, Indian muddiness of skins, smiles liquid and never Spanish. And Michael put his hand to his head, as if it ached—and snapped:

"Then I'll teach you."

Louise screamed, "For God's sake don't, he'll kill . . ."

But already Michael had swung at Guy's jaw, Guy had dodged, and then it was over before it hardly seemed to begin —dark low a vicious kick in the groin, wind punch, then a sledge hammer on the neck that knocked Michael's face clownishly sideways and dropped him like a puppet sprawled dead-still on the grass.

Standing over him Guy made two movements, both exactly at the same time—he put his bruised right hand up to his mouth and ground hard with his heel on the sprawled crutch beneath him. Then he turned and walked away. He walked with long strides not too fast, hurrying but not wishing to seem so—and then Prescott's stick came thrown wild and wide by his ear and he shot forward in a sprint, dodged around people, and was lost.

It had all happened too quickly. No one had time to intervene. Even then there might have played that instinct to leave two men to fight their quarrel themselves. Prescott alone had at last moved, and he for a soldier surprisingly slowly; but he was lame, unused to sudden movement—he had stumbled forward and too late thrown his stick circling at the back of Guy's head.

But now they were all gathered down around Michael's body. Louise raised his head, it slopped stupidly in her hands, and then undid his collar. The triangle of red at his parting showed like a bruise in the firelight. "He had a bad head," she kept repeating, ". . . he was ill. . . ."

A crowd had gathered and all were talking at once. Spanish rattled harsh and hard in argument. Then a short, compact, contained man pushed through saying he was a doctor. He bent down and sounded Michael. Prescott whispered in his ear where else to look, the doctor glanced up quickly and ordered the two women away, and then opened Michael's trousers.

His lips pursed, he looked around at Prescott and said softly: *"Ambulancia."*

Louise saw Prescott barge out of the crowd, muttering "ambulance" and in Spanish *"teléfono?"* to a man standing there. He was gone before she could ask him anything. She pushed through to the doctor: "What is it? Is he bad?" But the doctor did not understand. To placate her he simply placed his hand on her arm and nodded reassurance.

There was suddenly a commotion outside the ring of people who now no longer stared down at the body but talked and gestured loudly to each other. The body lay useless, disregarded. And now an angry gray-haired man stood there

141

with two children—a little boy in a gray cardboard sombrero, and a little girl dressed in a miniature Sevillian costume, hair piled up in neat black coils around a miniature comb, and who was now ruefully rubbing a big egg of a bruise on her forehead that seemed to grow larger every moment.

"Who threw that stick? Where is he who threw the stick?" the man kept shouting.

Those nearest him turned and explained all at once in high voices, while others consoled the child. The man still kept shouting. The little girl, till now fascinated by this new strange egg on her forehead, now broke into tears, so terrible did these big people make it seem.

"Why can't he stop? Why can't they move Michael?" Louise whispered. Then: "Poor sweet thing," and Madeleine hardly knew to whom she referred; she simply kept holding hard on Louise's arm, and thus they both stood above the body, waiting and unable to act.

A few yards away the gypsies were serving hot chocolate. Molly too stood some yards away, alone. Her eyes were still on the dark place where Guy had disappeared, she stood stock-still and her face shone with worship.

Now at last that angry father understood, but did not forgive.

"*Los extranjeros!*" he grunted. "Foreigners!" and spat. Then took his manikins one by each hand and walked away, less like a man with midgets than a wayward giant led by well-dressed adults.

The stretcher came, and with it the police. While Michael was being carried away, an officer began to question Prescott. Prescott opened his mouth and paused, perplexed. He looked hard at this police officer, at his taut gray uniform and his black-holstered revolver. His eyes shifted to the ground.

Loyalties take the strangest hold. Just as Carey had struck out at Guy with a "clean" left, automatically observing the educated decencies of civil combat—now Prescott found him-

142

self hesitating to put a personal acquaintance in the hands of the police. One would have thought, short of bursting a blood vessel, that pure disgust would have played strongly enough to give at least Guy's name and address. But no. Had Guy remained, Prescott might have tried to kill him with his own hands—and been near-killed as a result. But Guy had gone and here was this policeman. However disgusted he felt, Prescott felt a greater disgust in handing over a man who had once been a friend. He found it impossible. Friends, acquaintances can get away with a lot . . . with almost anything bar murder and large sums of money. By trading on "better feelings"? On the strange guerrilla impulse that protects against the legal forces of protection? But Prescott's impulse was simply that he should not be a sneak. Long ago his school had whipped into him strangely conflicting ideas—the rightness of authority and the rightness of banding against it. Even the masters and the prefects had despised a sneak. But so also, though they have to listen, do the police.

Thus on that distant Andalusian field the Major forbade himself to be a tattletale and stammered: "I don't know. A stranger. A drunk."

The officer took Prescott's name, and that, with its residue interrogation, suspicion, and supposition, was that.

At last he was free to leave with the others for the hospital. As they left they noticed Molly standing there alone. "You'll be all right? You'll go on home? Taxis are over there," Madeleine called, pointing.

Molly just nodded. A moment later a man from the crowd of onlookers smiled at her and gestured toward the *caseta* where chocolate was served. Molly looked away with deep scorn. For a moment she was almost Spanish. She was profoundly proud, from now on there was no man in the world but Guy, all others trash. Her judgment was at fault—but Molly in that moment was filled at last with something like an adult dignity.

In the taxi to the hospital there was silence. They were anxious, horrified, and ashamed. Louise put her hand on Prescott's, pressed it but still said nothing.

CHAPTER VII

HE next day at noon Molly was writing a letter when her mother, speaking to her dressing-wrap cord, drifted into the room. "Wicked thing," she cried, "what's come over you?" The cord had caught its tassel under the door.

Molly looked around scared, at that moment she had been engaged upon a matter now dangerous. Her hand grabbed out over the letter—but when she saw her mother struggling with the tassel, carefully paying out the cord, crouching like a fisherman with his line, she removed her hand and calmly closed the cover of her writing pad. She took up a hairbrush. She even moved clear away from the dressing table.

"Hello Mums, how's tricks?"

"She didn't have a very good night again, your poor ma. But there."

"It's the climate."

"It's your father," her mother said curtly. They exchanged a few more morning pleasantries, then Mrs. Owen gave her daughter a long sharp mother's look.

"*You've* been looking a bit peaky lately, dear. Feeling quite all right, love?"

"Right as rain, Mums. Whatever do you mean?"

"I only thought."

"But I look all right, don't I? Poo but it's hot."

"I don't know. It was just a little something about you."

"Old worry-guts."

144

"Were you out late last night, dear?"

Molly's voice instantly sharpened:

"And what if I was?"

The matter was an ordinary contention between them. Wisely, remembering that in any case this was a holiday, Mrs. Owen steered clear.

"Well you must tell us all about it later. Are you going out this morning?"

"I'm dashing straight off," Molly said, brushing hard at her hair, being suddenly busy so that her mother might leave, "to get those nylons before twelve when they shut."

"What, are they thinking of shutting then at that hour?" Mother soothed. And then: "Ah, my writing pad that I've been looking all over for."

It was indeed the mother's writing pad. And her hand had already grasped it. "I'll go along and get a line off to Auntie Frobisher."

A chill gripped in Molly. There inside was the half-written letter to Guy.

"Oh but Mums I'm just going to write. . . ."

"But you said you were going out!"

If she asked for her letter back her mother would open the pad and in a second read it, she knew her. If she snatched it herself it would look secretive, it would provoke a dangerous kind of fuss. And in the same instant her mind alerted by guilt remembered how writing on blotting paper can be read through mirrors, and it was a new pad with fresh blotting paper, her letter was imprinted there in permanence. She tried to be casual:

"Oh Mums, leave it for now. I'm going to write soon as I get back. I know, *I'll* start off the letter to Auntie Frobs."

"Now dear be quiet, your mother likes her own pad. You just ring down to the desk and tell them to send some notepaper up to you. Each to his own, you know."

"Oh Mums, *really.*"

She quickly went over in her mind what she had exactly

written, words that meant for her one thing, yet words she thankfully realized that gave nothing too much away. Something curdled inside her, she felt sick at the thought of her private words read by her mother—but even that was better than provoking by a fuss any larger meaning. Her heart was beating hard but she assumed instant nonchalance:

"Very well if you like, it couldn't matter less." Then she clattered up and down: "Now I must hurry!"

Mrs. Owen wandered out and along the passage to her own room, and there sat down with the pad at her dressing table. She then got up and looked all around for her pen, and then saw it right by the pad on the dressing table. She shook her head at herself: "Remember remember the fifth of November," she said.

Her mind filled itself with her sister, Agnes Frobisher. She saw Agnes sitting far away in Cardiff opening this letter from Sunny Spain. Then she saw Ag walking with the letter in her bag through the Castle Arcade, and then she began to wonder whether the green and cream wood there had been kept freshly painted, and how safe and cozy it had always seemed there under the glass—just like a rainy day always . . . *how* Father had loved it. . . .

Meanwhile her hand had opened the cover of the pad and Molly's letter lay right there before her eyes. But her eyes were far away, her pen poised thinking.

Yet a minute later she sighed and pulling herself together looked down. She was startled to see she had already started her letter.

"Whatever's coming over you? I don't know, really—"
Then she read:
"My darling darlingest,"
But however could I call Ag that?

And quite clearly she saw it was not her own writing but Molly's, of course, and alertly read on.

"I'm writing this in a hurry in case I can't see you at the hotel after last night. Guy, I'm afraid they'll stop me from
146

seeing you, but sweetest I *will*, all I want in the world is to be in your—"

There the letter broke off.

Mrs. Owen stared at it, all absent-mindness gone, but that mind now confused with a dozen new conflicting thoughts. Dear little Molly, her first love letter. Poor Molly, falling for such a man, besides he was too old for her. But me, for shame, sitting here reading her letter! Now I've done it— how can I pretend I haven't?—what should a mother do? And I don't like it, there's something about it, there's more than meets the eye. . . . "In your . . ."—surely Molly could not have . . . ? . . . no . . . but then, she's not really a little girl any longer. . . .

Mrs. Owen's face grew absent again with thought, her mind played with memories of her own first love letters. She remembered the boy distinctly, and then sensibly she brought herself back to Molly, carefully covered the letter up, rose, and went out to find her husband.

When Molly would come later to the bedroom she would say she had "dropped right off to sleep again, and poor Auntie Frobs would never get her letter"—and then give the child a chance to tear the letter off herself, as if it were unread—and meanwhile she would tell Dad to go along and have a serious word with Mr. Harrowby at his hotel. Much better than forbidding Molly, with all the bad feeling that would follow. Anyway, thank heavens they'd soon be aboard again for Australia.

By now it was nearly one o'clock, there was still an hour before the late Spanish luncheon but already Mr. Owen slightly swayed as he stood on the front step of the hotel. Three or four sherries had slipped his light head just across the intoxication line; and so he stood now in the hot shade of the portico feeling that all was well with the world—a barrel organ played the ceaseless *seguidilla* beneath the nearest of the great palms, three enormous motor coaches debouched a crowd of interesting newcomers from Portugal, and in his

147

hand he held a wire from London telling him that berths were booked in a ship passing through Gibraltar in three days' time. His mind moved with pleasure over the rattan sun blinds, like old brown mats, that hung down over nearby balconies. He liked this preoccupation with shade. It was a side line compared with rain: but one could see possibilities. All his working life, when normal people prayed for fine weather, he had prayed for bad: when others greeted each other with "Fine morning again," he had only truly smiled when the world was wet with rain. So this, in more senses than one, was a holiday.

Mrs. Owen found him thus smiling and swaying. He waved the cable at her and sang out that everything was right as rain. It was a family joke. But Mrs. Owen was in no mood, she clicked her tongue at him and went straight on to explain this new concern about Molly.

Owen's whole face darkened, furrows scowled deep clefts around his rubbery mouth. An hour before he had met a weary Prescott in the lounge and had heard all about the previous night's episode: and how Carey lay seriously injured in a hospital. Owen had been brought up in a tough part of the country, in the streets of Cardiff; he knew the worst of street-gang fighting, and he had always hated it. He heard about Guy with loathing. Moreover, Guy had borrowed five pounds' worth of pesetas from him the previous afternoon —on some plea of the cashier's office at his hotel being closed. He had not liked Prescott's wearily sarcastic laugh at this. But with his morning sherry he had already forgotten about it. Now he remembered.

His wife was saying: "So I think if you don't mind, Dad, you ought to go along and have a word with him." And then added, unsure of his condition: "Perhaps after your dinner."

Owen thumped the cablegram into his pocket. "By all that's holy, Ma, I'll see the bugger now!"

"Oh, Dudley, not before . . ."

His mouth went hard. His jaw stiffened, and a worried

148

look took his eyes: "You haven't heard all, Ma. That chap's a bad lot."

He walked straight off toward where Guy's hotel was, only once calling over his shoulder, "See you at dinner. Two sharp!"

The pavement along the noon-busy street was narrow, he kept having to step off to let others pass, and a small old lady followed him all the way whispering behind him: "*Señorito, Señorito.*" He stopped and gave her two peseta pieces. It was frustrating, he wanted to be carried straight on by the momentum of his anger. The sunlight was hot, white, hard. The need for a drink came, he crossed the street to a big busy bar and ordered two sherries. My Molly, he kept saying to himself as the warmth rose. "Two more," he said to the man chalking the price on the bar. He stood there, drinking now more slowly, staring at two A1 sauce bottles, bright exotics to the bartender, that had been placed decoratively one at either end of a fine long row of liquor flasks, feeling a true pity for Molly and a stern wish bred less of anger than a desire to wash his hands of Guy, as if he were simply unclean. Owen was truly pacific in his nature, and as such it never occurred to him that Guy, though so violent on the previous night, would harm him. He felt so instinctively his right that he did not even bother to foresee his opening words. He ordered one more to be on the safe side—but only one as a measure of discipline—and left.

The man at the hotel desk thought that *Señor* Harrowby was in. He went upstairs to find out. Owen was left in the dark vestibule among cane chairs and a smell of dusty leaves. He began to feel thirsty, but calmed himself. The man came down and said: "No, he is out."

But then Guy's face came over the banisters of the little stair well—he must have come quietly out to see who it was— and called out:

"It's only you, Mr. Owen? Come up."

Owen murmured his thanks and, unsmiling, climbed the

dark stairs. But Guy's room was suddenly sunlit, he stood blinking at the unmade bed and coughed.

"And to what do we owe this exceptional pleasure?" Guy was smiling. And then his eyes darkened amusedly: "Surely not to collect on our little loan? So soon?"

"No," Owen said, blinking to focus in the bright light on the man before him. Guy wore only his pajama trousers, there was a straggle of colorless hair on his chest and beneath his armpits, and this gave the crushed sheets a further intimacy. As with all small morning bedrooms it was like entering the lair of an animal. It should have smelled, but it did not. "No, not that at all," Owen repeated.

Guy had a cigarette in his mouth and let this flop down as he raised one eyebrow, staring then in question and saying nothing. Owen's expression was by now quite clear to him.

"To cut a long story short, Harrowby—"

"Yesterday you called me Guy."

"I'll not beat about the bush. I've come to see you about my daughter."

"Molly?"

"I don't want you to see her again, Harrowby."

Guy sprawled back on the bed, lolling easily against the crushed pillow. He put his hands behind his head, those armpit tufts stuck out obtrusively, he smoked his cigarette not moving it from his mouth, the ash falling. Meanwhile Owen was left standing in the middle of the room.

"But Owen—why? I'm very fond of little Molly. A bit."

"You'll not see her again and that's flat."

Guy smiled: "Aren't you being a little severe?" He peered suddenly hard at Owen, and gestured to a bottle on the washstand. "And won't you join me in a little drink? Fundador—good sherry brandy?"

Owen's throat in that sun-dried room rasped dry, his alcoholic veins ached. His eyes glanced automatically over at the bottle—but he got them back sternly to where Guy lay. He felt affronted by this sprawling nudity. He despised it, and

150

stiffened his muscles the more firmly within his clothes. But at the same time he felt vaguely like an inferior in front of some master at ease.

He said firmly: "I've just heard about last night—"

"Oh—that. . . . And did you hear that he hit at me first?"

"You've put that boy in the hospital, Harrowby."

"A lesson."

"You didn't fight clean. And I doubt you live clean. My God, if I were your age again, I'd . . ."

Guy gave a great sigh: "Yes, you'd knock the lights out of me. Really, Owen, you're getting rather tedious."

"Young man, I'd be careful what you—"

"Besides, your daughter's over twenty-one. Old enough to look after herself, I believe."

"I don't care tuppence what you—"

"In fact a lot more able to look after herself than you are." Guy threw down his cigarette and raised his voice impatiently. "Look at you, you old soak."

"What's that?"

"You poor old drunk—you can't even look after yourself, let alone the girl. Who the hell do you think you are, laying down the bloody law? When have you bothered to keep an eye on your innocent little daughter? You can't see straight in any case."

Owen choked. His worn blotched face surged with red, his eyes behind their water seemed dully to blaze, but he could only stammer: "You . . . you . . ."

"Look at your fat soaker's potbelly! Christ, I can smell your breath from here. You stupid old man—for God's sake get out!"

The drink had indeed begun to rise in Owen's eyes. And he felt weak and ashamed. He stared hard away from Guy, anywhere away from Guy and the bottle of brandy on the washstand. At the table by his bed. And found himself look- ing at four long red candles. Candles? How could any man

151

have such candles? Why? His eyes went up to the ceiling, and saw not one but two electric bulbs. Then why?

Guy was carrying on: "Get out you old clown. . . ."

But why candles? Owen nervously put his hand in his jacket pocket. He felt the cable—and made the last attempt to have a last word. But his voice faltered:

"Well, I'll thank heavens above we're sailing Saturday."

"Mmm," Guy crowed at him mocking like a schoolboy.

"And that's the last you'll see of Molly, whether you like it or not—"

Guy laughed: "I don't like it all *that* much, Daddy dear."

Owen suddenly paled. A fear so far unspoken rose, he looked helplessly at Guy's hard chest, at his rumpled pajamas —and a lump came in his throat. He said in a pleading voice:

"What—what have you done to her?"

Guy was lighting another cigarette. He looked slowly up at Owen, thought a moment and said levelly: "Nothing that Molly didn't want herself."

"What do you mean? I don't know what you mean . . . I . . ."

"Oh nothing," Guy said suddenly impatient, tired of baiting a beaten figure. "Nothing at all. Now please be off."

Owen had hung his head, he could get nowhere with this man who only made fun of him, and turned without a further word toward the door.

But at the handle Guy's voice stopped him, an abruptly reasonable voice: "Wait."

Owen turned.

"What if I do promise not to see Molly again?"

Owen simply shook his head in question.

"W-what . . . ?"

"I mean, you know. One good turn deserves another. Fair's fair."

"I don't see . . ."

Guy said: "I mean, how much is it worth to you?"

Owen could not believe his ears: "You mean . . . ?"

152

"Sure. Cash. You need a pristine daughter, I need a few——"

But Owen had turned away in sudden new fury and slammed the door.

After a minute or two Guy went to the landing and called down to the man at the desk. "I am sorry," he said in slow polite English, "to have changed my mind after you had given your word to that gentleman that I was out. It was deplorable. I do beg your pardon."

The clerk looked up and without expression inclined his head. He had been very angry for the past quarter-hour.

"But in future," Guy said, "I will be out to everyone. Everyone. Understand?"

The clerk again inclined his head.

In the big dark lounge at their hotel Louise and Major Prescott sat in silence. There was nothing more just then to be said.

They had spent dawn at the hospital, the Spanish doctors had looked grave. They had returned in the morning: an English doctor staying in the hotel had been called—on a plea of language difficulties—and he had come out with more sustaining news. A matter mostly of rest, he said. There had been a slight concussion, and some bad bruising lower down. A lot of vomiting, but that was a natural consequence. The only thing that really worried him was the patient's state of mind. The man refused to speak a word to anyone apart from the doctors, and to them only answered very shortly the pertinent physical questions. "Of course he's had a bad shock," the English doctor said, "but I do wish he'd perk up a bit. Do all you can to cheer him up."

For two hours they had sat by him, trying hard but getting nowhere. He had simply stared at the white enamel bed end, his head propped forward on pillows like a man hanged: his eyes looked larger, and in their vacancy had seemed to be very slightly crossed.

Prescott tried leaving him alone with Louise; and then

153

vice versa, to see if a male confidence would do anything. Only one sign of recognition did he give—when Louise left the ward his eyes followed her and a brief sign of life, or of hurt, came to them: then they turned back to the white bars at his feet. Finally Louise came back and both of them just sat beside him talking to each other, talking of plans for the wedding, talking of the present trip and of anything. They had no success.

"The medico," Prescott said for the tenth time, "seemed to know what he was talking about. At any rate he's physically on the mend."

Louise looked sharply at him as if he had said it for the first time:

"I'm not going this afternoon. He may need sleep. He may not *want* people."

Silence again. Porters and black-coated reception staff moved to and fro by the brass-gleaming doorway: behind them the glass door revolved like a round mirror emitting against the sun and glare the dark likenesses of people.

The Major suddenly punched one hand into the palm of the other, his black-browed eyes blazed around the lounge:

"By heaven, if I was a few years younger I'd give our Mr. Guy a lesson! I've half a mind—"

"You've shown a very sensible restraint so far, it's the best thing."

The Major bent toward her and all over again enumerated his thoughts:

"And what exactly is the good of restraint? But then— what exactly can one do otherwise? The *Guardia*, of course —it goes against the grain, but I've half a mind—"

"Father dear, do stop having these half-minds, you were quite right not to," Louise said, lightly, impatiently.

The Major tapped with his stick on the tiles:

"But what else can you do? That's what I'd like to know. I could've gone round this morning and taken a poke at him. Satisfying. But he'd have put me in the hospital too—that

154

wouldn't have been very clever as I seem to be the male responsible for this trip of ours. What else? Hire a couple of thugs? Nonsense. The point is he's got us all around. *He* can use whatever tactics *he* likes—but us, we're left in the ridiculous position of protecting the fellow." The Major gave a forcibly loud tap on the tiles. A fat Portuguese passing gave them a sad look from eyes of thick oil.

"My God!" the Major said loudly, "I wish I'd got the fellow in England. . . ."

It is scarcely to be believed, but just then the Major had conceived the idea of getting together two or three of his more athletic ex-comrades-in-arms and kidnaping Guy, not to beat him up but to deposit him in some public fountain without his trousers on. Yes, the Major grimly dreamed of debagging the man.

Sunlight, paled and dusted from the glass dome above them, shed a conservatory light down on the cool tiles, the leather sofas, the big brass spittoons, and palms of that late morning lounge. Such a light reflected the watered-down sentiments of those two seated with their frustration. Unable to take action, with their anger thus weakened, their minds themselves took a kind of independent action and began to look all around the affair free-wheeling: so that finally both in a wayward moderation—though they would never have admitted it—thought less harshly of Guy's behavior. Moderation was the essence of Prescott's extraordinary impulse to debag him. Now he wound up by opening his hands and repeating: "What can you do with a chap like that?" One might have listened almost for a chuckle.

And within herself, from some most recessive layer of the mind, there came to Louise a feeling rather than an admitted picture of Guy's sudden onslaught—but now vaguely romanticized, so that it was really a sense of two men fighting alone beneath the southern sky and she herself standing there the pale prize. It did not last. She blacked it out and repeated:

"If only he would speak. He doesn't speak."

They went on sitting there.

That resident matador came in through the revolving doors and slipped quickly over to the elevator, followed by eyes and whispers of admiration; then was discreetly gone.

Less discreetly Owen entered. He was recovered: that is to say he was no longer shaken and sobered, but erect and stumbling. Several brandies had restored his fortitude. He came over saying:

"Well, I gave the bugger a piece of my mind."

"The—?"

"Harrowby—who else? Told him what I thought, the dirty skunk—"

Prescott looked at him and said wearily: "Very satisfying, I imagine. But do you suppose it will do much good?"

Owen's mouth half-opened. Only the brandy had boasted; he had been shaken, he was worried, and he said in a suddenly small voice:

"Nay, I don't suppose it will at that." Then he asked: "But how's the poor young fellow?"

"Not good."

Owen grunted. Then:

"He's been seeing too much of my Molly."

Louise kept very quiet, her heart beating hard.

"But we're sailing Thursday, so that'll be the last . . . ah, there they are."

Molly and her mother were coming out of the elevator. The elevator boy was taking the opportunity to practice his English: "Good morning, madam. Thank you. Okay," he said joyfully.

But the faces of these ladies never heard him, Olive Owen's more desperately anxious than ever, Molly's tight-lipped and serene. They had been having an intimate talk. Every hint of Mrs. Owen's had been denied: the denials had been so strong that now she knew.

"We're just talking of that Harrowby," Owen said straight

156

out as they came up. And to Molly, "There's been a fight. . . ."

Molly raised her eyebrows and sighed overwearily: "I know."

"You know?"

"I was there."

Owen lost his head. "Well I'll be . . . well you'll not see that fellow again, my girl!"

Molly raised her eyebrows further and said only: "Won't I, Father?"

Owen shouted: "And take heed what I say!"

"Shh, Dad," his wife said.

And Prescott, as was his self-elected task, once again had to intervene: "I think it's time we ate." And firmly he piloted them all to where food would calm their troubled minds—at least occupy from time to time their mouths.

In the hospital Michael Carey lay and watched the end of his bed.

While he still spoke to no one, a single voice spoke to him in his mind, one phrase and one only grumbled repeatedly at him as it had done ever since he had recovered consciousness. He had awaked as people whom he did not know were settling him into bed. Vaguely their voices came to him. Half-dreamed, airily distant the guttural Spanish came to him: "By God, I'd be sorry for the mother of his children."

And a voice had answered, it seemed crooning, high, high and far away: "Never to be . . . never to be."

These voices had said nothing more—whose were they, the stretcher-bearers'?—and he was left to the nurses. But the words went on echoing in the strange high roof of his waking mind. Only later, with the advent of pain and the doctor's examination, did the meaning come to earth.

As his mind became clearer, so did the implications. Pain gritted at him as the words grumbled round and round his brain, at times it rose to a razor agony—and then the mes-

157

sage rose also sharply intense, so that the very words seemed to take on the plastic form of letters and go tearing at the round dark dome inside his skull.

That pain made him want to cry out for confirmation: Is it so? Can it really be so, really, with *me* . . . ? But an extraordinary sense of shame kept his lips tight closed: for how could one ask such a question? The answer was too terrible to risk. His mind, almost delirious, knew that it might be delirious. But the memory stuck out so clear: and he suddenly found he could remember the long, dark hairs whorling in watery shape on a wrist that had smoothed his pillow. That proved he had been quite conscious.

So the hours, the white hours had passed. He lay alone with the white sheets, the passing white-coated doctors and the white-cowled nuns, the white enamel and the dark thought growing harder in the kernel of his brain. Once, alone with the English doctor, he had tried. In confidence he had screwed up a kind of casual tone and whispered: "Doctor, shall I— you know—be all right?"

The doctor, pleased at this show of interest and wishing to promote it, had replied in too suddenly a jovial tone:

"All right? Of course you'll be all right. All we want at the moment is a good week's rest. We'll be up in no time."

Carey simply did not believe him.

The doctor's cheerfulness only increased his certainty, he saw in it simply an exaggerated bedside manner, a deathbed jollity, the limp of the last smile. From then on he distrusted the doctor. His mind became obsessed, and his distrust expanded to cover and despise the whole world.

At times, though, another sense of shame came to him— but different and perhaps not so profound: at least he was able to try to battle with it. It first came to him by chance as he noticed a new long-spouted water jug that was brought in and set by the door of his ward. It was a white enamel jug edged with a thin blue line, a jug reminiscent of a sickroom at home. It may have been the mood of England that this ob-

158

ject provoked, or it may just have been the moment's abrupt distraction: but whatever it was, he suddenly began to think of Guy and the fight. And from then on, whenever he chanced to glance at the jug, his thoughts went to the man who had injured him so. It lifted him from his main depression, it gave him a certain strength. He felt ashamed that Guy had so easily knocked him up, but this time it was a shame of fury, he wanted to get out of bed and get at Guy and show him. It was not pain that impelled him, it was shame. Shame of his own failure, shame of the figure he had cut—but also shame of Guy's tactics. He was fiercely resentful, he wanted his revenge—he even felt a pleasurable taste on his tongue as he thought of what he might do. This was thoroughly unusual in a man of Carey's fair and placid character: as well as wounding his body, Guy had had his effect on his mind.

Though Carey was not naturally so placid. He was unduly sensitive and of too uneven a temperament: years before he had faced this, and in defense against himself had assumed a placidity that had in fact grown in on him. It was thus in essence artificial: so he had the fewer real resources with which to combat his present predicament. When he thought of Guy he grew murderously angry, when he thought of his own condition and of Louise he fell into deep and hopeless despair, and his two shames, and their confusion, occupied him absolutely.

But shame turns easily to disgust, to self-disgust, but also to disgust with the cause of shame. And this, since he was powerless to take action, was what overcame Carey. He lay weak and disgusted. From time to time he vomited physically. He was nauseated with himself, with Guy, with the way fate had left him physically finished. Once, in a rise of sudden anger, he threw a glass at the blue-rimmed water jug: it fell short, and the effort cut him with abrupt and awful pain. He sank back exhausted, weaker than ever.

Whenever now he thought of Louise, her own image and the image of their future together lay dreadfully separate.

159

That is, he imagined he was thinking of the future: in fact it was far worse, he was thinking of the past, and the future as seen from the past, and suffered the greater hopelessness of what might have been, of something now unattained forever. Whenever this came to him he could not help the tears. They came in great sobs, heaving at his chest. But the heaving hurt. He had even to cry quietly.

He refused to speak to her when she visited him; he could not bear it, he wanted to get back to his thoughts. Even they, in their terrible way, were a relief.

But later, on that first long day, he asked for a paper and pencil. He began to write a note. Yet stopped, unable to go on. He lay for a long time with the paper and pencil in his hands, one to each side, beaten and hopeless and lost.

That afternoon Louise went for a walk alone in the park. It was simply a question of waiting, there was nothing one could do. The Major, after offering to accompany her, had wandered off to the bulls. The only decisions taken were negative: not to go near the *Feria;* nor the hospital, which they now only telephoned, leaving messages to simulate attention. Robbed of the possibility of action, time hung more heavily.

The green rose-draped park was as beautiful as ever. It was midafternoon and empty, and wandering along paths coined with sunlight fallen from the high green leaves Louise felt the great consolation of gardens: her unhappiness became translated into an endurable melancholy.

Once she passed by the café where she and Michael had sat only a day before. She stood and looked down the green lane of tables, all now empty, and her sadness deepened. But with it came a sudden sense of inquietude. Why was that? Her mind puzzled, and in concentration destroyed the feeling itself. It would come back. She passed on.

Further along the path the trees thinned and a wide space opened to reveal a number of enormous brick buildings designed in exotic Moorish and Spanish styles: the palaces, she

160

brought to mind, of a great trade exhibition held many years before. They sat scattered about like a herd of giant gas stations and museums. But somewhere in the center a flock of white birds rose and fell, and toward these Louise walked. They were doves. A broad square of paving stones was their daily feeding place, and now a hundred of them fluttered and strutted and pecked surrounded by their equipage of seed-sellers, park rangers, official cameramen, and tourists.

At that moment a bald man in a glossy suit stood with his wife and three nestling children, doves squatted all over them, being photographed. One dove sat high on the father's bald pate like the eagle on a war lord's helmet. The camera clicked, and with a gust of giggles the group collapsed and the doves blew off in a cloud as though they themselves were laughter. And that was all. Nothing more happened. It was a lonely time, with few tourists; and a lonely sight among those huge shuttered buildings.

Yet as she stood and casually watched those doves pecking, some pale brown and almost pink, Louise saw that, in fact, much more was happening. In that peaceful struggle for existence at dove level—simple enough, but made to seem of great urgency by the bustling movements and hurry of the birds—tragedies occurred. One unhappy mother dragged behind her a crushed, half-laid egg: it was broken, still attached in some way to her, and while she pressed herself to go about the business of feeding, there seemed to be in her ruby eyes a weariness, as if this burden of both loss and attachment would never be forgotten. But how could emotion rule such predatory eyes of dark red? Louise told herself: Idiot. And looked away—and saw something even more disconcerting.

And up on the human level. Under the eyes of the park ranger, a figure of authority with his red-and-yellow cockade, the old men who sold dove seed plainly had to clear up empty paper packets dropped by their customers. There was an obvious hierarchy on those pavements—the lordly park ranger, the middle class of uniformed cameramen, and finally the poor, the seed-sellers. Now these old men sold seed not from bags but paper twists, and here and there over the pavement discarded white cones of these twists lay scattered. But a light breeze had sprung up: the cones had filled with air and now, among the doves, blew along like white clowns' hats. One man, very old and bent, had concentrated on one particular paper cone that strutted in spasms right away off the edge of the pavement. This man alone with his cone bent down to clutch it: but every time his fingers came near, the wind hurried the little paper clown further on. The old man straightened, followed, then racked his bent body down again: again the wind laughed and blew the cone a few cruel feet further on. This happened two, three, four times. Louise had a tragic vision of the old man following his dreadful little cone away down one of the long avenues forever. She could not bear it. She hurried over and easily picked up the piece of paper and handed it to the old man. The old man thanked her and glared: his pride was hurt.

She turned away and left the park. She walked home by the gardens called Las Delicias, a name that was famous and that had touched her for its beauty. But across the road and parallel ran a black steam railway track. Everything that afternoon turned sour: a secret eye in her heart found buses and chromium, ugliness and squalor, poverty and distrust where none had been before. Not a balanced view—that eye sought out the sores.

She returned to the hotel, hoping for a message from the hospital. There was none. There was still nothing to do. And there were several hours yet until dinner: mealtimes, though unenjoyed, are the only saviors for such a day, the only punctuations in the passage of the hours. So that without much reluctance, for there was little alternative but the faceless bedroom, she agreed to go with Madeleine and the Major to a café. Madeleine went out of her way to be cheerful; she felt that any lonely lowering of spirits would be bad, and besides she was bored herself. The Major had been to the bulls and

162

had seen some very good fighting. He had thoroughly enjoyed himself, but on leaving had remembered and felt irritated with himself for such high spirits: but now he was glad to see the two women in what he presumed was a more cheerful mood.

They sat at a large café on the Quiepo de Llano, opposite the cathedral. Madeleine chose it for its size and movement, passing crowds and the glitter of nearby shops might take them out of themselves. She also insisted on tall frosted cocktails, and almonds and cheese, not shellfish, and it was before these that the three of them sat and tried to talk of everything under the sun but Spain.

Despite these devices they remained in Seville. The pavements grew every moment more crowded at this time of the *paseo*, the shoe-cleaners flocked at them. In a few minutes the Major gave in: "My advice is to have a shine-up while the going's good." A shoe-cleaner squatted down—how eagerly, what life on an empty stomach!—and started to go around the three of them, brushing, flicking, rubbing the brown cleanser that hena-dyed his palms. Occasionally Louise looked down at his head bowed so vigorously before her and felt uncomfortable: but now she was too listless really to mind anything, and finally the effect, like a massage, was soothing.

Madeleine had taken from her bag an old Spanish phrase book and was chattering: ". . . after a bit one forgets the Spanish side. You just can't help reading on. The plots! Listen to this . . . it's called '*A Social Visit.*'"

With that plum on her tongue, her eyes wide with horror, she read with mounting excitement; hissing the final words of tortured melodrama:

> "It will soon be two o'clock.
> "It is almost two o'clock.
> "It is *nearly* two o'clock.
> "It is half-past five!
> "*Let us return home. . . .*"

163

"What on earth do you think they did? That stroke of conscience at the end. . . ."

The Major watched his wife and chuckled. He ordered more of those cocktails, and Louise smiled a little as Madeleine said hoarsely: "Madness *'At the Shoemaker's'!*"

> "They are too low!
> "They are too high!
> "They are too large!
> "They are too small!"

She paused, lowered her voice and said slowly:

> *"They fit me very well. . . ."*

She fluttered her eyelids dreamily: "What hands the man must have had." Prescott put his finger to his lips and pointed to the shoe-cleaner's head:

"Might be infectious," he said. And then handing the cheese plate: "Mousetrap anybody?"

The shoe-cleaner had by now got around to the Major. He had never risen, simply shifted around on his stool with the movement of those crippled beggars who creep the streets with legs dragging like flippers. Madeleine was going on, and now her voice rose higher than ever, she cried in abrupt horror: "But really! Listen to *'In the Suite'!*"

> "There is a knock!
> "Come in!
> "You are the chambermaid? What is your name?
> "Gertrude, sir.
> *"Please shut the door."*

"Well!" Madeleine gasped.

This time Louise laughed with her. She had listened half-amused to what had been said before—the laugh, the absurdity made her feel better. But now it was the Major who no more than smiled. He bared his teeth as if he had heard a knife blade drawn across glass.

164

"Sour-puss," Madeleine said.

"Just seen that bastard," Prescott grunted.

"Bast—?"

"Guy." He shifted angrily as if he wanted to get up, then subsided. "Best to ignore him."

They had all looked around automatically, and there was Guy standing in front of the next café along the street and obviously searching for someone.

"Don't expect he'll come near *us* in a hurry. Don't all gape."

Guy, careless as ever, hair tousled and hands slewing his jacket pockets, stood at ease roving his eye over the people ranged in front of him. His mouth at rest hung a little open. He stood with his loins jutted forward, resting back on his spine—a corner-boy attitude that might have been assumed, as he had assumed the habit of talking with a cigarette stuck to his lip, during his time in the ranks. He had the chameleon gift of some actors, and assumed such attitudes automatically.

He seemed to have digested that café and moved now toward theirs. Madeleine suddenly began to compliment the shoe-cleaner. That is, she raised her foot at him down there, and repeated nodding big smiles: *"Bueno! Muy bueno!"* The others glanced down, and she went on instantly to call attention to the stitching of her shoes and compared this unfavorably with Louise's. Louise disagreed. They argued. All heads in fact were bowed down to the ground, faces hidden, which was what Madeleine wanted.

But Guy was looking for them and of course he found them. He came straight up.

"I've been looking everywhere," he said. "I wanted to ask—"

The Major cut him short: "I don't think we need your company, sir."

Guy's face creased itself into an expression of apology: "I'm sorry to intrude. I wanted to see Louise. Lou, I want to

165

apologize to your Michael. Must have been out of my wits. But I don't know where he is. . . ."

Louise said nothing. She bit her lip and looked away. She began to breathe fast, her brooch rose and fell.

"He's not seeing anyone," the Major blurted, "least of all you. Now will you please leave us?"

Guy stood there and went on humbly:

"But really . . . I heard it was a hospital—I don't know which . . ."

The Major burst: "Get to hell away from here."

He clutched the table to rise, his jaw stuck out furiously— but the shoe-cleaner still gripped his foot. He spoke sharply down in Spanish.

Guy smiled: "Very well. If you can't be ordinarily civil . . . I can wait."

The next table was empty. He moved a step away and sat down at it. He sat facing them, amusement in his eyes, and drummed his fingers. Then called the waiter and ordered a beer.

Madeleine started on her shoes again. But now Louise could not speak, she was only able to hold herself steady. The Major paid the bill and motioned them to leave. They rose and went out into the crowd. None of them spoke a word.

At a café further on, well out of sight of the other, the Major stopped. "Damned if the fellow's going to spoil our cocktails!"—and rapped hard with his stick on the iron legs of the table. Waiters came running at the noise and the cocktails came quickly. Then Guy sauntered in and sat at a nearby table, smiling and still drumming his fingers. As soon as a chair nearer to them was empty he moved to it. He was perfectly at ease. He sat there chewing a toothpick, mouthing amusement.

It is a commonplace that adults at play like to behave, beneath some sort of grown-up veneer, as they did when children. Too often one can hear in their moans of mockery or their cries of delight straight echoes from the playground.

166

Unconscious attitudes—but now Guy was playing such a game consciously and in the provocative open. If he liked he could follow them all over Seville. He could herd them absurdly back to their hotel. He had the patience and the skin for it. He had adopted the role of the worst of all bullies, the bully of ridicule. And it worked. While Prescott sat in fuming silence, or speaking most forcedly only to drop into silence again, Guy sat at ease and smiled. However, tempers were rising.

An "icy indifference" is supposed to be a safeguard in this kind of a situation. But such an indifference is never cold inside—the effort is out of proportion to the bully's ease. Nor is wit, nor sarcasm nor irony of any help against a thick skin. There are only two defenses and both are attacks—one to play the ridicule back, the second simple violence. The first was unthinkable—they all felt too deeply. And with the second they were at the mercy of good manners: as moneyed people they had learned restraint—order goes with money, disorder runs away with it—and this was the stronger since they were visitors among a courteous and dignified people. By their virtues, in fact, they were made to feel foolish; while Guy in his aggression sat pretty.

But what can be done against a thick skin and a steady nerve? Right often becomes might, when you feel in the right you can strike successfully at a most formidable enemy; and best when that enemy feels in the wrong: Guy did not, and his personality was too strong and cold to bear down upon. The Major clenched his stick tight as if to hold it to earth. For once his eyes were still, they remained fixed on the table in front of him. Once he glanced at Louise, he saw that brooch at her throat moving fast, and it infuriated him. She sat bolt upright, and in this way with her arms to her sides somehow sacrificial, and that made it worse. He thought: "Hell, I'll put them in a cab home." And raised his glass to finish it—when he saw Louise suddenly grab forward at hers, and it was plainly not to drink.

The drumming of Guy's fingers had got into her brain, drumming up darkness more than sound, stifling her breath like hot dark wool. She no longer saw the yellow trams belling by, the *paseo* crowd, the gray cathedral beyond, but now only Guy's face as it had been a few minutes before, posing humility—an act she knew well from the past—and his face as it would be now if she dared to look—composed and mocking and goading, well known and hated. And because of all this she had these memories to bear as well as what for the others was unbearable and so she was the first to break. She caught up the glass and turned to Guy.

"Louise!" Prescott shouted. He shouted it loud and because she had not herself spoken what her mouth was even then opening for, he stayed her a second, she stopped in a moment still, hand raised and listening while he went on quickly: "Louise, I've got something to say, something important . . . here, listen to me. . . ."

He did not know what to say, he only knew he must go on speaking to hold her—but this effort itself broke what had been hypnotic. Suddenly he could think freely—and the answer instantly slid in with ease: Guy did not speak Spanish—then simply call the manager and tell him this stranger was annoying his women.

Still with his eyes on Louise he raised his hands and gave a loud clap, an explosion in good *flamenco* fashion. Waiters came hurrying. But also a passing policeman turned—and the Major changed his mind and went into action at the same time. He waved away the waiters with one hand, and with the other beckoned to the policeman. This was a lean brown *Guardia Civil*, black leather Bonaparte cap and field-green uniform, automatic rifle slung, cartridges and revolver at the belt—he came over frowning as the Major stood up to meet him.

Prescott spoke to him in rapid Spanish pointing at Guy. The *Guardia* looked sorrowfully at the Major, then bulled out his neck toughly turning toward Guy.

168

Guy had half-risen from the table. He was staring at Prescott astounded, "What the devil are you telling him?" he swore. He was plainly, righteously angry.

"Enough to settle *your* hash."

Guy stared astounded: "You mean you've told him about last night—?" The words came mouthed with slow indignation: he could not believe it.

But the *Guardia* was moving toward him speaking in Spanish. The *Guardia* knew this was a foreigner; he was not out to hold him, he was telling him to get himself away.

And Guy was already going. As the *Guardia* closed in he glanced around for escape, gave Prescott one last look now of derision—and went out fast through the tables.

Madeleine gave a shriek of joy. The *Guardia* looked annoyed, but the Major thanked him with full courtesy and saw him on his way.

"The righteous anger! The nerve of the fellow!" he chuckled as he sat down.

But Louise seemed still upset. "What did you tell him?" she said quietly.

"What? Oh, that he was a crazy English annoying you, that's all."

"Oh." Her relief was obvious.

The Major looked at her sharply: "Hey, who's side are *you* on?"

She smiled and said ashamed: "It's just that there's been so much trouble I'm glad there's no more."

Then they all felt a little better. The Major was pleased with himself and this communicated itself. A moment of triumph in this small affair overshadowed all that was still most seriously wrong.

As they left, the waiter asked for payment for Guy's beer. Prescott indignantly refused. Did he not see them fetch the *Guardia* for the man? But Louise managed quietly to put a note on the table without him seeing.

The mood of triumph was naturally as short-lived as it

169

was lightly conceived. Prescott was of the opinion that Guy was now "on the run," that he would surely leave Seville for good and all. That was something. But when they returned to the hotel there was still no message from the hospital. They telephoned and heard that the patient was no worse, but still seemed not to wish to speak to anyone.

They had a quiet dinner. From the street came the sounds of singing and clapping as groups of young people passed on their way to the *Feria*. A barrel organ stationed itself outside and played on the scented night air that same insistent *seguidilla*. The whole wide warm city was waking to a further life. The hotel gradually emptied. Louise hesitated at the door, then turned up to bed.

CHAPTER VIII

*O*N THE morning there was a telephone message.

"Mr. Carey would be grateful to see Miss Abbott, alone, this morning." And the address of the hospital.

This was the first the management had heard of their guest being detained in the hospital. They made polite inquiries. They were worried, particularly at this, the height of the *Feria* . . . the radiant pleasure on Louise's face reassured them.

She had been wandering about the lounges, now she went instantly upstairs to get her bag and some books for him— and as the elevator rose so did her spirits, that swift mechanical elevation matched exactly what she felt. At last action, at last release. A woman's patience under pain or at some defined task is a byword: but then patience itself is the action. But the last twenty-four hours had been no more than a vacuum, at every point Louise had simply had to contain herself.

170

Now all this restraint flooded free. She sang out loud in the taxi to the hospital. The day seemed absurdly fair. It was already hot, but she felt the air fresher, clearer—and the taxi went fast. The sun that usually soaked the old plaster walls seemed to sparkle: and she suddenly caught a breath of the north and of England. She saw in the sun's slanting spring light the slant of a September sun—it was the same angle of light, and there came a memory of freshness in the air, of September in England, when the season is neither summer nor autumn but mysteriously cleansed by a lighter, brighter air and a hint in the wind of frosts to come. She thought of paler skies and soft white English clouds, an airplane studding them like a small black clove and sending aerially down its windswept distant throb. Now all this beckoned from the future. Spain would soon be forgotten, Michael was getting better and the dark patch, Guy, was at last settled with. She felt life squared again, a hundred times magnified she felt the pleasure of parcels tied and sealed, she saw with love Michael's smile and in the cool taxi smiled with him.

"Michael!" she said, standing at the door of the ward. "*Dear*est!" And ran to him.

Michael raised his eyes, but never smiled. He was pale, he had been retching again. He waved his hand to a chair by the bed, and followed her with his eyes as she crossed the little room.

Louise sat down with the books on her lap: "Oh, it's so good to see you again . . . you did worry us when you kept so quiet."

Michael said nothing. His eyes were back on the bed end.

"The doctor says you're getting on fine. Did he tell you?"

Michael looked at her again, a long look of plain painful reproach.

"You're tired," she said, smoothing a hand on the sheets by his chest, "don't speak, darling, just let me talk. Look, I've brought you these to read."

"Louise," something like his voice suddenly said. It was

171

choked, it sounded like a voice through a telephone, instant but terribly separate.

"Darling? Yes?"

"Louise, I had to see you. I had to speak to you. I couldn't just write a note. . . ."

"A note?"

"Louise—I want you to go away."

"But Michael! I've just come, dear!"

"No, I want you—I mean—to go right away, away from Seville, Spain, I don't know . . ."

"And leave you here?" She gave a light nurse's laugh. "You must be out of your mind!"

He went on in the same tone, evenly, mechanically, pausing to review each word:

"I don't want to see you here again."

"Now darling, we wouldn't think of leaving."

"We? I mean you, Louise. It's difficult . . . I can't say . . . but—I don't want to see you . . ."

"Michael!"

". . . ever again."

"Ever? Darling, whatever are you saying?"

"It's all off, Louise."

"Michael—you're not quite well. . . ."

He suddenly urged himself up on an elbow: "I'm quite clear about this, Louise, I'm sorry. You see. I've been all wrong, I couldn't tell you before—but Louise, I—I don't want us to be married after all. . . ."

Quite abruptly his face crumpled, he turned it away to hide what tried to be tears. The sobbing hurt, he fell back on the pillow. "Go away now, please . . ." he whispered.

She watched him terrified. The morning sunlight shone fresh on the white sheet, the clean enamel. A cart creaked outside in the courtyard, the clatter of a pail echoed on the paving stones—yet inside in the white closed room everything tightened and the head turned away sobbing on the pillow had a greater presence of sound than all the wide

172

streets. She did not know what to do—to ring for a nurse? She did. But she said softly first:

"Michael, don't worry, you've had a bad turn. You're not yourself yet, darling. I'll go just now . . . you sleep, you'll wake up feeling—much—better. . . ."

Michael did not look around, she went quietly to the door and made signs to the nurse as to what had happened. She shook her head to show worry: the nurse only nodded and smiled.

She got down to the street again, shocked and hurt with pity for him. The pavements no longer sparkled, they were heavy with the weight of noon. She wandered along in white glare and black shadow, her mind scrambling with questions. If he was delirious, why should it take such a form? Did one speak the opposite to one's real wish in delirium, as dreams are said to go by opposites? Dreams and opposites— an old wives' tale? Her mind rambled on: delirium tremens, *in vino veritas*, truth coming up? Suddenly she remembered the Maria Luisa park, how they had had that quarrel in the arbor café, and the balloons that had appeared there and the balloons again where Guy had hit him. Could there be a connection—a coincidence deranged and grown large in his sick mind? She picked at any idea however wild. Then she found herself isolating all too clearly the little quarrel itself and wondering whether perhaps this had been the first evidence of something he was trying to say to her. . . . Had he really found himself mistaken about her? She walked along shutting such thoughts away, trying to feel instead a tenderness for his sick and troubled state.

But beyond all this, walking along that sunny street, walking she knew roughly toward the center and passing much that otherwise would have delighted her, she was left more than anything simply waiting again. As with Guy, so with Michael. About none of them could she do anything. The impulse was to turn about and shake Michael, to shout God-sent words that would jolt him out of whatever he was in.

173

Impossible. Nothing to be done. Simply face another dull, bright, endless day. The street was the street, the hospital the hospital, wherever she looked life went on and everyday usuality grated in like a curbstone not to be crossed. On a curbstone just ahead a carriage drew up, from it alighted a dwarf admiral in white uniform followed by several ladies in motherly black. A boy dressed in admiral's uniform for his confirmation. Gold braid and white silk and brown excited face, he stood there a moment in full command, his first, of the ladies who were commanding him. Louise scarcely noticed.

Back at the hotel she told the others nothing of what Michael had said. He was still very quiet, she said, perhaps a little delirious, certainly still shut up with his depression: he seemed to have wished to see her, and then not felt up to it. That was all. She lied—but it seemed unfair to repeat to others words spoken from a sick mind: it was not only senseless but disloyal.

She went to while away the afternoon in the Alcázar gardens. Wall and tile and flower and myrtle shut out the world. Only the high blue sky proclaimed an outer existence. Within the high outer walls, inner walls: then inner gardens within gardens, and others sunk within those. Fountains, courts, trees of feathered black and weeping green. It was paradisiacal, a Moorish beatitude, but as a paradise it weighed.

Also, it was empty. It should have suited Louise's mood. For a while, and certainly at first sight, it did. Its privacy was overwhelming. But exactly overwhelming it continued—such an immaculately proscribed place matched too closely the state of her mind itself. Within its walls there was planted a complex artifice—an artifice similarly began to seed itself within her. For when she had hidden from the others what Michael had said, instead of convincing herself further of it —as one may state a thing and convince one's own ear—the opposite had happened. By hiding it she had created something to hide. And so the possibility that Michael had meant

174

what he said took on presence, she wandered alone in those gardens with doubt taking root.

It was terribly still. The thick-growing plants weighted the air with scent, with smell of leaves. Against the sky a high black tree blazed its darkness, absolutely still against the blue, no tremor among the leaves. Between low squat palms and an iron grille a single pot stared its deep dark Arab blue, motionless in polish. In places there were set long tiled benches, beautifully worked in orange and blue and white tiling: these, so bright against the feathered green, began to take on a fearful stridence, they hit the eye like overcolored jazz patterns. So much in the heat so still—it seemed finally that not only was the city shut out beyond the walls but all moving air, as if the gardens were not real but etched in some fearful mirror stuff. Her mind saw Michael in his white room with its green afternoon light filtering through the jalousies: it grew unbearably hot in that room, and there too nothing moved.

She grew more and more restless, saw that this state of mind was no good, and left. Once more she found herself leaving a place of most peaceful beauty without regret, with almost dry disgust: and the noise of outside traffic, the cloppering of hoofs and the metal grinding of trams, sounded only welcome and relief.

She returned to the hotel and telephoned the doctor. His voice sounded oddly constrained, all the bedside cheerfulness gone. At first she blamed the wire, then heard the voice say that in future his patient would see no one at all. Was it the patient's own expressed wish? Yes—but as a doctor he himself wished it too. This morning's visit had for some reason proved a big upset. Physically he was on the mend—but these mental relapses were a nuisance. Whatever had happened—well, it had better not happen again. The doctor was sorry.

Later, before dinner, she got Prescott to use his Spanish on the hospital and find out whether there really was a message forbidding visitors. Prescott came back looking puzzled.

"Yes," he said, "he's not seeing anyone. But the funny thing is the way they say it—it's almost as if they suspect . . . as if they think we had something to do with it."

"Do with it? What?"

"Well, I suppose the fight. That we're responsible." He coughed uncomfortably: "No reason they should know any different, of course, but still . . ."

Louise felt her face whitening, the whole doomed day seemed to clutch at her stomach. A puffball of sun and black shadow and hot plaster had been rolling since the morning, gathering force throughout the day with her lie of omission, the silent comment of the Alcázar, and now this final authority echoing near but impersonal from the telephone instrument— as though the wall itself were watching and speaking.

"Louise—for God's sake what's the matter?"

Madeleine leaned forward and took her wrist.

"It's all right. Only I . . ."

Madeleine looked hard at her: "Lou—what *did* he say to you this morning?"

She looked up into Madeleine's eyes and saw their searching intuition. She had no defense. A small voice said from her:

"He—he said he didn't want to marry me. . . ."

And then she told them everything.

At the end Madeleine said calmly: "Quite absurd. He's delirious. He's sick. You mustn't—"

"But that's what I thought. That's why I didn't tell you. But now, after all this time—"

"Well, it's plain we must do something."

Major Prescott had listened with some embarrassment— he felt this was a matter for them alone—but now he coughed and started to get up:

"I'll rout that doctor out right away."

"No—please. . . ."

"Louise's right," Madeleine said quickly. "It'll do no good tonight. We'll see all about it in the morning. But definitely."

176

There was security in her voice, for a while Louise felt that something had been really settled. But that passed quickly, they were all simply faced with another long evening of waiting.

Except that a few minutes later Owen came across the lounge trailing all his family. He stumped across breezily, his mouth already working words before he got near:

"Here we are, here we are, *here* we are again!" he sang. "Here we are to be wished Godspeed."

"Yes, that's right," Olive Owen nodded beaming at his side. Molly stood saying nothing, trying to smile.

They were off early in the morning for Gibraltar. It was a welcome disturbance. Prescott was glad to have to get to his feet, and for a few minutes they all chatted about the journey, the ship, Australia. But then Owen suddenly clapped his hand to his forehead:

"But I'll be forgetting my own funeral next. I haven't asked . . . how's young Carey getting on? How's the patient?"

There was a moment's hesitation, an awkwardness, and then they assured him that Michael was doing as well as could be expected.

Only Molly stood saying nothing. Once she looked at Louise, their eyes met and she smiled. Perhaps this was simply because they were both the youngest there, perhaps some sort of understanding passed between them—for, in fact, Molly was exactly as unhappy, as frustrated as Louise. At a critical moment, at what seemed a turning point in her young life, she found herself helplessly in her parents' charge. They were going to Australia, she had no option but to go with them. Only a day ago, after hours of wild-beating thought, she had made a decision terrible for her who had never thought of such a thing before. She had decided to stay with Guy. She had decided to use her majority against any argument her parents might put up—or better, simply to leave Seville secretly. She had discussed none of this with Guy—but

177

the evening before with decision in heart, courage high and determined, she had gone to tell him. They had already fixed a meeting at a café behind Guy's hotel. But Guy had not turned up.

She had waited half an hour, her heart slowly dropping. She had gone around to his hotel. The porter had said he was out. She had left a note, a most urgent note, and returned fearfully to the café. By now the barman recognized her, put his own construction on a young woman out thus drinking alone, and greeted her with a too knowing eye—this too she had to withstand. She asked whether Guy had appeared, gesturing Guy's height and saying *"Ingles,"* and the barman had shaken his head. She waited another twenty minutes—then returned to the hotel. Before she spoke to the clerk she saw her note was gone. Yes, *Señor* Harrowby had been in and had gone out again. He had read the note? Before he answered her eye had glanced down at the floor—a crushed ball of paper lay there. Had Mr. Harrowby said where he was going? Certainly, to the *Feria.* He was with some other ladies and gentlemen.

Molly had made a further attempt to see him the next morning. She had been told again he was out. She had crossed the street, and waited guiltily in a doorway watching his window. She stood there for about ten minutes, saw him come to the window, stand for a moment looking up at the sky, puff once at a cigarette, then—it seemed at terrible leisure—recede into the room's upper darkness. She had crossed to the hotel again, assured the clerk she had just seen him. The clerk had simply repeated: *"Señor* Harrowby is not in."

She could do no more. She had left. She had gone to her room in tears. But after hours of thinking it over this way and that, she had concluded that somehow Guy was in trouble, or that some mysterious business matter—he was still in many ways a stranger to her—had made this behavior necessary. She came to this conclusion humbly, from an innocent belief in him—and kept to it at least because it was the

178

most comforting. She wrote him a long letter saying that whatever had happened she would understand: saying that she was helplessly without money and in her parents' hands, and that they were leaving the next day: saying that even if he came at the last moment she would stay with him: saying that though Australia was so far they would not stay there more than a few months, and what were a few months in a lifetime, and that anyhow she would always keep herself for him. Yes, even at her age, when a few months looked indeed like a lifetime, she was able to write that. And now she too had the dreadful evening to face, among a grief of scattered clothes and filling suitcases, hopelessly hoping.

While her father, boisterous and glad to be on his way, was making a farewell that would never end, going over and over each stage of the journey, reveling in it, while all the others nodded and laughed—it seemed they overlaughed, and why was that?—until finally he got to Australia itself and put the flat of his hand to his mouth and whooped, beside himself in error for an aborigine, like a redskin.

"Dad!" called Olive Owen in horror.

"Coo-ee" suddenly crooned Major Prescott, probably to put things right.

"Father!" Madeleine whispered.

Prescott looked awkward. But only for a second—for then abruptly Owen changed his tone, the skin around his eyes crinkled and their pale glaze softened and he extended a hand to Louise, bowing almost as if to kiss hers:

"And you, my dear," he said, winning and soft, "I wish you all happiness in your life you've got before."

"We all of us do," his wife said from her heart.

But this Molly could not join in—in the quiet that for some reason suddenly dropped, among a sudden awkwardness of eyes, she turned away to hide the dreadful mouth of tears that dragged at her.

It was never noticed. Louise was swallowing hard against the lump in her own throat. She found herself staring into

179

Owen's smiling eyes, and looked down unable to say a word. This was taken by Owen as a gesture of most charming modesty. He chuckled, archly put a finger to his lips and as if on tiptoe led his family away before Louise could find her voice of thanks.

However awful this had been, it had the effect of loosening the tension. They looked at each other and, a little painfully, managed a grin. "Cooee indeed!" Madeleine snorted.

But it also reminded Louise that the Prescotts were on holiday. She yawned and said how tired she was—but insisted that the others straighten up and go off to the *Feria*. None of this deceived Madeleine. But she agreed, no purpose would be served by sitting together gloomily, companionship is not always the help it is held to be. And what else was there to do?

Louise hardly slept, but she was up and by nine o'clock had left the hotel. It was not too early, the hospital's day would be well begun, and she entered and walked past the concierge's desk firmly ignoring him.

She was nearly successful: she was already at the stairs when the concierge called after her. There followed a difficult argument, neither knowing the other's language. But Louise persisted. She pointed to the ring on her finger, repeated and repeated Michael's name. The concierge grew weary of shaking his head, tried silence, found this too difficult and at length picked up the telephone. A long argument, a wait, and still holding the receiver he looked at her and again shook his head. Louise measured the distance to the stairs, drew in a breath to run for it. But then suddenly the man was saying "eh? . . . no? . . . eh?" in surprise and turned to ask her to wait again.

It seemed that above there had been an inquiry, a refusal, and now after whatever deliberation ensued, a change of mind.

Then suddenly the man turned and nodded. But now she climbed the stairs tensely apprehensive of what she had to say—an apprehension echoed by the bare corridors, the silent passing nuns, medical machines, and the light ominous smell of disinfectant.

Michael was propped sitting up more easily against his pillows, and looked altogether in better color and fresher. He gave her a smile as she stood hesitating a moment in the doorway.

"Come in, Louise."

But it was a smile of politeness, and passed like a cipher. Her Christian name, unendeared, sounded strangely impersonal. He had been writing on a pad of paper, and now put this aside with one hand and motioned her to a chair with the other—all composed gestures that showed he was better and in charge of himself. Despite some curious chill of formality, it gladdened her. So she kept what she had come to speak of for the moment and simply pleased said:

"Darling—you look so much better! You look *well* again."

"Yes. I'm straightening up a bit." He did not look at her, his eyes were fixed on the pad of paper he had put aside.

She laughed: "When I think of you yesterday—"

"Yesterday?"

He neither smiled nor looked at her. Pajamas and the white sheets wrapped him away and fixed him apart: she was simply a visitor with shoes and the breath of pavements. She felt all the sickroom visitor's unease—what to do, to sit on the little chair or walk about the too clean floor? Where to put the hands? To smoke?—and she bit her tongue to keep back what now, nervously, she could not help.

"Yesterday you said—you know, such things." She tried to smile it away easily, she reached for his hand. "Oh, Michael, you had a bit of a fever you know."

He slid his hand away from hers.

"But, you know, I had no fever."

"Now really, darling. . . ."

"I meant exactly all I said."

He twisted himself up a little on the pillows. A frown of

181

pain crossed his face, she leaned forward instinctively to help, shocked, not understanding. The morning sun had not yet come around to those windows, it was cool and bright in the little room, quiet and too fresh and clean for such words. But he went straight on.

"Louise," he said slowly, but still not looking at her, looking past her head to somewhere over at the white washbasin stand, "what I've got to say is very difficult. I was going to write. I thought it would be better. I was writing when you came in—but now you're here . . . well . . . I'd just better go ahead. . . ."

He turned his eyes to her, stared, then looked away again.

"You're not going to think much of this—"

"Michael, whatever . . . ?"

"But that can't be helped. So here it is. It's something I suppose I've found out here, perhaps something that got knocked clear in my head the other night. I told you yesterday that I wanted us to part. For good. Louise, I meant it. But I don't think I told you why. I suppose you thought me—well, out of my wits?"

He actually smiled. Then seemed to sneer the smile down and went on slowly, as if he were writing the words on that quiet, morning-fresh air:

"For all these last days, I mean all the days we've been in Seville, since Gibraltar, there's been something worrying me. There's been something wrong. I tried to avoid it. I didn't want to face it, even find out what it was. It was something that concerned you and me, and deeply. Well . . . now I've had—I suppose—the jolt I needed, and a few hours alone with myself to look the thing straight in the face. Louise, it's got to be faced—I asked you to marry me for all the wrong reasons. I wasn't in love with you."

He paused and then spoke louder, and quicker:

"You won't like this, but I've got to . . . you see, I was sorry for you. I wanted to help you."

"Michael!"

182

"No—please—it was something you had—a lost look, I don't know how to say it?—and knowing Harrowby had let you down . . . I wanted to help you, and anyway you swept me a little off my feet, and the business of being on that ship, things happen on the sea . . . all this taken together . . ."

She got up from the chair, she stood wanting almost to stamp her disbelief on that iodoform floor: "I don't believe you, you *couldn't*. . . ."

He stiffened his face and looked at her almost sourly: "It was pity."

She choked out at him: "You're mad, people don't do such—"

"Yes they do, and I was, if you like, mad. It was indefensible."

"For God's sake, Michael . . ."

"It's no use saying I'm sorry."

He stared at her with a sudden hopeless look: "Oh, my dear, I'm sorry, but there it is."

She picked up her bag and turned toward the door. The shock had passed, she was angry.

"I don't believe you."

The hardness was in his eyes again, and his lips moved into a bitter smile: it was almost as if he were finding a dark enjoyment in the taste of it.

"Well, there it is," he said, casually stretching.

She hesitated by the door, half-turned back, then opened it. Her shoulders seemed shrunk and slack.

She just said: "All right, Michael." And left.

She went straight home to find the English doctor.

The battered old taxi shook and shivered over the lines and cobbles, it seemed to lurch anger out of her. Her pride told her she ought to be angry—but still she could not quite believe it. It was preposterous . . . and through the window a sudden basket of pink crayfish, a cluster of palms, a wall of huge red-and-yellow bull posters all fused madly—on such foreign streets nothing could seem truly real.

The doctor was naturally surprised to see her. When she immediately said: "I've just been to see Michael Carey" he clicked his teeth with outright impatience—and was plainly going to lose his temper—but she went straight on to tell him what had happened, that Michael had broken off the engagement, and she spoke with such candor and urgency that he listened and said nothing. But when she finally asked him: "Doctor, what *is* wrong with him?" he still said nothing.

Or could say nothing new. He simply repeated the facts of the case. As she had seen, the patient was altogether much improved. But he added, with a curious glance at her, that never really had there been a reason to suspect any delirium. "It's only plain, too plain," he added, "that he was brooding over something. What that something was . . ." He shrugged his shoulders. Then suddenly began to ask her about their relations together. But this she could not bear, she answered shortly, and left.

She was more afraid of Madeleine, her confessor, than anyone else. She left a note at the hotel and spent the day wandering the back streets—untouchable, noxious, afraid to meet anyone.

But when in the evening she finally returned to the hotel, and found there the letter that Michael had been writing when she had disturbed him, a letter that in cold inked words restated exactly and clearly all he had said in the hospital, a letter whose first sentences were in pencil but whose bulk was in ink, so that he must have completed it systematically and at leisured consideration after she had left, a letter terribly of apology and one that ended with the word "Good-by"—when she found this she simply handed it to Madeleine and went upstairs to pack.

Much later she took a last look around at her bags set in the precise and irrevocable order of packing, the folded squares of clothes in their neatness final, and walked out onto the shallow balcony. There, for the last time, lay the wide old Plaza Nueva. Feathered palms and the baroque-roofed city hall showed black against pink light rising from commercial streets beyond, and from the even greater glow that fanned out across the indigo night sky from the distant, music-throbbing *Feria*. And all around rising with the scent of orange flower and freshening leaf there sounded the love cries of traffic, the plaintive horns hooting serenade and answer, the belling of trams warm with night blood, and the distant screech of tires as somewhere in the canyon of hidden streets a contact had been made: all swallowed in the hot heavy air, forlorn as any sound on the summer night.

But down in the quiet intimacy of the square, on the broad avenue that ran between her balcony and the first wall of palms, a bare electric light turned its neighboring tree acacia-green. And here beneath it a single carriage turned in the quietness, a dark open carriage with red wheels. It bore on each side the yellow flame of an oil lamp, and almost in silence its shadowy horse turned, lost itself in other shadows so that only a carriage with red wheels seemed to be turning by the light of old lamps beneath a strangely pale green tree. Nothing else. Once a figure a distance away crossed the wide cobbles, it moved slowly over that broad place. Then nothing. And slowly swaying, with a fading clopping of hoofs, the carriage moved off and was lost along the street.

Days of carriage and of promenade, long-ago days— Louise's heart in its own loss felt the passing of time, the tranquil age of this great old city stretched around her. Sadness discovers beauty, a saddened heart has time to feel. But as if these warm things touched her spine with a chill, she shuddered. And the next moment she was shuddering again —the moth-soft scents of the evening receded, she felt suddenly the Seville of great iron dredgers and its muddy slow river, of rotting slums and desert ruins in Triana, of tourist windows desecrating old Sierpes, of black locomotive smoke on the Delicias, of all the corrugated hardnesses her mind now exaggerated in hatred for the place. This city had brought her from the greatest happiness to the lowest misery and hu-

185

miliation. It was animate against her, she forced a superstition on it. Bitterly alive to the loveliness of its night, hating it and afraid, she banged the windows shut and turned back to her well-lit room, to the crying piles of luggage.

CHAPTER IX

*M*AJOR PRESCOTT drove fast down the flat road to Jerez. His foot pressed love into the accelerator, his black hair frizzed back and his face squinted its eyes in the smack of the wind. At last, the engine roared, we're going somewhere.

He had been bottled up near to bursting, he had found himself wanting to wring Louise's neck. Why in God's name didn't the girl *do* something? Couldn't she have kicked? Couldn't she have shouted? Even that Molly Owen had kicked over the traces in the end—some shemozzle about flinging into Harrowby's hotel on her last night, opening the doors all along the corridors, barging into one room after another until the porters had got hold of her and telephoned that old soak back at the hotel. Hadn't come to any good of course. Harrowby'd been out—he'd heard from the porter there'd been some trouble that night in one of the "houses," something about Guy insulting a whore, and by God the pride of a whore's something to contend with, let alone a double-strength Spanish job—no, Molly'd not found him—and now she was well shipped off. . . . But at least she'd tried to *do* something. While this Louise . . .

But, in fact, he was simply transferring his own impotence —he still felt guilty about letting Guy go scot-free. He knew very well how powerless she was to act. You can't slap the

186

face of a man lying in a hospital bed, and nothing sensible comes of spitting in the eye of a man like Guy: and so on. He felt for "the hole she was in"—but his years added an easy "she'll get over it in time." He turned around now and grinned at her sitting with Madeleine in the back seat— somehow to make up for what he had been thinking. Madeleine waved his eyes back to the road in alarm. He straightened and pressed down that rubbery resilient accelerator. It was as sensuous as pressing flesh. Anyway—now action! Like a fierce boy he began to play the part of a man of action devising a difficult escape maneuver, indeed an escapade.

Plans were fixed, watertight. First down to Jerez for a few days' business. These days to be filled socially—with all the enormous *bodega* families they would never be alone, no time to brood. Then he had to take this car of Echevarría's up to Granada, meet E. at Granada—and then more of the social round. Granada a fresh scene too, breath-taking. And afterward? Anywhere—train up to Valencia, perhaps. Barcelona. Keep moving at all costs. They'd just buzz off across Spain, plenty of new faces and places to absorb them, and then England, Home and Beauty. He hummed satisfied at the wheel. They were in the vine country now, it did him good to see it.

And it all went as he devised. Jerez received them into its golden arms, into its rich dark vaults. Louise allowed herself to be led from ranch to small palace, from farm to ample town house, around bellying dark casks ranged royally among cobwebs and around black-shawled old women, aunts and wives and grandmothers and their vast families of sons and daughters. What indeed else was there to do but accept and let people imagine they were taking her mind off things?

But her mind had its own way of healing itself. Slowly, stage by stage, it found methods of new sustenance.

A few days later, for instance, at a lavish dinner party after a long day, and openly in the patio of their host's house, she broke into tears. She let Madeleine hurry her away, while

187

the Major explained that she was not very well. She wept all the way home in the taxi, and in the room Madeleine nursed her while slowly, ending in silences and sudden sobs that shook her whole body, the tears ebbed to a stop. It had been a small hysteria: but she felt afterward tired and cleansed, better.

And the next day Madeleine had posed a question which had been at the back of all their minds, but which no one had liked abruptly to raise.

"Lou darling—we haven't talked of it before, but don't you think you ought—I mean wouldn't you like—to go home?"

Now Louise had been keeping herself from thinking of England. That first fresh morning taxi ride to the hospital had stayed in mind—a moment of joy when with the air blowing through the window and the promise of seeing Michael again she had imagined an English spring and their new life together, years it seemed of fresh air. England then had meant a lace of hawthorn draping the tall grass, high May nettles and moss-dripping stone, the feel of summer silk, the smell of talcum in a bathroom, the pips of a wireless in a windless dusk. Now England signified no more than the same old mews flat and the reassembly of old routines; a sour and dull prospect.

But also—and she only half-admitted this secretly to herself, as one admits against all common sense a superstition—she could not bear to leave Spain while Michael was still there. Somehow that would seal the break. Absurdly she could let herself travel hundreds of miles away over intransigent Spanish roads, further away in time than an air passage from England: but it was impossible to leave, in terms of the map, that peninsula.

"It's going to be hard wherever you are," Madeleine repeated, "but at least back home there'll be more to occupy you." And she thought "occupy"—how on earth does one say such things?

188

"No. I'd rather stay."

"We could take a plane together," Madeleine persisted.

And this Louise grasped at with relief. She saw that Madeleine would never let her travel back alone: and remembered how important this trip was for the Major's business. Any splitting up and journeying home would upset everything. She could never allow that. It was an excuse to stay—and a rational one. It made her responsible, it laid a core of positive behavior.

So once again and finally she was able to say "No. No, it's sweet of you, but no. I'll be all right. Promise." And to mean it.

And again a few days later, in Granada, she had to pull herself together and exert responsibility. Both the Prescotts seemed to have got out on the wrong side of the bed that morning. They were sulking when they came down and this fanned up into a plain, speechless row.

It was an ordinary engagement of bad bile—but its effect was to make Louise peacemaker. All the way up to the Alhambra, under the nightingale elms and along the Moorish battlements, in the Court of Lions and through hidden gardens of myrtle she soothed them—and felt much the better for it.

And it was in Granada, too, that a moment of unique and again strengthening vision came to her. This time she was alone, again up among the great red towers of the Arab fortress. It was a particularly clear spring morning, the valley of the Darro sparkled in sunlight and the white and orange houses on the opposite Albaicin hill seemed to echo their colors in the fresh air. Sounds echoed too—it was a morning when sound came free and sharp and seemed to sing up into the bright air. The gentle Albaicin slope spread out a map of life across the valley, everywhere small movements could be seen—a train of three mules plodded slowly up one street, a woman hung out a line of bright washing, somewhere a man made a thud of ax on wood, pigs squealed and grunted,

189

and regularly there came high and wide on the windless air the long crow of a rampant cock, a sound as domed as the bell-clear sky itself. So many scattered fragments of morning vigor, so many patches of color and of sound—yet all wonderfully separate from each other, each unseen by the other but embraced in a whole by the watching eye above. A picture of morning . . . but something else too? Louise felt exhilarated as she shaded her eyes against the sun dazzle . . . a pain of pleasure at some other unremembered scene pulled at her—and then she realized what it was. The map of this hill of houses resembled so much a chart that had hung once years before on her schoolroom wall. A colored drawing of a French village, with a pond and a house and farmyard and a field and a road, a little French vocabulary illustrated. In this picture, which lived in a clear spring light of sharply-drawn figures and clear-washed colors, there strode about— but dead still—a life of blue-trousered peasants, aproned farm wives, yellow ducks, brown-spotted cows, pigs, dogs, cats, hens, cocks, horses, and all the rest of the farmyard scene. Hour after hour, whenever the words of her schoolbooks had dried in her mind, she had fed and refreshed her eyes on this picture. And its unique quality, now matched exactly by the Albaicin panorama, was that all these diverse men and women and animals acted quite separately. They were magnificently independent. Nobody seemed to see what the next was doing. It was like an extraordinary village of the deaf and blind.

So this picture of freedom so deeply instilled came true before her eyes. A morning for the ring of buckets on the stone, a morning for the shine of washing on a line . . . and up there on the Moorish ramparts she stood and breathed this wide and hopeful air, air of morning hope, of the childhood of the world. Yet still it saddened her. On that last evening in Seville unhappiness had evoked beauty and now the reverse occurred, beauty bore sadness. But it was a sadness alive, a strength of melancholy, a living and powerful taste.

190

Sadness, when the heart is freed from facile joys, discovers new sensibility: life is felt more keenly, more profoundly than ever before. "Dulled by sorrow" is seldom true for long.

So the days passed. She was never quite free from a kind of hopelessness, the melancholy remained; and the mind abhors a vacuum, and of course those days could not seem anything but aimless. This hanging about Spain was a kind of marking time. Though they tried indeed to make a strenuous time of it. The enormous and delicate Alhambra, blood-red in the sun against the great snow mountains above, a miracle device of hot palm country against ice, was in itself a considerable exercise—let alone the grotesquely mixed city of concrete skyscrapers and adobe terraces beneath. And under Echevarría's guidance they again lived a full social round in the patios of his hospitable Spanish friends. To the end that man was courteous and generous, restrained and thoughtful: no one had told him of any trouble, but unobtrusively he went out of his way to look after Louise, he seemed to smile out his own leathern resources for her nourishment. And the Major was all for keeping moving. As soon as the tempo of interest in Granada seemed to be slackening, he booked seats on the Valencia express. And so the sixth day saw them up early and settling into their compartment for the fourteen-hour run through to the orange coast. Another stage in the "aimless" journey. But already they were the aim for others.

At about the time they left Granada two matters took their predicted course. Guy received a hoped-for telegram from London: and Michael Carey was discharged fit from the hospital.

"But—you mean—get up?" Carey sat up in bed stupefied. The doctor had spoken with the casual air that doctors assume for greater precision. Until this moment Carey had still believed that all the doctor's previous assurances—"You'll be out in a day or two" and "We'll see tomorrow"—were said only to hearten him. Yet here was this man giving an explicit order—it suddenly seemed extraordinary that he was there at all, casual in a gray suit, a smell of soap on his hands, out and about, probably up for hours, breakfast inside him, now going off somewhere else.

"Of course I mean it," the doctor was saying, while Carey studied his bottom waistcoat button with wonder, "you're fit as a fiddle—that is, take it easy for a couple of days, of course . . . but otherwise—" and he clicked his fingers in a final gesture.

"Doctor," Michael said slowly.

"Yes?"

"Doctor—am I absolutely all right?"

"Now old man, I've told you that."

Michael studied him carefully.

"You mean—in every way, in the future . . . ?"

"You've nothing whatsoever to worry about."

"But . . ."

"Now what?"

"Am I—you know, complete, like any other man?"

The doctor sighed and gave Michael a mock stern look from under his brows—peering over invisible spectacles.

"Complete? I don't know what you mean. I do know if you go on like this I'll be of the opinion you're a bit wanting in the upper story. 'Course you're complete."

Michael swallowed and then blurted it.

"I can have—I mean, I can make children?"

The doctor swung back, hands in pockets, and bellowed with laughter.

"Hundreds!" he roared.

Michael closed his eyes, "Oh God," he said and sank back on his pillow horrified and grateful.

Much later he left the hospital. He had told the whole long and difficult story to the doctor, whose manner had instantly changed—he had known something was wrong, but nothing so profound as this. Immediate and sympathetic advice: "Go after her. Quick as you can. All cards on the table. At all costs don't hesitate."

Which was exactly what he wanted to hear. And so he spent an immediate hour with the hall porter, trying to telephone Echevarría, telephoning the offices in Jerez. The total answer was vague—that they had left for Granada, address unknown. But it was known to Michael—frantically he searched for an envelope on which they had all previously jotted an itinerary home. Granada was on it, with a suggested hotel. He was not too well supplied with money, he considered the idea of a plane, then decided to play sure and conserve all his resources. He booked a seat in the morning bus.

Afterward he walked out and up to where the *Feria* had been. A dragging curiosity took him there—mainly to see again the exact spot where the trouble had occurred. He found the wide Prado a wreck. The *casetas* had been struck, workmen were clearing away the last torn canvas, wood partitions, the mass of wire, and dead electric lights. Torn paper, wreckage, litter of every kind—and curiously, for the backs of things were exposed, all of this was gray and white, all color was gone.

He found the spot only by the gypsy fires. He stood and looked at the muddy grass—there, exactly there it must have happened—and looked around him. Nothing was recognizable. What otherwise would have seemed a forlorn and miserable scene filled him with joy. It showed the thing to be a dream, a picture of no importance, a matter of the past. But the words he had confected at Louise were no dream. They tolled miserably down inside him. He shuddered. To be capable of inventing such a thing. . . . Would she ever be able truly to understand? He tried to decide, with misgiving, that she would.

In another part of the city Guy received what he had hoped against hope for—a big offer from a large film company. It was the first time. It meant a lot of money in the pocket and a certain security if the film was unexceptional enough to draw a large public. The end of small parts in the theater, the battle for broadcasts, walk-ons in films, and all the loitering in between. Guy had no great love for his art: the life suited him, he had his ephemeral enthusiasms for this part or that. He liked a sudden access of money, but he got on easily enough without it. And though he lacked enthusiasm for the fine pinnacles of his craft, he lacked also the dreadful earnestness that prevailed among so many of his fellow professionals.

Though however much he might have despised the monotony of actor talk, he most certainly wanted to talk about himself at the moment. Not so much to receive congratulations as to share the exhilaration of the jackpot. But there he was, with his ship come home, in a city of strangers. The white walls of his bedroom were not to be endured, he went out and walked fast along the street with the telegram folded live in his pocket. He cursed all these dark men standing around talking their incomprehensible tongue: they should have been dancing for his joy, teeth flashing only wonder at this all-embracing news. Then suddenly he thought of a huge international hotel along the way—there would be English and Americans in the bar.

There were. He soon got himself talking to two crew-cut young men busy at their morning Martinis. And after a decent interval he suddenly doubled the usual order and announced his celebration. The Americans were polite. They raised their glasses with formal geniality, their well-shaven lips uncurling over good American teeth. "Jeeze, that's swell!" "Sounds like you're on to something, fellah!" But their eyes were cold, they had heard of films before, and soon they were back talking what they wanted to talk—clichés of church architecture and all over again the mystery of the bullfight.

He went out and into a bar in a side street. He sat listening to the Spanish all around. He thought of the group of

194

French-speaking Spaniards he had gone out with on the night Molly was looking for him—there certainly had been trouble, he wondered whether he should telephone them, realized it would be no good, and for once cursed himself for not behaving better, he should have had more common sense. Suddenly he realized someone was talking to him. A cheerful man wearing a black mourning band was leaning over with a bottle of sherry—explaining something and smiling, obviously offering him a drink for good humor's sake. Possibly this bastard also had a contract? Guy managed the word he had learned *"Extranjero.* Foreigner," and found himself absurdly pointing his finger at his mouth, mouthing: "No speak-a." But the Spaniard laughed, put a warm hand on his shoulder, poured a drink, and, as astoundingly so often happens, went on speaking to Guy in Spanish.

That bar was called Los Caracoles and along one side was a glass wall-tank filled with the little snails themselves. They slid slowly about, their pale putty stomachs open and clutching at the glass, and these Guy found himself watching as the interminable Spanish words cracked and gurgled about his ears. It was too much. The snails, the Spanish—it could go on forever. Suddenly he made his mind up. He rose and, abrupt as usual, concerned only with his own purpose, left.

There is occasion and there is cause. The snails, the Spaniard, the two Americans, and this indigestible triumph of his news together fanned the occasion of a quick decision. The cause was much deeper. It was unforeseen. It was loneliness. To travel alone had seemed a comfortable way of passing the period of his quarrel with Louise—which he never doubted would blow over: a new country, a holiday from the old face—what better? But for once he found he had not the resources in him to amuse himself, He had to face it—he needed her. Badly.

He had to think quickly. The question of returning to England was attractive but impractical—there would be weeks of waiting before the studios would call him. But he had no exact idea where Louise might be, he had no itinerary, no list of possible hotels as Carey had. He went straight to their hotel and asked at the desk. The hall porter who had helped Carey telephone remembered. Jerez and Granada. But no hotel names, no indication of the next stop. Guy weighed it quickly—Granada meant striking east and probably then north: Barcelona was one way out. Possibly Madrid and Irún? Possibly—but the Mediterranean appeal was more likely. At any rate Barcelona was his own way home.

He left for the ticket agency.

And deep in the lunar foothills of the Sierra Nevada, the curious blunt-nosed *rápido* wound its way Valencia-wards. Like a blind scent-busy beetle this single coach of blue and silver, this diesel eccentric of the railroad, turned and re-turned as the track made its way through moonstruck mountains brown in the sunshine: so tortuous this nosing about in the crevasses and cuttings and ravines that at one moment the great sugar-line of the distant Sierra might appear to the north, the next southward, and then suddenly to the west dead straight on from where they had come. It was perplexing, mad. And then, when a wide plain of broken loess suddenly opened out to reveal the town of Guadix, the earthen field became scattered with white pimples like bright puffballs, chimneys of a great assembly of caves. Even the names that passed were difficult to believe: Iznalloz, Guadix, Baza.

But unsettling as this mirage protested to be, the journey in essence was settling to the spirit. There were fourteen hours of it. The coach was crammed with passengers and baggage, Louise had her one seat and little else for a day and an evening: a box of a wine bar took up a miraculous few feet at one end of the carriage—but this was not the place for a lady and in any case a bother to reach. There were several half-hour stops for meals, but for the greater part of the journey there she was, settled, undemanded of and unable to demand, a captive of the seat and her thoughts.

196

And among much else she thought of her past life—and pictures of Guy sometimes recurred, vividly, and by the way she developed and tasted them in her mind's eye, in some way still preciously. As usual, the past isolated its pleasurable moments: as usual, the instinct to avoid pain dulled its memory. Particular and always golden times imposed themselves—a moment in October in London, a good clean morning with yellow leaves crisp on the pavement and a premonition of frost keen in the nose, when they had walked past a shop window glittering in the angled sunshine and she had seen their reflections, two together, for a perpetual second: and another time, above a railway freight yard in some suburb (why were they there?), stopped by an enormous sunset making a remote lost land of islands and estuaries in the sky above the real lost land of grimed tracks, and she had looked up at his profile lost in these lost lands and seen all the wide magnificence around reflected there. When such pictures came to her she tried to fix them in her mind, to fix and find more in them, as one might dwell on a treasured photograph reconstructing more and more of the past from it; or, after some party, try to relive it again in the unhurried dark of one's bedroom, bringing to mind forgotten conversations and episodes lost in the general excitement. She remembered exactly how she had been dressed on these occasions; and how Guy had responded to things she had said: and above all she felt again the wider, immaterial sense of blessed participation in each other. Time and again, in exasperation, she put such thoughts away. But it was like closing a box of forbidden sweets.

Past Baza, past Lorca and lunch. The day settled in. Prescott and Madeleine had fallen asleep: they sat crumpled together a few seats away. A magazine was gently slipping off Madeleine's lap; Louise watched it without moving, long ago they had all given up the exhausting grimace and call across seats. On one side the cream-colored blinds had been lowered against the sun: a half-haze of hot siesta darkened the coach, and above the lounging shapes of bodies cigarette smoke barred itself bright blue in a lonely shaft of sunlight. Louise was quite alone, quite awake, and the ceaseless stream of the country, now here, now gone, flowed like the backward stream of her own thoughts.

It was now a whole day since Prescott had telephoned the hospital in Seville to find that Michael had been discharged. Unexpected news. It had seemed for a moment as if he were now free to come to her—then the moment passed and she was left thinking: "How quickly he's recovered now I've gone." Now his freedom only seemed to seal him further away. Later that morning she had written to the doctor in Seville apologizing for her abrupt behavior. And that letter, too, seemed an act of resignation, a cutting of final threads.

Resignation, too, last night. Part of resigning is to begin afresh, and they had all, in Madeleine's phrase, decided to clear the air and "beat it up." So to a gypsy cave on the Albaicin. They had had several bottles of wine. The atmosphere had been amusing. Such prosperity—the cave spotlessly lime-washed, the walls ablaze as a Devon teashop with copper pans and fire irons; for once the price of wine was high; one cave along the way was even known to have a tiled bathroom. Yet none of this could spoil the quality of the dancing and singing itself, these survived as gravely pure and exotic as ever. Later they had driven home and gone on drinking in Louise's room at the hotel. To the amusement and apprehension of some of the hotel staff they started to stamp out the gypsy dances themselves. They made a lot of noise and laughed a lot. Louise had got herself drunk on purpose. It did no good and she knew it. And she knew it more definitely in the packed dry carriage the next day.

The train gritted hotly on. Her mind began to ramble. What was she? What had she always been? She looked down and saw her hand, and past it her calf and ankle and foot. Well-known fingers, trying to taper and never quite succeeding: ankles in fine new stockings, good slim ankles hoping

198

their bones were not too prominent: shoes new, disconcerting, but in them feet that were hers and only hers. All parts of her. In fact there she was, exactly *there*, sitting below herself. Same hands that had picked the skin of these same toes in the dark of her girlhood bed; same feet that had felt the bruise of hard ridges on the seaside sand, same that had danced themselves sore in their first high heels. And this same head that was thinking of this . . . what had gone on through that head all this time? Summer mornings, winter frosts, dripping autumn afternoons—what had it truly been after, been at?

Just then Elche appeared at the window—a dried river course overhung with white houses, first spouting of African palm plantations, and glittering in the center a glazed dome of deep royal blue whose blueness dazzled and overcame everything. Louise watched abstractedly, only the deep blue dome made its impression—and her mind wandering in the past chose to link this with a memory, it brought back a bright blue glazed pot that had sat, perhaps still sat, on the book-case of the room where she had begun the first work of her— could one call it so?—career. Well, that had been something, she had preferred this ill-paid serious work of archaeologic research to a more lucrative and glamorous job offered at the same time. That was something, or was it? Was it even consistent? She might as well be two-headed as well as a two-handed creature—there had been sad lapses in between. A night-club period, the time of the "happy tramp" when to slouch and slop became an ideal, a number of odd romances that had drifted her in different directions. Lapses—but were they so sad? They left a residue of experience. However . . . it all boiled down distinctly to two persons, not one, operating. And that, my sweet, is a truism. That is known the world over. People are always two people, if not more.

But truisms cannot just be spoken and believed, they must be felt to be known. The wise old words wind very easily round the brain, winding—but wait till a years-old adage stands stock-still and is! . . . Wait till it fits, hits you between the eyes! Well, she thought, so I am just a girl who wants to eat her cake and have it? Yes. And is this unusual? No. And can one go on like this? No. Then must I, young as I am at twenty-seven, sit down and make up my mind? You might as well start early.

At that point the *rápido* entered the enormous Elche palm groves, and mile after mile of elephant-hide trunks dazzled by like stout railings. A gap, a vision of salt lands straggling to the sea—but always the palms closed in again. The train whirred on, the palms whirred dazzling by . . . and perversely Louise's mind grew clear. It was almost a clarity of impatience—dazzled by the flickering palms, hazed by hangover, packed in with smoke and bodies and baggage, muddled by introspection, pure impatience seemed to clear her head and suddenly start making up her mind. But it was more than that. It just happened to be the moment when the resources that had been regathering in her over the last days sought an outlet, a decision, a purpose. Quite coolly, and firmly, and with no surprise—for unconsciously this impulse must have been growing all the time—she decided to get Michael back.

Get him back. Get him. Behind those moth-soft eyebrows the mind hardened, grew very hard and alert indeed. Plans came from nowhere instantly, her brain rode smoothly into action as if all the time it had been prepared and housed, oiled and waiting. And as this happened, though what she thought was not always pleasant, her lips lengthened slightly into a smile, a longing predatory smile like the taste of food.

The train drove into Alicante bay and stopped. Silence suddenly. Silence and the sight of the sea, a palm-lined promenade, a beach. Then the engine gave an oily cough and started off in reverse, shunted through the town along the side of the road, turned past a high engine shed round as a bull ring and gathered speed for the northward journey.

Madeleine woke up and stretched, cursed the magazine dropped so long ago on the floor. Then exclaimed at the changed scenery—for now the land had grown suddenly green, now for miles they plowed through wide orange and lemon orchards, and the rich scent from these gusted through the open tops of the windows and filled the coach. She called to Louise over the people between, pointed out of the window. But Louise only nodded. No more landscape for her—she was interested from now on only in people.

Michael Carey arrived in Granada the day the others left. Rain had fallen overnight. The gutters ran with mud. He left his cases at the station and took a tram up to the center of the town. From there he was directed up a hill street wet with chalkish mud to the new-built hotel whose name was penciled in his old itinerary.

He did not hesitate. He went in as, all being decided, one might walk into a hospital for an operation.

He gave her name and the porter nodded amicably. "The English," he nodded, with approval.

Michael's heart rose instantly. The good luck to have found them so easily! In a minute, in a few seconds . . . ! It suddenly occurred that she might be out, and after all this time the thought of having to wait for half an hour seemed unbearable.

But then the desk clerk was shaking his head, looking automatically back at the pigeonholes behind for a message, shaking his head again. "They left this morning."

The little hotel hall subsided to its bare morning emptiness, Michael saw he was simply standing there in a hotel hall alone with a porter and a desk clerk. The sound of an electric sweeper whined from a room along the corridor. Probably from her own room, cleaning away the last of her. He stood there imagining the clatter of luggage, the excitement of coats and bags and taxi as the group of them would have left, filling the corridors one moment with hurry and the next gone away.

Gone. The hours ahead revealed themselves. He tried to

pull himself together, made inquiries and discovered they had left for Valencia, and then went down to a travel agency.

There was no seat on the Valencia express for two days. Perhaps one might try at the station . . . there was always —the agency man waved his gray-olive hand to embrace all the world and all time—a chance . . . or call in again in the morning? *Mañana, mañana*—the old joke as always quite true, endearing and exasperating. He stood there helpless, no way out, islanded on the plateau of this city.

But there was a way out. The very delay gave him a moment to pause and reconsider his immediate instinct. Better, after all, not Valencia. Better surely to get one step further ahead and make sure of things. He booked through to Barcelona. He would find them somehow.

The danger was Majorca. Palma was suggested on his list —though at least it carried a question mark. Were there boats from Palma straight to France? Planes? Could they get home missing Barcelona altogether? And in any case what were they doing? What state of mind were they in? Would Louise now want to stay out of England or get back? He suddenly envisaged her spending weeks, as it were recuperating, on the Balearics. But still Barcelona was the surer bet. In any case, he could never seriously imagine her needing recuperation after his insignificant demise, he simply felt her to be a creation superior in every way, her life would naturally resume its sure course.

He was confirmed in this when he returned to the hotel and booked for the night. The boy who brought his luggage was very merry about those English departed. In the hotchpotch French that served for all foreigners, he described with glee the party of the previous night, particularly the behavior of one of the ladies. He even danced a few steps of a *zapateado* in demonstration. But when Michael, thinking of Madeleine's light-colored hair, gave him a kind of smile and said: "The blond?" the boy shook his head positively and

202

said no the dark one. There could be no doubt who had been so funny dancing.

A confusion of hopelessness and jealousy filled him as he then opened his attention wider on the boy. Painfully he asked again for all the details. Another page boy of another nation might have closed up at such evident questioning—but this one was innocent of innuendo, in fact proud of his guests, and was most pleased to re-create the scene in the greatest detail. Michael was in a mood to believe anything: his heart sank.

He went out into the town. The plane—for that had been his rash decision—did not leave until the next morning. There were hours to fill in and a hotel bedroom, where at the best of times a disturbing life is led between the basin with its stuck drain and the window with its exasperatingly limited street view—a bedroom was no place for him at such a time. He went out and walked up to the Alhambra, and then above to the gardens of the summer palace only a few yards higher, the Generalife. There he mounted an obvious lookout tower, a tower with a celebrated view, and placed his hands on the very balcony rail on which Louise's hands had rested the day before. This was no coincidence, it was a natural apex for the visitors. Gazing out over that extraordinary perspective of palace and hill and plain he thought of this, imagined her there, and looked down at his own hands with fearful curiosity. His guilt, even at such a remote contact—or was it simply the sight of his hands? came riling back. Once more he went over the enormity of what he had said to Louise. It was truly terrible. How could anyone, ever, think of forgiving . . . so far he had blindly followed her, buoyed up by the doctor's words, trying not to dwell on what he had said, only wishing to get there and speak it all out quickly and straight. But this delay . . . he wanted to write, he thought even of writing the same letter to all the hotels on their list. But it was impossible to write even one letter, such things did not go down on paper.

He stood above the myrtle gardens and looked down at the delicate Arab arches and the silver play of fountains and felt guiltier and guiltier. The gardens were many, small and walled, like a dozen London back gardens interlinked with steps and grilled gates. They looked from above like a hive of damp prison cells. And here the Arab kings used to wander against the summer heat, the snows like sherbet against the hot blue above . . . yet what king knew what assassin stood with the long knife behind each turn of these walls? Guilty himself, he saw intensely the terror resident in those gardens. The paradise smacked of blood. Among the dark cypresses, themselves like shadowed figures, a single nightingale sang. For the rest, silence, sunshine, dark shadows, a silence of treachery.

He turned away, he had been deliberately giving way to his nerves—and left that uneasy place. He walked slowly down the long elm walk to the level of the town. He took trams at random, sat in café after café, searching the street scene to divert his attention. He sat opposite ancient Moorish walls and modern concrete skyscrapers. He noticed how even the most modern building still had its sky line planted with obelisks and urns, and began to make a counting of them. This was bad, again giving in to nerves—he began to walk. The idea of Majorca occurred to him again. It assumed a dreadful significance. If they did go there, he could wander for weeks. He walked faster—away from the idea of Majorca. Dusk found him in the busy old Plaza de Bibbarambla, its blue lanterns gloating slyly among the green leaves, and the *paseo* was again upon him. All Granada was out: everyone greeting each other, no one greeting him.

He wandered, lonelier and lonelier, had dinner, wandered again. That night a great storm hit the city. Lightning flashed purple on a slate-black sky, huge façades of white concrete or the distant pale mound of the Sierra showed suddenly violet and vanished. A great downpour flooded the streets. In an empty intersection of roads in the center of the town a number of quail flying from Africa were forced down, drenched and exhausted. The little fat birds trotted about in the puddles, and men walked after them knocking them dead with sticks. Simply with sticks. Tobacco-sellers, lottery-sellers, anyone who was about made their kill. A brisk market began.

Michael went up to bed.

Guy landed at the Muntadas airport the following day. The same storm that had hit the Granada tableland never caught up with him; such a storm was a strange visitant for that time of the Spanish year, its great gray-black clouds rolled out fanwise across the dry land and headed slowly north, catching Louise at Valencia and appalling the Valencians, many of whose farmers, despite their love of rain, crossed their black smocks in superstitious fear.

But Barcelona lay bathed in hot spring sunshine, the great port rattled in the sun. Guy's first move was to take a room at the station hotel: in fact, to station himself there. He planned to hang around and watch the trains come in. In case they came by air, he arranged for the hotel porter to send a runner round the more obvious hotels to inquire— Barcelona runs with the poor and a few pesetas bring a deal of service. The alternative watch point might have been a café on the Ramblas, foreigners must sooner or later meet on that celebrated avenue of trees and flower stalls milling down to the port: but the Ramblas is too busy, too easy to miss someone there. Better the station.

So Guy settled himself into the life of stations among the station-livers. Restless, he sat among the restless. His news still undigested, he lived among other people preoccupied with plans and projects. Every main railway station in Europe knows the businessman who knows no more of the town than the station: his precinct is the buffet and the cabstand, he smells of engine smoke and paper towels, his ears are full of the owl hoots of engines behind great glass arches. Of Milan he knows nothing but the red salvia beds and Musso-

205

lini's travesty of concrete; of Geneva no blue lake, only the pale gray *brio* of the cafés in the station yard; of London no more than the lounges of the Grosvenor. Of Barcelona, the same. Yet he is envied for seeing so much of the world.

With all the other station dependents, and among the hinter-life of peak-capped hotel runners and prostitutes and pimps, Guy took his place. Against the grubby façades of thin ter-minus hotels or in the big buffet he drank his cooling beer and waited. Now and then he went in to watch the trains empty themselves; or wandered along to the Ramblas and the busy port streets. But mostly he just sat and drank his beer and watched, fuming his inactivity, eyes constantly on search. They not only sought Louise. They sought anything. In this they were unlike his friend the Major's eyes in their habit of glaring: with Prescott the impulse was to assure him-self that everything was all right, shipshape—but Guy's search was a prowl, he had the look of someone wanting to pick something up, or break it up. He belonged to station life.

Yet this life did offer one further advantage: it offered a changing population of foreigners who spoke other lan-guages than Spanish. Apart from Louise, Guy was plain bored lonely. Exercising his usual charm, he was soon able to make a passing friend or two. But as easily as he made them, a restless canker moved him after a few hours to alien-ate what he had found. He found it impossible to compromise with the polite illusions that make life tenable, under a mild cloud of whitish lie, among people of short acquaintance.

Thus once he singled out an elderly lady by her clothes and her large low protruding behind as probably Dutch or Scandinavian: these usually speak English, he went forward and helped her shut a suitcase that she had opened on the buffet floor. She thanked him and they talked. She turned out to be English, he had not properly marked the make-up on her face. He listened while she told him where she had come from, where she was going, and a fair outline of her

206

family life. When at length he told her casually that he was an actor, and in films, she was genuinely impressed. But she had not seen any of the plays in which he had taken part, she could not, in fact, identify herself with him, and rather skittishly, for she was one who plainly considered herself young for her years, excused herself with a joke:

"Us old ones don't get around much, you know."

Guy looked at her carefully. "No," he said, "I don't suppose you do."

The lady started, then tried quickly to pass it over.

But Guy took trouble not to. He threw himself into a long, carefully condoling expiation of the disabilities of age. "But in *your* young days, life must have been so much richer than ours. . . ." And he carefully named a date before the turn of the century, a decade before what could have been that lady's evident spring. And again: "But how nice not to have to exert yourself so much—I'm always glad of a rainy day when one *can't* go out, when one can close the windows and really relax. . . . I suppose it must be like that . . . ?"

Finally he smiled good-by to a lady much disturbed and several years older.

On another occasion he fell in with a Swiss gentleman—a traveler, as might too easily be expected, in watches. This in itself was lightly exasperating. And the man seemed, sitting there in his proper gray suit with his gray rubber coat neatly folded on his knee, to be too self-provident and through his rimless spectacles too severely benign. Guy soon got onto watches, and thence to all measurement. The Swiss naturally praised exactitude. Guy argued against it. "As soon as you measure something, it disappears," he asserted, and exaggerated at length on this theme. The Swiss defended: Guy scoffed. The Swiss was an intelligent man, and knew there were all sides to all problems. But he was not intelligent enough to remain unmoved, he grew angry. It was that deeply galling anger at injustice—and he finished by losing his temper. Guy answered with irony: the upshot was that the Swiss gentleman rose abruptly and left—and remained on edge for the rest of the day.

But on yet a third occasion, in between trains, when Guy had ventured along to the Ramblas and the sun shone on bird stalls and flower stalls and gold-lettered signs saying, amid a freckling of plane leaves, SIFILIS Y LAVAJES Y VIAS URITANIAS —on this occasion he showed himself in a somewhat better light. It happened in a small, afternoon-empty bar. Two young Englishmen were drinking; it did not need their gray flannels and tweed coats to define them, they were loud-voiced and blatant, holiday-makers in their twenties and very sure of themselves.

Two or three beggar boys came and stood near, at the door. Their heads were cropped against lice—one, sharp-cheeked and blown-bellied, was in fact a crop-haired girl. Then the oldest of them, plainly half-witted and an object of display, began to bark like a dog. He came barking up to the young Englishmen holding his thin hands up to his chest like paws. He stood there, and like a little mad wolf-thing howled. The Englishmen leaned against the bar and laughed: they exchanged a look—somehow self-congratulatory—and laughed. Then one of them spoke in Spanish—so they were not, after all, holiday-makers?—ordering the boy to lift his leg like a dog against a chair. The boy did this. In fact, he himself was laughing. Finally the little "clown" held his hand out for money. Suddenly looking grave, the Englishmen felt in their pockets. But instead of putting the pesetas into the boy's outstretched hand they threw them away on the littered café floor, shouting: "Fetch!"

Guy got up and went straight over:

"Pick 'em up," he said.

The Englishmen raised their eyebrows and laughed to each other: "Oho!" they said and: "Who have we here?"

Guy stood there and repeated louder:

"Pick those pesetas up!"

208

One of them growled: "Who the hell are you?"

The other said: "Leave this to me," and took a step forward.

"D'you want to make something of it?" he said to Guy.

Guy looked him up and down.

"Yes," he said.

A pause. The beggar children had scented something and stood huddled and frightened by the door.

The young man said less decisively: "Well, if you want to make something of it . . ." He tapered off uncertainly.

Guy said: "I do."

Another pause. And he repeated sharply:

"Well—are you going to pick them up?"

The young man shrugged his shoulders and muttering "No use making a bloody mountain out of a molehill, no bloody sense of humor . . ." went down on his heels and picked the pesetas up.

"Now hand them properly to that boy," Guy said.

The dog-boy shrank back as the pesetas were handed to him: then he took them, but now furtively, all fun gone. The voice of authority was about.

But the voice of authority only turned back to the bar without saying another word. The young men, awkward but pulling themselves up into a sneer as they got near the door, left.

The children, now frightened, left too. And once again Guy was left, however fair his momentary instinct, and however brutally low the level of fun he had spoiled, in a funless, empty room.

CHAPTER X

UY was in Barcelona on the third of May. On the sixth, Louise and the Prescotts arrived. One day later, on the seventh, Michael Carey's plane touched down at Muntadas.

Guy need never have worried about posting himself at the station. In fact, he missed the train on which they eventually arrived. But there is another place where visitors to a city are apt to meet—the head post office. And there quite casually he ran into them.

They were standing in a crowd at the stamp counter. On this last lap of the journey they had spent the afternoon remembering friends at home they had forgotten—now they stood with post cards fanning out in their hands like playing cards, silent and waiting, listening to the echoes of the great post hall, feeling how insecure all those papers looked lying about among the fingers of southern clerks, wondering whether one was allowed to smoke, and so on. Into this impassive assembly Guy broke like a small storm; like a playboy on a *plage* more than a man in a post office and in disgrace.

"Louise!" He took hold of both her arms and stood grinning down at her.

One moment the echoing post office—then this well-known face, unbrushed hair, tie askew, smiling all teeth and strong eyes twinkling, plainly pleased and expecting pleasure. It was only noticeable that he had called her "Louise"—not Ludovica or Lulu.

Her heart jumped—but a very little. She answered coolly, feeling hard inside, unmoved enough even to be amused by his absurd resilience.

"Guy! And where have you sprung from?"

He told her. And how he had been waiting for days. And how much he had longed to see her and tell her some great news—but that must wait. He never stopped speaking, he poured words all over her as if nothing at all had ever happened in the past weeks, and at the same time he was nodding and smiling over her shoulder to Madeleine and Prescott.

But Prescott turned away. And then Madeleine came over from the counter with a streamer of stamps in her hand. Ignoring Guy she said to Louise: "Got 'em. Let's get the things posted."

Guy was not to be deflected:

"Now look, Mad, I've got the most terrific news . . ."

"Are you coming, Lou?" Madeleine repeated.

And then swung up at Guy: "Apart from everything else, for Christ's sake don't call me Mad. Ma-a-d," she mouthed.

Guy pretended exasperation:

"Oh . . . can't we let bygones be bygones—just this little once?"

"Is that a song or something?"

"Oh, I know—I *know*. . . ."

"I'm glad. Now we'll be getting along. . . ."

But Guy insisted: "Look, you simply must come and have a drink. I tell you, what I'm going to tell you is . . ."

Madeleine turned away impatiently: "Louise—are you coming?"

But Louise did not move. She stood thinking, feeling oddly calm and casual and finding in this a strange comfort. Madeleine looked at her astonished. She thought of Michael—and then of course remembered that there was no more Michael. But surely the little bitch couldn't . . . ?

She appealed simply: "No! No . . . Lou!"

But Louise turned to her and nonchalantly, a new hardness

showing on her lips as she pursed them, almost considera-
tively, she shrugged: "I don't see why not."

And coolly to Guy: "Where?"

"Oh . . ." Guy waved his hand exuberantly at the post-
office wall, at all Barcelona, and then curiously said, and
very heartily: *"Irgendwo!"*

Louise smiled to hear the German word, he was not quite
certain of himself. She did not feel exactly triumphant—she
was simply enjoying this new sense of detachment.

Madeleine said coldly: "Well, be seeing you at the hotel. . . ."

Without looking at Guy she went across to her husband
and left.

He took her to a café in the drooping old yellow Plaza
Real. At least one could sit quietly there, a few tables stood
under arcades peeling the memories of better days. The plaza
made its own deep shadow, its tall shuttered houses cloister-
ing a few palms that stood about tiredly like long-legged old
featherless birds. Lampposts surmounted by black iron hel-
mets stood like the skeletons of armored knights. About everything there hung a vague smell of compost. But in a corner
occupied by a restaurant a golden-brown chicken turned over
a bright charcoal fire.

Not so many passed through this square, though it abutted
near to the Ramblas themselves. Its solitude emphasized a
new kind of constraint that Louise noticed as she sat there
close to Guy—the propriety of an old lover: it was like sitting with the husband of a good friend.

". . . so there you have it!" Guy finished. The skin on
his face, usually so dry-looking, glowed with a physical enthusiasm. His eyes mirrored himself in pleasure: "God knows
where it'll lead—but it's an end of the old life. More of everything, my girl, and no more lip service."

His eyes narrowed: "Though the old life wasn't half bad,
was it . . . but you're looking rather strange Lou?"

"Aren't you, for that matter?"

"Naturally enough." And then he pretended slyly: "Jealous?"

She was able to look him back straight in the eyes. She wondered casually at this, which had never been easy before: even at their most intimate, his eyes had made her shy.

"No, Guy," she said, "why should I be?"

He suddenly thumped the table, the little sugars rattled in their bowl.

"But for God's sake I'd forgotten—why are you alone? Or are you? What's with your Michael—?"

"After all you've only got one film."

"Oh Lord," he said suddenly serious, "he's all right, isn't he? I should have asked—"

"And you know yourself—you're very capable of breaking it all up."

"Breaking what up?"

"The great chance. But it's wrong of me"—she managed a wry kind of smile—"I'm very glad for your sake, Guy."

"You haven't answered my question. Where's Michael?"

"Michael?" As if she had heard him say the name for the first time. "Oh, Michael's following on," she lied. "Michael got stopped by a nave or two."

"Business before pleasure—funny time for that?" He added, "But there's something else funny in that quarter."

"You mean?"

He took up a *palilla* and began picking at his teeth, over his face came the vacant look this gives. "Nothing. I'll tell you some time. . . . But how is he?"

"He's fine. What did you mean? I don't like mysteries."

He smiled at her again, suddenly affectionate:

"You know I've missed you a lot, Lulu. I think I saw for the first time, down there alone in Seville, how much . . . it's all such a damn mix-up . . . and only too late you see how much you need, I mean *I* saw how much I needed you . . . hell, we could have done such a lot now. . . ."

213

He looked downcast, and down at his fingernails. She said again steadily:

"*What* was it you were going to say just now?"

"Oh . . . you probably know anyhow."

"*What?*"

"Something I heard about Michael. As a matter of fact, I wrote home to an architect chap I know."

"Wrote home?"

He leaned forward sincere:

"You know, in a way I do feel a bit responsible for you, Louise. I just wanted to find out something about the fellow." He smiled. "Didn't want you to make a bad choice."

She was suddenly frightened. Guy's sincere moments were not to be trusted; but she was frightened. All the sense of nonchalance went.

"You had no right to do that," she said.

"I feel I had. I didn't want you to make a mistake." He added slowly: "As it seems you may be doing."

Louise said nothing.

Then Guy seemed to make a decision against his better self. He drew in a breath between his teeth and spoke coldly:

"It seems Mr. Carey was corespondent in a particularly unsavory divorce matter—"

"I don't want to hear anything about—"

"The husband being overseas in the field of battle—or rather off it, a Jap prisoner in Burma in fact—while Carey was nice and comfortably set up in London. With the lady-wife."

"He was a pilot." She bit her tongue for bothering to argue. "Anyway, I don't want to hear another word."

"Just as you like. But it was quite a case in the press— you probably read it yourself at the time. In point of fact, I have here"—he reached in his pocket and brought out a letter and some clippings—"the documents. Like to refresh your mind?"

"Put the filthy things away."

214

"Anyway, Carey'll be here soon, you can have it first hand, eh?"

She said before she could help it:

"He won't be here."

"But you said he was following."

"Oh the hell with you, Guy. He's not. There's been a row."

Guy took the toothpick from his mouth and his eyes opened wide. He beamed. He was like a father pleased at a prize his daughter had brought home:

"Why—Lou!"

She nearly laughed at his enormous complacence. But he caught himself:

"I mean . . . not so good in a way of course . . . on the other hand . . ." And his eyes under their dark short lashes were still flickering pleasure.

Louise looked at him amazed: then around at the quiet old square, and then fixed on the chicken still brightly turning on its spit. Nothing just then seemed quite real, everything stood out separate, isolated, and unbelievable. Could such atrocious self-satisfaction be possible? Had she really lived with this for so many years?

"That's very kind of you, Guy," she said. "But there's no other hand, not at all!"

"Yet it's a little too early for a row—or isn't it?"

"The row will be patched up."

"But Louise, honestly . . . do you think you can be sure of a fellow like that . . . not after—"

"Everything in the garden will be lovely. And now I'm going."

He finished: "—not after this divorce business and God knows what else. . . ."

She stood up abruptly. What he had said could be despised —but it left its mark.

"Good-by. It's been bloody seeing you—"

"Now Lou . . ."

"As usual," she smiled.

Guy spoke fast: "Lulu—tomorrow! Let's at least meet to-morrow! We *must*, it's—I haven't told you—my last day. I've got to go sooner than I thought. Can't we paint this god-awful town up a bit tomorrow? Say *yes*. Last time!"

She laughed.

"How charming! No, Guy, there'd be very little use." She was casual again. "Besides I'm busy with Madeleine. And you know how she loves you. . . ."

He took this for weakening. And then snorted with laugh-ter: "I'd like to see her face when she hears about that con-tract."

"Have a good trip."

He got up amused.

"See you tomorrow, then."

"Good-by."

"Till tomorrow."

So when the next day came and the receptionist telephoned up that a Mr. Carey was there to see her, she thought it was Guy being funny. It was before ten, she was only just dressed and breakfasted.

She could not be bothered with any of this—and she put the receiver down with a brusque morning finality. But the next moment she felt less certain. She sat looking at her fa-miliar things hung about the room—suits and dresses well known and nearly hated, and with her mind trying to press the collar of a dress slipping off its hanger began to wonder suddenly if—perhaps—it were not Guy at all? She tried to brush it aside. But, again—just possible? A chance in a thou-sand? If it were Guy, it was again a kind of schoolroom trick that succeeded: it was infuriating how there was no defense against these simple attitudes. For there wasn't, she couldn't be certain it wasn't Michael. And obliquely then, to excuse herself, for she was already at the door, she thought: "Well, it *is* Guy's last day after all."

But again, if it was Michael . . . her mind began to work

216

above her heart, she began to calculate. Refuse to see him. Keep cold. Show him these things were not so simple. She had already refused on the telephone—if she went downstairs she would simply be walking down the hall of her hotel on any normal errand, she saw herself asking the porter the hours at the opera.

She held her breath on the stairs. She thought this was to keep herself quiet: but her heart was beating fast and it seemed loud, she felt her breathing could be heard. There was a mirror at the foot of the stairs, a great old gold-framed monster that took in half the lounge. She held her breath and went further down to where she could see most of the lounge reflected: cane chairs, a pattern of tiles, a table of green A B C's and the pink bullfight paper, a family of luggage herding itself, but otherwise nobody at all, absolutely empty— then suddenly a voice came up the stairs, in the emptiness no more than a loud whisper, and Michael's voice:

"Louise!"

Her heart rocked. She looked hard at the mirror, at the tiled stairway walls. Empty. But then Michael came forward into the mirrow-view with his head turned up at her on the stairs—of course he had seen her feet and bless him recognized them, and then she ran down the last stairs, all calculation gone to the winds, shouting loud his name.

But Carey's eyes were anxious, his smile grave, he had been stiffening himself for this meeting and could not unstiffen whatever her welcome: and so her smile half-died and they stood awkwardly in front of each other, without even the touch of a hand.

"Louise, I've got to talk to you. I'm miserably ashamed, I didn't mean any of those awful things I said, you've got to give me a chance to explain. . . ."

But she was just then purely delighted to look at a well-known bushiness about his eyebrows, the implicit smile marks in lines by his lips:

217

"But of course Michael . . . here, there's a sort of lounge place. . . ."

"No. Not here."

"But why . . . ?"

"D'you mind—out somewhere—alone—"

She looked around the empty hall and through to the empty lounge and half-smiled at him: "Alone?"

"Please. I can't explain . . ."

"But wasn't that what you wanted," she tried to laugh, "to explain?"

That failed too, he gave a smile that would never work, he was stiff with his anxiety.

"Right—out then," she said, and led him out through the door.

It was raining. "Rain," she said.

This was extraordinary. She stopped astounded. All through the last weeks of spring there had been those fixed blue skies, rain was a forgotten element—yet now these metal-dark clouds and the first heavy gray drops splashing the pavement piebald. "Well, it's raining," she repeated.

But Michael took her arm and led her hurriedly into it: "I know, it's been following me everywhere."

She laughed at this: "Oh Michael, that's too much. . . ."

The big drops fell gray all about them so she hurried him into a back street. The hotel faced the quay. Nowhere to sit there. She made exactly for the same plaza where Guy had taken her the day before—it was all she knew. They hurried through the dark crowded Escudillers and up into the square, getting into that arcade café just before the sky burst the full force of its southern water.

It came down vertically, curtains of shivering metal chain shutting in the arcade. It was early, and no chicken yet turned on the restaurant spit. It all looked wet and drafty, a thousand miles away from the warm dry yellow of yesterday's shade.

But Michael persisted with his anxious speech. He had been

218

preparing it for days. It had to come out in spite of Louise's now obvious welcome.

"I don't know how to start," he said, who well did, "except that I don't know how you can ever forgive me. But Lou darling, dearest—listen—

"I'd better come straight to the point—what was at the bottom of it all. Lou—it was that . . . I thought I couldn't give you any children. Ever. I thought I'd got a wound that washed all that out forever. It was something they said when they brought me in, I don't know, I was hardly awake, but I'm sure they said—"

He looked suddenly puzzled at the pavement by the table, and repeated to himself: "I'm *sure* they said it." He lowered his voice: "One of them said: 'I'd be sorry for the mother of his children.' And the other said: 'Never to be. *Never to be.*' Do you see? *Never.*"

"Oh Michael . . . !"

He went on impatiently: "I can see now I might have misheard . . . but then I was so sure I even refused to check up with the doctor. Anyhow I didn't trust him. I thought he'd think I wasn't in a fit state to know."

She had reached forward for his hand. She held it trying to cover it with hers so much smaller.

"So there seemed only one fair thing to do. . . . And there I was cursing you and loving you and worsening what I had to say, and then having to act it at you . . . at *you*, Louise! And then"—his eyes wandered a moment, frowning—"a dreadful thing happened. But it doesn't matter now. . . ."

"No, Michael, tell me."

He looked suddenly ashamed, but still trying to puzzle out something unbelievable:

"I—I found I was enjoying it," he said. "I lay there and enjoyed it, I began to taste the words and I watched the look on your face—"

He waved his hand wearily. "God knows what the mind

219

does to one. I was just beyond everything. I suppose it was the only way to get it done and something bad, something truly bad, evil came up and helped it. I cried about it afterward."

"Oh my darling, poor—"

"I just want you to see, Louise. And now . . . understand what I felt when that was all over and done and you had gone and the doctor came bowling in and told me to get up. And get out. Go. Fit. Fit as a—my God, his word, *hundreds* he said."

"Hundreds?"

"Oh hell—of babies!"

They looked at each other a moment, a long look of mirrors, a look of eyes behind eyes—and then both started to laugh, a giggling hysterical laugh that then opened out until nearly the tears came.

Then suddenly stopped.

And in wonder again Michael just said: "I'd never have believed it."

"Hundreds—I should think not. Think of poor mum."

"No, I mean you—here—looking so glad."

"Same to you, my darling," she said. And then murmured half-ashamed: "You've taken the wind out of my sails too. You know, I was all set to get you back—in England."

And so they sat and talked on together and gradually the old warmth, ease, surety returned. The rain poured down, rattling the gutters, streaming from a broken pipe, curtaining with wet the dry arcade. But even then the place was brighter than the day before.

Then a little later Louise made a mistake. He had been on again about the hospital and that part he had played—and then of the dreadfulness and pity of all deception—and finally said: "At any rate that's the end of it with me. In future, no secrets." The phrase clicked in her mind, she was in a sentimental mood, her emotions rose to the myth of the clean slate and she blurted out suddenly—as she would never

220

have dared or wished—what had yesterday left a sting of discord in her.

"And talking of secrets, Michael—"

"Yes?"

"At least it's not a secret, but—"

"What's all this?"

"But I wouldn't like you to think I didn't know."

"About what, for heaven's sake?"

"Oh, I know you'd have told me, but since I know already I might as well say so and—"

"Really darling! What?"

"I mean that divorce business of yours."

"*What!*"

"I don't want you to keep that a secret. That's all. No more to be said. All over and forgotten."

"How the devil . . . ?"

"Now—no more! Finish."

"But Louise," he said gravely. "What did you hear? How?"

"Oh, some business in the war, anyway it was the war, people parted . . . don't for heaven's sake think I blame you. I do understand, Michael."

"You don't. You've heard it was a soldier's wife, haven't you? And that he was abroad fighting? It makes a pretty picture, doesn't it?"

"Please—Michael—I'd never have mentioned . . ."

His voice was hard:

"You'd better hear the rest of it. It's true her husband was overseas. And it's true we had a kind of affair—I was on leave, I was far too heavily on leave. But what she never told me was that she was married. Very much the opposite, the tale went. Nor that she had arranged for witnesses. The bitch wanted a divorce. I was the lucky culprit."

"But Michael—didn't you say that in court?"

"No."

"But—why ever not?"

221

He shrugged his shoulders:

"You can't very well do that."

And added: "Anyway, it would sound silly."

She looked away from him, out at the rain, low and humiliated, low and odious as the woman herself. So that when he said: "However did you find that out?" she said without thinking: "Guy told me."

He lost his temper, he had been losing it before at the memory of that case:

"Good God, that bastard again! Is the fellow everywhere at once? How in hell did he know?"

"He—he wrote to London."

"How thoughtful! At whose request?"

"Michael, don't!"

"Well?"

"I didn't mean to mention him."

"But now that you have? Is he here in Barcelona? I suppose you're all chummed up again?"

"*Please* Michael! None of us thought we'd see him again— but he followed right up here, he turned up yesterday—"

"And?"

"And I just thought the best thing was to rise above cutting him, better to treat him as of no particular importance. And then, well—he seemed to be behaving reasonably for once, but then out he comes with this letter from London about you, he'd heard from a friend—"

"This was apparently some grave concern for your welfare?"

Louise suddenly flared: "Yes, I suppose it was."

But he hardly noticed, pushed his chair back: "You'd think the bastard had done enough already, it's like keeping company with a running sore."

Louise stood up:

"That's enough Michael. If you can't understand—"

He looked suddenly startled, as much at himself as at her.

222

"Oh hell, Louise," he said softly, "I'm sorry . . . it's just . . ."

"I didn't want to see him. I didn't want to hear anything. I just—I just—"

She wasn't crying. She was dry with tears, swallowing hard. He got up, suddenly frightened:

"Please darling, I shouldn't have—it's ridiculous—"

"It's so awfully unfair to you, it's beastly for you, it's—"

She was sobbing. They still had the table absurdly between them. Michael tried to push it aside to get to her, but even that played against them, it was weighted to the floor, he had to stumble and nearly fall as he took her in his arms. She buried deep in his coat, nosing under the lapels, crying and shaking. He simply held her tight, saying nothing, feeling the smallness of her bones and her small warmth and the shaking and looking down on her hair over which he then put his hand to press it closer, while his eyes looked gravely beyond at the pouring rain as if he would protect her against that for a start.

Her sobbing slowly changed to a sighing small laugh at herself, and she looked up, hair caught flat and wet across her face:

"I don't care," she smiled.

He bent down and kissed her deeply.

Then suddenly he laughed:

"D'you see—this is the first time we've done this? Touched each other? It took our friend to do it. . . ."

There is the expression "jump for joy." But one can neither jump about in an adult arcade, nor kiss too long even in the empty rain among the Spanish proprieties. Yet action was needed badly—and just then Michael saw they had started to roast a chicken on that spit, a gleam of golden warmth in the rain-drafty arcade.

"Ours," he swore.

And dragged her laughing into the restaurant and harangued with the waiter to let them have the chicken, wrapped up and half-cooked, just as it was: and may it do them good, the poor half-baked ones, the waiter prayed.

They had returned, and were sitting in the lounge over-looking the street when Guy came in looking for Louise again: he had been there already once that morning. It was still quite early.

They were sitting together at a small table near to Madeleine and the Major, who also sat at a small table—the four sat watching the rain through the plate glass as at some theater show, the gray-wet street was framed by plum-dark plush curtains and an old brass rail ran along the sill like the curtain rail of an orchestra pit. But thus separate Guy was able to come up to Louise and Michael ignoring the others.

He was there before they knew it, as he crossed the lounge he had time to recognize Michael's presence and quickly revise his attitude—for he only nodded to Louise and spoke instantly to Michael:

"Look, Carey, I don't know how to apologize," he said, breathing hard as if he had run there to be able to say this, jaw working humbly. "I did a damned awful thing pitching into you like that. Went completely off my head. I'd've come to the hospital, only they kept me out. I feel like hell about it."

Carey looked up at him coldly: "You're not the only one."

"I know," Guy said, humbly taking it, "I don't blame you."

A pause. Guy put his hand up to that hairlock that fell over the hard bone of forehead. It was difficult for his dry hard face to look ashamedly apologetic: but he managed it, lowering his eyes and letting his lower jaw fall.

"Well," Carey said, "is that all?"

Madeleine and the Major were reading too quietly; no pages were turned. Louise sat awkwardly looking straight in front of her out at the dark stone of public buildings opposite. It was the signal, made quite plain, for Guy to go. But of course he stayed.

224

Just then, however, a boy came over and tapped him on the shoulder. *"Teléfono,"* the boy smiled, making the motions of answering a call and pointing to the desk.

Guy said "Excuse me" and went over to the telephone.

"Excuse me's good," Michael said.

Louise nearly laughed. It was after all a day of good humor, of celebration, an expansive day. Indeed, the celebratory chicken, a trussed-up parcel now letting a little oil, still lay on the table in front of them. The rain hardly mattered at such a time. Guy could be disregarded.

"Pray God it's his nameless film company," Madeleine mouthed from her paper, "pray God they've sent him an airplane."

Major Prescott flicked a hand, too imperatively, at Louise:

"For God's sake get rid of him," he growled, "today at least." He added, a little surprised at himself, to soften it: "Bad enough with this merry old Mediterranean weather outside, you know."

Louise said in a small voice:

"It was different yesterday. Michael wasn't here. I was only trying to smooth things."

Michael smiled to cover her:

"I don't think we should bother too much. He'll go."

"He won't," Prescott snapped. "The man's got the skin of a leech."

Michael frowned. He may have hated Guy, but he disliked even more any criticism of Louise. And he could not forget how this morning he had brought her to tears more or less on the same matter. He reproached himself, he resented Prescott's interference. Oddly too, he still regarded Guy as a friend of Louise's, a kind of appurtenance with whom she should at any rate have the privilege of dealing privately.

Also the physical hurt Guy had done him had lost its bite, it was as difficult physically to feel as the cold of winter on a summer's day. He decided to try to be reasonably polite if Guy returned.

225

And Guy soon returned:

"Can't understand it," he was muttering as much to himself as anyone. "Consulate? What the devil does the consulate want?"

He looked at Louise and Michael and said: "That was my hotel. Something about the consulate telephoning. Couldn't quite get it, very mixed English the chap speaks—however I said I was here if they wanted anything. Mind if I—?"

He pulled a chair toward the table and sat down. He made no apology, he had dropped his mood of humility and was now simply concerned with his own affairs. No one spoke, but that he never seemed to notice. One arm slung over the chair back, sprawled down at ease and as vitally untidy as ever, he began to talk of what was instantly in his mind. His train that day. The time it reached Paris. What did the consulate want? And Barcelona was a stinking hole. He gestured a hand at the window: "Might as well be in London already."

It did look very much like London. The dark gray stone of municipal buildings streamed with rain and soot. Pavements, curbed in the English fashion, shone a slush reflection of low gray clouds overhead. Black umbrellas milled and jibbed everywhere over bowed, hurrying shoulders. A steamer from the wharves boomed its wet complaint. But most telling of all were the red double-deck buses that passed to and fro against the gray. And over everything—umbrellas, buses, pavements, gutters—the rain streamed down unceasingly, wetting the whole world, seeping like liquid mackintosh into the veins. It might have been a wet Monday at the Mansion House. Then a deliberate engine came pluming black smoke along the quay and pushed it all further north to Liverpool.

Guy talked on, then took to asking questions that needed an answer. That became too uncomfortable. Louise was about to say she must go upstairs to write some letters—when again the page boy came up and tapped Guy on the shoulder.

"*Señor* Harr-ow-bee?" he asked, motioning toward the desk in the hallway beyond.

226

"Christ," Guy said and rose to follow him.

They all looked at each other, papers lowered and chairs shifted in a great sigh of relief.

"I can't stand it," Prescott said.

Michael whispered tentatively to Louise: "Darling, don't you think you could do something?"

She shrugged, it seemed hopeless: "He'll never take a hint. . . ." Then pursed her lips and sat up impatiently looking for her bag: "The only thing is to escape. Let's go for a walk in the beautiful rain."

Madeleine stared moodily at the passing umbrellas. "Pity old Owen's missing this. There's the chap to cheer you on a day like this."

"Shall we go, Michael?"

"Mind you take your Rattan Partridge Crook."

Prescott worried his paper and grunted: "At least that's one small mercy we've been granted. Probably stewing in the Red Sea."

Unconsciously Madeleine's eye may have recognized the shape of Owen standing far back in the hotel hall by the desk to which Guy had been called—though such a preposterous message would never have reached her brain. But now suddenly Louise shouted:

"Talk of the devil!"

They all turned and saw that indeed Owen stood there.

He was talking—it seemed effusively—to Guy. Olive Owen stood a little way away silently watching.

Prescott raised his eyes to the ceiling, there was nowhere left for him to look: "The end," he murmured and shrank behind his paper.

Madeleine yelped with delight. "So here we all are again! How *very* cozy!"

Michael put a finger to his lips and took Louise's arm: "Quietly, now's our chance. . . . It's an ill wind . . ."

Owen was sober.

He stood, feet firmly placed apart, and faced Guy's tall inquiring smile.

"I've been looking all over for you," he was saying fast, sentences spluttering over each other, "I left ship at Port Said, I've flown all the way back here. And now I've only found you thanks to the consul—"

Guy raised his eyebrows and nodded. "Indeed? All most interesting. But what exactly inspires this great honor you do me?"

"You'll know soon enough," Owen snapped. He stood there in some attitude of authority, or of defiance: but it was plainly an effort, he looked tired and those legs planted so squarely were pathetically bent, the thin legs of a drunkard weak beneath their potbelly.

"What I've got to say's private," he said, glancing around. "Come over here. . . ."

"Isn't this a little imperious?"

But Guy allowed himself to be led away from the desk and into a corner of the hall away from the stairs, a kind of alcove where a telephone booth stood among notices and a sudden planking of dark wood.

Owen spoke low now, looking away from Guy, hating what he had to say:

"I'll not beat about the bush. It's about my Molly. She's in —in a certain condition." He paused and looked up at Guy almost as if he were in search of advice.

Guy said nothing.

Owen almost whispered, "That'll be news to you?"

Guy's eyes flickered:

"A certain *what?*"

"Condition, I said. Molly's going to have a baby."

"Oh."

Owen looked at him hard. Neither said anything. Owen snapped suddenly:

"Is that all you have to say?"

228

"Well—of course, I'm sorry to hear about it. In the circumstances."

There was another pause. A bell rang suddenly in the telephone booth.

"Well?" Owen said.

"I'm afraid I don't . . . ?"

"What are you going to do about it?"

"Me?"

"I don't have to tell you who's the—who's responsible."

"I'm supposed to know?"

"You know damn well it's you, nobody else."

Guy smiled: "This is indeed news."

Owen's jaw stiffened, he thrust it out, it was not used to this and stopped there quivering.

"I'd not speak like that to me, young man. Now come on!"

"But by what magic do I become a—daddy?"

The bell went on ringing urgently muffled in its glass box.

Owen glanced at it and lowered his voice again. He spoke tenderly, sorrowful for his daughter: "The poor girl's told her mother everything. You—you ought to be ashamed of yourself. But I'm going to see to one thing." His voice rose: "You're going to make a decent woman of her, Harrowby."

Guy said one word only:

"Difficult."

The older man swallowed, he pretended not to hear:

"She's my only daughter, Harrowby. You two have got yourselves in a—a fix. But what's done's done. So here and now—I want to say I'll give you her father's permission. I wish I could say blessing. I can't."

Guy stared at him unbelieving. The old fellow—he said afterward—looked like a senator facing the firing party. He tried not to laugh, there was a cold smile in his voice:

"Look here, Mr. Owen," he said, "I can see you're upset, very upset"—he watched Owen's face quaver, the more upset for being told it—"and it's pretty awful Molly's being pregnant, I can understand, believe me—" and he saw how the

229

word pregnant hit the older man—"but what I can't get is why you accuse *me* of being responsible—"

"Accuse?"

"Mr. Owen," Guy said in what he made a kindly voice, "I'm trying to help you."

"My God!"

"I'm afraid," Guy said, he was unable to resist it, "you'll have to look a little further Father." But then to cover it he turned and swore loudly at the ringing bell—it was no good going too far.

"By heavens, do *I* have to answer the damned thing?"

"What?" said Owen.

A clerk came hurrying from the desk.

Guy looked down at his fingernails, he considered them with an air of reticence, as though he did not like what he was going to say but on consideration felt he had to.

"Mr. Owen, it's unpleasant to have to add to the burden you're already carrying"—he thought, I didn't even mean to say that—"but I feel it my duty and duties must be faced. I think you ought to take your mind back to that ship, Mr. Owen. I wonder if you can remember any of the stewards—say particularly the one on B deck, the one attached to the end cabins of your own corridor?"

"Steward? What ship? I don't see what you're getting at. This is all getting off the point—"

"Then you don't remember him? I'll have to enlighten you. (I'm sorry to do this, by the way.) Good-looking chap. Curly hair, kind of dimple in his chin? Great smiler, spoke a little West Country? You don't get him?"

"What I don't get's what all this . . ."

"He used to take Molly her breakfast."

"Breakfast?"

"And if you'd taken the trouble to step out on the upper decks of an evening you might have seen quite a friendship forming—between Molly and this young fellow. But you spent most of your time in the bar, didn't you?"

230

Owen's face flushed—an ill red band crossed part of his face. He struggled: "Are you insinuating . . . ?" But Guy went straight on, coldly and kindly:

"Come now, Mr. Owen—it's very natural. A shipboard romance. Molly's not an unattractive girl. And it's also natural enough, now the worst has happened, for her to—shall we say, dissimulate on the nature of her gentleman. A steward! No, much better to pick on one of the passengers. Me, for instance."

Owen suddenly blazed: "My girl couldn't do such a thing! And she's told her mother . . ."

Guy too raised his voice and now snapped:

"In fact, your little girl's quite a little snob."

"You—you . . ." Owen clenched his fist.

A gabble of Spanish muffling from the telephone suddenly changed to firm exasperated English: "No! Madam will be at the bulls."

"A rather silly lie," Guy said.

"You call my daughter a liar, you bloody—"

"I mean about the bulls, Mr. Owen. It's raining."

"I know it's raining," chanted the clerk into the telephone, "but Madam said she was to the bulls. This is all I know."

"Look here—listen to me . . ." Owen said, but his litigant mouth that never otherwise seemed to stop went on now moving without words—it was plain he did not know what to say, already a doubt in his mind.

Guy saw it and now struck hard.

"Why don't you go back to Port Said and find your blasted steward and for God's sake give me a little peace!"

Droned again: ". . . to the bulls, sir."

Guy caught sight of Louise passing almost a yard away, head turned away: "Besides," he said, "I've an appointment."

Owen said suddenly loudly, desperate now:

"But she says you're the father, she *says* it."

Louise stopped dead. She stood there, head still averted, but listening.

Owen saw her and stepped forward, his hand outstretched in appeal: "Miss—Miss Abbott, you're an understanding person. . . ." And stopped, miserable. Of course there was nothing he could say.

But Louise now turned and looked at Guy. She said in a low voice:

"Molly?"

Guy shrugged his shoulders.

"Molly," he said. "But nothing to do with me."

She lowered her eyes, her shoulders fell hopelessly: "Oh Guy. . . ."

Michael had come up and not knowing took her arm: "Come along—"

She looked from Guy to Owen, lazily, the look almost of a sleepwalker, and then saying no more simply let herself be led away.

Guy nodded quickly to Owen: "Apologies," he said, and hurried with his long stride to the revolving doors.

"But . . . but . . ." Owen stammered after him.

But Guy was gone.

He walked sadly over to where his wife stood by the desk. She raised her anxious eyes, dried of tears.

Owen looked at her somehow in surprise. And said, as if this were inconceivable, a sudden and hopeless gift of surprise: "He—he won't listen to reason."

Guy caught up with Louise and Michael, he had on a raincoat armored with military flaps, he walked with hands deep in his pockets and those long, muscular arced legs trod surely into step beside them.

There was no surprise in Louise's face, at first she scarcely seemed to notice his appearance but simply walked forward too straight and blindly, head bent forward against the rain.

Then Michael took her arm and purposely turned down a side turning to get away from him.

232

Guy followed. Michael stopped, his patience, his effort of politeness finished.

"We want to go for a walk," he said, "alone."

Guy smiled:

"You don't exactly own the pavement, do you old boy?"

Louise said quietly:

"Darling, let him stay."

Michael looked at her amazed. Her voice had meant plainly that this time she wanted Guy there, it was no show for the sake of peace. He closed his lips tight, he grew terribly alert.

They were out then on the wide gray quay, the rain had dropped to a drizzle. The enormous word TINGLADO appeared written in letters across the side of the great customs sheds, belying the look of London. And then abruptly between gray stone buildings there flashed out a strange brittle wave of ironwork and stone painted orange and blue, the urgent etiolated nightmare of a Catalan modernist. Michael took this in, responding automatically to his profession. He hated the work of this Gaudi and his school—but in any case there was a grotesque strength in it, a hellish groan that struck at the nerves. Looking at it he heard Louise say to Guy:

"What are you going to do about it?"

"About what?"

"For God's sake don't pretend. . . ."

He said carelessly: "I don't see what I've got to do with it."

"You sound stupid. At least you're not usually stupid." She spoke angrily, but then her voice trailed off: "You might as well know I know . . . I even heard . . ."

They were intolerably close in something. Michael saw Guy look down at her. He caught up and just heard him say: ". . . a little trip to the Indian dentist to have it out. . . ." He had to try to break in.

"Is something the matter, Louise?"

She took his arm, and made to hug it: "I—I can't say just now, Michael. I'll tell you later."

His lips came together again. He was excluded. He pur-posely dropped a little behind—she did not even seem to notice. He tried to take it lightly, to be generous. It was no good.

They were then at a junction of roads. The pavement had narrowed. A great many people crammed it, umbrellas and hurrying soaked shoulders filled the pavement. He had to step off the curb—and so, a few yards ahead, did Guy. He saw Louise's head a little bent forward, she looked fragile in that bleak rain, and something in the set of her shoulders told him more urgently than ever before that there, inside that coat, was all that he loved and abruptly his hatred of Guy ceased to contain itself, an access of hot poison flared and clouded his head, it boiled in his head, his head swelled like a sac of hate, he dug his nails into hands to hold himself, but as he walked on, his eyes fixed on Guy's back, the feeling swelled and swelled.

And just then, at the very moment his hate grew uncon-trollable, he felt a giant shadow behind him, a low-chorded horn sang, and he had just time to leap sideways to the curb as a limousine, silent and of enormous proportion, glided where he had been walking an instant before.

The second hung, he had been covering Guy's back, his mouth opened to yell a warning—enough time even in that second . . . but instead he held his breath, he stood poised on the curb, hoping, hoping hard, hard as the light that whipped a sudden orgasm of bright pleasure into his eyes . . . while the great car skidded by, perhaps out of control, perhaps simply autocratic—it was a dark bull of a car, a matador's black sleeping-hearse but empty, as empty as the horn that never blew its warning, until it was too late . . . almost . . . and then it did, a sudden bellow as the heavy chassis slewed aside and Guy leaped for the curb, swinging himself around and left for a shocked second suddenly alert and facing backward at Michael.

Their eyes met. Michael flushed with pleasure, smiling ex-

234

citement as one might smile at the end of a race—and Guy crouched tense a second from death. There was no question of what had happened, Guy saw it quite clearly. And slowly over his face there crept a knowing, bitter, and almost loving smile, a smile licking a dark secret—and he nodded at Michael.

A man on the pavement, seeing the inch between the mudguard and Guy, laughed a sarcastic *"Olé!"* The car like a wind of leaves was gone. Louise, who had seen nothing, turned and frowned, impatient with the rain.

"Thanks," Guy called. "Thanks very much."

He turned and caught up with Louise.

Michael pulled himself awake. His heart beat fast with fear of himself, the pit of his stomach soured, guilt rose and gulped inside him. And as instantly tried to cover itself. It hadn't really happened. He'd only imagined it. A hundred times on a rainy day cars skid. It was nothing. It was normal. He'd never wished it, his mind had raced ahead of the moment seeing what might have happened, a kind of paralysis, it was nothing to do with wishing it to happen, all understandable, excusable . . . if Guy wished to make something of it he could just go ahead, what the hell was there to care about? But he knew the truth. And he could not just then face Louise. He went plodding after them, careful now not to catch up.

Somehow they were back near that post office again, and the rain took on a sudden, pointless acceleration as if some great thumb pressed a tap above the cloud curtain. The drizzle hustled into a heavy stream of water. The whole street broke into hurry, cars swished through sudden deep puddles with the sound of swimmers diving into baths, there was a run for the shelter of doorways and a run on the post office.

They stood panting in the post-office portico, and when Guy said: "We can't spend the whole day buying stamps" Louise rose for a moment from what seemed still like a walking sleep and said: "Couldn't we get one of those buses?"

For a moment they looked uncertainly at the great red double-deck buses herding to go on their unknown routes, then Michael said suddenly: "Barcelona!"

Guy looked at him sourly: "Quite right, my boy."

"No—there's a subway." He wanted just then to be off the street, away from the sight and thought of cars.

Guy grabbed Louise by the arm: "Make a dash. It's just down there. . . ."

They ran for it down the steps to where indeed the concrete entrance and its crowd announced a hole in the ground.

"Now where?" Guy said.

"I didn't say I knew which way—" Michael answered, and cursed the apology in his voice.

Louise said nothing. She looked still dazed, deeply abstracted—and now stared blankly around at this new underground street as if it might not be real. Such sudden white walls? Such white glazed tiles after the dark mess of rain and quay outside? No color, no advertisements, no decoration on tiles—in Spain? Only a sense of electricity abounding among the bright-lit whiteness, a silent powerhouse—sickening cleanliness, the quiet whine of power, wheels moving faster than movement. . . . They got tickets and descended.

Michael made a desperate move to rescue himself, he went up to the wall map to find a route—anything to pull himself together and help. Appalling Catalan words faced him: Llull, Güell, Putxet. And Craywinckel. But he managed. Then suddenly thought this an opportunity to ask Guy where he was going, no reason surely for him to come back to their hotel? But he could not bring himself to face Guy.

A heavy square-doored train came clanking in. The rain-soaked crowd surged at it, the doors slid open, the carriages smelling of metal-dust became instantly urgent with wet clothes and faces and shoulders and hands all talking and moving at once. Into this they were sucked, pulled, buffeted.

236

Yet there was no need—the carriage arranged itself, and they found themselves sitting three together in a row.

Louise sat in the center: facing her mostly men, the wetter for being brown-skinned, two large motherly women in shapeless black dresses, a frowning beautiful girl alone and expertly catching no one's eye: a usual Barcelonese lot, poorly dressed, most carrying a parcel or some old leather bag—there was even a sea-food seller with his huge basket empty and dripping. Now these all sat against pale-painted steel, against glass dark from the tunnel wall, in a clean steady electric glow—they needed sun to bring out the color of drab overworked clothes, they made a wet ghost-clan doomed and drifted forever from sunlit memories of the acacia avenues above.

They echoed the state of Louise's mind, she sat quiet and dead in the eyes as the most live thoughts drummed in her mind, as the words repeated themselves: "Baby? . . . a child? . . . Guy's?" The train rocked with the words, she frowned to get hold of them. A simple enough image. . . . Then suddenly she visualized with horror Molly, plump and blonde Molly with her young scornful eyes, her growing airs —and saw these innocent airs suddenly collapsed by what had now come to her, she saw all the pitiful terror and misery the girl must be feeling and her heart shrank. But other voices edged at the pity as dimly insistent as the train's nagging wheel-rack—voices that edged in louder and louder until the pity was lost and a desperate disgust took its place. Disgust at the silly little bitch throwing herself at Guy, disgust at the clumsy way a child had come of it, disgust at them both: but with a hatred of herself for having prevented that same thing happening before in her own years with Guy. What had happened now was fact, incontrovertible, it had been done and could not be undone. A kind of race had been won, and she had lost it.

And what would Guy do about it? She had been shocked at his apparent dissimulation—but now, was she so sure?

Wouldn't it be better if he did manage—however sickly the business might be—to have no more to do with it? She tried to think of Molly as some vague and troublesome idea, as "the other woman," as an "unfortunate misadventure," something to be kept in the back streets and not mentioned. And then above all she had to think—what concern, after all, is it of mine? None. Apart from the first normally decent wish to see that Guy acted rightly in the matter. Otherwise—no concern of hers. But her whole body was tense with concern: she sat there dull with envy.

Suddenly she remembered that she had left a few things, clothes and a pair of earrings, in Guy's flat—she saw them plainly, two dresses on hangers pushed to one end of his wardrobe—and felt abruptly comforted.

The train drew into a station, a sudden bright-lit platform sent in more people, the door slid to and the engine sucked up a groaning draught of power and pulled off again into the tunnel. One word persisted through all the Spanish, repeated and repeated like a tragic truth in a chanted chorus, the simple word no longer simple: "*Llueve*. It is raining."

Once again, as at other times and on that longer train journey from Granada, images of her past with Guy suddenly imposed themselves. The happy pictures—that autumn reflection of the two of them in the plate-glass window, that moment of magnificence above the sunset railway yards—these and others flashed up into her mind. In seconds, as a long dream may take place in only a fraction of time, they asserted themselves and passed. Previously she had played with these pictures, but pushed them aside exasperated with herself—the box of forbidden sweets firmly shut. But now she made no attempt to shut it.

I've got to snap out of this, she thought. And how do you "snap out" of this kind of thing? Then at least—you *do* something? But what exactly is the thing you do? What indeed can you ever do if it's no concern of yours? If it's no concern of yours you can stop bothering about it. But . . . a

238

child? Sentiment rose in her as if it were an excuse to go on bothering, she thought of the child itself, the baby not wanted and unloved. Then she remembered that whatever happened it was likely to be loved. She shuddered.

Suddenly she realized that Guy beside her was laughing out loud. She looked up. He was laughing to himself, a deep laugh, shaking with it. She saw him glance—it seemed almost archly, he rolled his eyes sideways trying to keep a straight face—over her head to where Michael sat.

She frowned: "What's so funny?"

"Oh," Guy laughed, "a little secret." And then put a finger to his lips. "Michael knows," he said.

"He *knows?*"

Guy nodded wisely.

"But he can't know. . . . Whoever told—"

His laugh petered out, he made a casual gesture: "No, not about all that business. No, Michael knows about something else. Don't you, Mike?"

Michael must have been listening, he blurted too quickly: "I don't know what you're talking about."

She turned around quickly and saw he looked strangely ill at ease. What on earth was going on now? Her brain tried to shake itself awake.

Then abruptly all the lights went out. Sudden blackness— and the train slid to a stop.

The air churned alive with cries, questions, imprecation:

"Ay!"

"*Hola!*"

"The lights!"

"The lights have gone out!"

"The train!"

"The train's stopped!"

No more the low litany of "*llueve*"; no Cockney voice to bellow: "Where was Auntie when the lights went out?" —these people took their misadventure as a serious matter.

And gradually that carriageful of passengers found them-

239

selves sitting in the dark with the seconds turning to minutes. The first voices of surprise faded. Now on all sides explanations were made, technical knowledge freely exchanged. Most still sat simply wondering: "What has happened?" and beginning to fear. And there hung behind the fear the ominous knowledge of so much out-of-season rain. Yet somebody said: "But rain makes electricity. We'll soon be off."

Those voices struck in the darkness from every direction, now it seemed from the roof, now even from behind. Despite the clamor Louise strained to listen to what might be happening outside. Outside was the place—but how silent it must be out there, out in the clean tunnel muffled by such a weight of earth, yet alive, with mice sounds ticking and dripping in the quiet? It was dead black. Hadn't there been tunnel lights? Had they too failed? The great weight of earth pressed down from above, they lay trapped there in a worm hole, inside what was no more a great carriage but a tight metal box. All around wound high-voltage cables alive and waiting, coiling dangerously along the track and the dark subterranean walls.

But above all Louise sat listening for the grumble of another train pounding blindly along the tunnel behind them. . . . Yet this was a modern railway, there were safety devices? But what was ever foolproof? There was always the hundredth chance. . . . Somebody somewhere might have left something undone. . . . And the idea of a chance in a million, a thousand, a hundred grew monstrously certain in the dark.

She felt a hand fumbling for hers, for a moment her sense of direction slurred, she felt an absurd fear. Then: "Michael?" she whispered.

"Yes. All right?"

Someone along the carriage struck a match. Perhaps because of a rigid no smoking rule no one had thought of it before—but now this single flame flared and made a great yellow cavern. At the sound of Michael's voice she had turned toward him and now saw his face clearly lit, it was

240

recovered from whatever had been wrong, and smiled down at her reassuringly. It reminded her of Guy's laughter. And now she realized that he was still shaking with it, silently, on her other side. He sat there in the dark shaking with silent laughter.

Others started to light matches, there was a constant flickering, a going and coming of flame and shape and shadow as they flared and went out, and all those faces circled in the gloom, with their dolorous dark eyes and the leathern set of their features, began to look like the faces of waxen martyrs considering their votive candles in a dismal grotto chapel. Or like miners entombed.

It was then that somebody smelt the first faint smell of burning. A sudden hush fell on the carriage: everyone was sniffing at the dark air. It was unmistakable. A hot smell, a bad smell of burning paint or oil. It seemed to creep about in the air, one moment perceptible, the next gone. But it always came back. And it grew stronger.

The smell of so many sulphur matches? Petrol fumes of lighters? Possibly . . . ? But not—it was definitely a hot smell coming in from outside. Now people strained to peer through the pale smoke of their own lighted matches at the glass windows fearful to see the first sign of fire glow in the black outside. The carriage had grown uncomfortably hot, it was terribly enclosed, it would soon be difficult to breathe, the blackness and shadow stifled like a warm woolly cloth. So many warm bodies enclosed? Or was the outer steel of the carriage actually growing hotter?

Michael gripped her hand hard. He tried to be reassuring:

"Oil on the axles," he said in an offhand tone. "Friction heats it. Normal. You can't smell it usually."

She nodded, wanting to agree; or simply not to have to speak—she sat dazed, so many things had somersaulted, nothing seemed to have any reality, even the hand she grasped seemed to be nothing but a hand, nothing to do with a body and Michael, a hand, no more.

241

The carriage began to shift. People had risen from their seats and simply stood up waiting; or hustled to the doors and looked fearfully at the handles; or held matches to a corner of the ceiling and up to some kind of emergency appliance, levers quiet against the smooth high paint. The young girl opposite had lost all disdain, now she talked urgently to two young men: one held on to her arm, responding to some last need of contact before facing whatever might have to be faced. Others comforted the two older women, big black eyes now wide like owl eyes: *"Madre, madre"*—or were these comforting the men, their sons? And still the burning smell grew stronger, the pale smoke thickened, the air grew sicklier. One man opposite sat twisting his hands, his face twisting with fear bubbling up inside him, his skin beading with sweat.

Yet Guy went on laughing, he had said not a single word, he just sat silently, vastly amused.

Michael was saying: "I hope to God they keep their heads. It can't be long. Any minute for sure—"

And then the first scream came. A single sudden cry like a dog's whine rising inhuman among the deep urgency of other voices. It stopped, poised and high, then broke down into sobbing, hideously out of control. It was infectious. It began to echo everywhere.

"Hell!" Michael said.

Then: "What we need's a proper light. Pity Guy hasn't got a few of his famous candles—"

Louise stiffened. Candles! She had forgotten, clean forgotten!

Michael was going on talking for talking's sake: "I once knew a man who ate candles. He ate wax of any sort. He loved honeycomb. Why I don't know. He just liked to eat wax. . . ."

Louise sat suddenly paralyzed, appalled. Michael was saying, perhaps to jolt her: "God, he'd have eaten the wax from his own ears. . . ."

242

But her hand pulled itself away and she turned all of her-self to Guy. By matchlight she saw him. He was not laughing at all. He never had been. He was shaking with fear. He had lost all grip. He was shaking like a shell-shocked ghost of himself, drained white, teeth chattering stupidly, knees jerk-ing out of control, hands shivering as he lit, one after the other, in a prodigality of little flame, match after flaring match.

"Guy—for God's sake Guy!" she cried. "Don't worry, I'm here, get hold of yourself—"

And she put her arms around him, half shaking him, half embracing.

Michael was leaning forward and around. "What . . . ?"

She swung around a loud whisper: "It's nothing, noth-ing—"

Then she lowered her voice, secret: "It's the dark. He can't stand the dark. . . ."

Guy looked at her, the yellow flicker of his eyes dull with terror, no more eyes but sockets of fear bruised and hurt in the drawn white skin of his face, and suddenly he lurched across with a small cry hiding his face in her breast while her arm went protective above and around his shaking shoul-ders. A lighted match fell and lay burning on the knee of her coat. Michael brushed it off.

"There," she said, looking down at his head, "there—"

The knocking began. Someone began knocking. A heavy sound of iron on iron, someone had got a mallet or heavy stick and was pounding at the steel door. Metal gonging, muffled as the air itself, a futile sound showing only how much more muffled it would sound out in the emptiness of the tunnel—but insistent, steady, and wild, the very drum-ming up of panic.

Louise whispered, "He can't help it, it's something he can't help. He had it as a boy. And then in the war . . ."

She went on talking, not so much excusing him as speak-ing words that went with each stroke of her hand on his head, while Michael looked down horrified and sickened, he had never seen a man so collapsed.

". . . he had to leave his—you know, his parachute outfit in the war because of it . . . he was very brave, he went for all the worst jobs—but he just couldn't stand the dark, it's not fear, it's—"

"Panic," Michael said quietly. "Bloody panic," he swore, suddenly standing up.

That man opposite who had sat holding in his great fear had stood up too, his eyes rolling, his arms raised to the ceiling like a tortured man drowning. His mouth began to open, wider and wider it opened, some dreadful sound gathering, when Michael's fist crashed into it and he collapsed no more like a man but a slopped clothes bundle lumping on the floor.

"Perdon!" Michael shouted down at him, more accusing than apologetic. Then louder turning to the whole carriage *"Perdon!"* and then began to speak loudly, in stilted Spanish, but with a coolness of authority:

"There is no need whatsoever to fear. I am an English engineer. I know this railway. I know how it is built. What you can smell is only hot grease, any workman knows it. Believe me—we will soon be starting. . . ."

They had mostly stopped talking; his voice, strange in the dark, caught and held them. He could not be seen clearly, but the foreign accent and the tone of certainty surprised and for a moment impressed. But that knocking went on—it wavered only once, and the wavering was worse. Perhaps it was this that broke the spell. At any rate, eyes peering at him close in the gloom recognized the foreign-dressed man who had only a moment before struck another, for this had all happened in seconds, and a murmuring of protest began.

Michael knew he must go on talking. He had picked up that man, and as he leaned forward to set him comfortably in his seat, somebody thought he meant to hit him again. Or was hitting him. It was difficult to see—even matches were

244

now running out. Voices were raised, a hand came down on his arm. He flung it aside and stood upright again:

"For the sake of God keep quiet, don't be foolish—" and then louder—"Stop that knocking!"

But this time there was no response, the voices rose harshly around him, once more that high whimpering howl rose eerily at the end of the carriage now darker than ever, and in the dark hotter, and he stood listening hard through the knocking for some other knocking outside that would mean the breakdown gang or the fire gang. Someone had loosed his bowels in fear, the smell fouled the air further.

A hand caught at his arm again, then another: with no way out they were turning their panic need for movement onto him. One or two started arguing for him and only fired and confused further the blackness of sound—and even then, in the gloom of some last match he had time to look down at Louise's hand stroking Guy's head, and not resent this, but feel it part of an emergency that would right itself later— and then he pulled himself up to a last effort and shouted:

"That knocking—stop—that—man—knocking . . . !"

But the knocking only quickened, it accelerated with the dreadful growing insistence of a drummer intoxicated, the beats falling over themselves in rising excitement to get there always faster—it seemed suddenly that there was also a knocking outside, men with lamps and crowbars were there, he stretched his ears and almost heard the first breaking of glass as the outside world came blundering in, smashing a heavy way into the foul air, freeing them. . . .

But suddenly all the lights snapped on and after a thoughtful moment, as if to allow time for the shock of the lights to be observed, the train groaned, gathered itself and purred heavily off. No warning whistle, no hoot of triumph—it heaved itself into motion simply and casually, as if nothing whatsoever had happened.

And that is what in the first seconds of blinking struck into the minds of the passengers—the exact nothingness of what

245

had happened. It was exactly the same carriage as before. Nothing had changed: the lights sent their same clinical glow over seats, windows, supports, smooth steel panels. It was like waking from a dark dream into a familiar room: relief was soon followed by a sense of deception—everybody felt cheated.

There was no stupefied silence, they did not stop talking, they could not—but they all in their own way realized that the only change had been in themselves, they saw how they were standing, what figures they cut, and slowly subsided once more into formal passengers: formal and brave. The man who had belabored the steel wall with his stout country stick looked uneasily at the great scars he had made on the paintwork—and turned quickly away. The girl clutching the arm of an unknown young man stared at it in surprise, and thoughtfully, her face slowly assuming its old disdain, disengaged herself. Those who had argued on Michael's side gained supporters and cried in satisfaction: "See—he was right! The foreigner was right!"

But the man who had been hit maintained only that he had been hit, pointing to his face and glaring hatred at Michael. In vain Michael tried to apologize: he could not think of the word "panic" in Spanish and substituted the word "mad." Madness was infectious, he said, and much against his will he had done this thing. "I am not mad!" the man swore, getting angrier. But he was quietened, people had had enough for the time being—and Michael sat down heavily on his seat.

Just as Guy tore his head away from Louise. For a moment, while he pulled himself together, he sat with it in his own hands. Then when he raised his face he looked at Michael swiftly—and it was somehow a look not of shame but of accusation, as if blaming Michael for being there at all—and then simply muttered: "Sorry, Lou." No more explanation was needed, it had happened between them before.

When the train drew into the next station, they all three rose to go. So did every single one of the other passengers.

246

Irrespective of destination. None of them, apparently, felt cheated enough to stay on.

Whatever had gone wrong with that train neither Michael nor Guy nor Louise ever knew: or bothered to find out: or even discussed on the long wet walk home to the hotel. They slushed through the rain in silence, all occupied with their own thoughts, their own exhaustion. Along the easier broad boulevards, past modern mansions writhing their serpent stonework, past the gray block of the Ritz smoking its great squat chimney like a battleship. No one touched the other, no one took an arm. Their only occupation in common was to look out for a taxi: none of them really cared, it served only to excuse, now and again, the silence.

Michael had assumed a command and as soon, by the absurdity of the train just starting up again, lost it: he had made an urgent effort in what had proved to be a bubble, the bubble had burst and now no one would ever think of what might have been, it was an absurd anticlimax. He felt intolerably let down—instead of comparing himself with Guy, who had lost his head completely, he went the other way and suspected himself vaguely as being an alarmist: an old woman who cries "fire" at the smell of pipe smoke.

Worst of all he lacked confirmation from Louise. She said nothing. She seemed entirely bound up with thoughts of her own. But she would be shaken . . . then he remembered how she had comforted Guy, she had not been so shaken then. He saw her hand again on Guy's hand—perhaps now quite clearly for the first time—and his heart sank. And above all the thought kept recurring: two bloody accidents, two in no more than half an hour! But after all—were they accidents? A car too selfishly driven? A short stoppage on the subway? Surely—normal metropolitan risks? It is the people involved that make the accident. He tried hard to think of this—he wanted to avoid the moment when he had watched the car smashing into Guy's back, barely short of murder attempted.

247

Pretending to peer across the road for a taxi, he glanced carefully at Guy. The man still looked shocked, his face was white and set hard—and his coat collar up against the rain made him look all the more like a man walking alone with his illness.

But he was most certainly not walking alone—certainly not. Why was he still there at all, why was he still following? Why not back to his own hotel? He looked down at Louise—was she inviting him . . . ?

Then at last they were in through the door, a sudden crowd of three shaking raincoats and stamping, then turning to the lounge—where a strange sight indeed faced them.

For everything was as they had left it.

The Major and Madeleine still sat looking out at the street. Owen and his wife still stood uncertainly behind them. A few others, visitors and waiters, seemed to be facing the same positions as emptily as before. Even that chicken lay in its wrapping in the same place. With all that had happened—they might never have left the hotel! The lounge had the feeling of a waxwork set, more than real, far too usual.

Even when he read a paper Prescott's eyes were on the watch, and now he looked up, waved hello to Louise, saw Guy, and looked pointedly down at his paper again. Madeleine yawned and stretched her arms lazily, managing a wave as she did it. She could just have awakened from sleep, perhaps they had all been asleep, perhaps there had been no subway, nothing. . . .

For the moment, then, of crossing the lounge this strange usualness added to whatever was already confusing Louise, it was like walking from one dream to another—at any moment the tiles might change to soft carpet as soundless as . . . what . . . apprehension itself? She tried to shake herself free, impatient of what must plainly be some relapse of nervous tension: one doesn't face burning in an underground train every day. But still a premonition held her, it was like a sound felt before being heard; or as if she were somehow a derelict fascinated by fast waters flowing toward a weir, the waters flowing faster as they drew nearer, while the weir and its great drumming and the plunge made a giant mystery hidden, waiting, soon now to be tremendously revealed. She could hear her heart beating. Yet here in this hotel . . . so ordinary . . . ?

But then the Owens stepped forward and between them they revealed at least one new element in that dream-bound lounge—Molly was sitting in an armchair just behind. Produced like a conjuring trick, she sat there in her armchair, as though invalid, those guardian parents shielding her. And —terrible thing—she looked already fatter: but that was because her poise had collapsed and with it all hard and supercilious lines, now she sat softer and rounder, all sharp defenses down. She looked up at Guy miserably, with a face shaped for crying but dry of it; and made no other move. She looked what she felt—an untouchable.

"Christ," Guy muttered quietly, "can't they for God's sake arrange this themselves . . . ?"

It was not old Owen who then came up to him, but his wife, her anxious blue eyes now hard with pride, her chin stuck out firmly, an unsteady hat with a large single feather like an insect's antenna bobbing above her. Yet a strong sense of purpose about her overcame that absurdity; nor could her overfirm jaw seem mock heroic—it was, simply, heroic.

She was not wasting time; no formality, no "Mister Harrowby."

"Guy," she said, looking him straight in the eye, "I've brought Molly along. I think she wants a word with you. I would like to talk to you too."

Guy raised his eyebrows, he tried an expression of polite surprise. But that small plumpish woman, her face somehow baring its tired wrinkles and her unfortunate hat bobbing, stood and outstared him and he dropped his eyes. Perhaps a certain nobility at last embarrassed him: or perhaps he was simply exhausted, and wanted to postpone the moment: however that was, he seemed abruptly to give in, he said in a quiet grave voice:

"I can understand how you must feel, Mrs. Owen. Your husband's told me about it. I—I can't say how sorry I am. But look here"—and he spread his arms, hanging his shoulders dejectedly, opening the palms of his hands toward her, wrinkling his forehead and letting his whole face slack open humbly and honestly for her investigation—"I'm in a fix just now. I've got to leave for London today. I'm sorry, but it's imperative, I have to go. Now—here's my address, my card. Why don't you come around and see me there, as soon as ever you get back, and we can talk seriously, without all this . . ." He waved his hand around the lounge, as though it were crammed with a watching crowd.

"*You've* got to go to *London!*" Her voice rose, it was a mistake—this was no longer a noble sound but the boom of propriety outraged.

"Yes," said Guy evenly. "I've got to go to London. In any case," he smiled, "we can't actually do anything here, can we?"

Mrs. Owen bit her lips together, she took a deep sniff of air—she became no more than a woman deeply offended, a well-known face. People have only a small repertoire of faces in their lives: Olive Owen had this one for moods of disapproval in hers, it was the only one she could produce that came near to matching this present and grave situation. It fell grotesquely short.

That might have baited Guy—at another time. But now instead he drew himself up, passed a hand quickly down his cheek—almost as if he had finished shaving—and spoke definitely, and loudly, as much it seemed to the whole lounge as to that woman before him:

"Then I'm sorry. I can't help you. I've no time. I'm off. I'm going—in fact I'm going *now*."

It was final. He must have been absolutely weary. His

nerves had been badly shaken and now boredom cleared his head. He was finished, he was definitely off.

He turned to go, not bothering even to wave a vague farewell to the others.

Mrs. Owen gave a little cry, the little white visiting card still held out in her hand, as if it was a ticket and she had been refused entry.

Then suddenly another cry came—Louise was hurrying across the lounge after him.

"Guy! Guy!" she called, her face radiant, laughing as she called him.

"Guy—wait for me!"

He stopped, stood still with his back turned for a moment, then slowly brought his face half around to where she came running. He might have been stopped by the pull of a rope, not by his own will. She had to go around him to speak: and stood looking up like a schoolgirl addressing authority.

"I'm coming with you darling . . . darling, wait while I get . . ."

He stood stock-still, said nothing, and no change came over his face. No surprise, no shock, no disbelief: he seemed only to look harder at her, peering as a man might peer at a well-known landmark on a journey, not surprised to see it but for a moment necessarily studying it, letting its presence sink in.

While she looked up now breathlessly smiling, cheeks flushed now, eyes alive and bright, standing it seemed on tiptoe to him, eager and excited and radiant and the words scattering out of her:

". . . get packed in a moment . . . when does the train? What time? . . . Oh *Guy.*"

"Louise!" Prescott's voice rapped out deep and angry across the lounge.

She scarcely heard. Only this deep warm enormous flood of relief ran through her like new blood—while she looked up at Guy's well-known face with wonder, and an exasperated voice rang inside her: Blind, blind, blind.

251

Blind all these amazing days running away from him, blind not to have seen how impossible it would be, blind not to see how greatly, deeply, absolutely she loved him and only him forever, whatever happened, always.

Her whole soul inside her rose to welcome him. With relief and more than relief, the rediscovery of what was truly secure and real, as if lost in a strange city a corner is suddenly turned, and there, there all the time, is the street.

Unbrushed hair, grittily shaved cheek, cleft in his chin . . . she ate at these things with her eyes and broke out laughing, still stumbling out words:

"Tickets! . . . I'll get tickets . . . darling. We'll bribe half Spain to get them. . . ."

A waiter standing by the desk began to smile too; the bellboy joined him. They could not understand what words were said but what they saw they knew, they saw a happiness of two people and it warmed them to see this in their lounge, their dismal old lounge.

But no laughter from others.

"Louise!" Prescott came limping over now, his dark brows frowned in one deep line of anger:

"For God's sake pull yourself together girl! What's got into you?"

But Louise never even turned her head, her eyes never left Guy's face.

The Major had limped fast, as always he seemed to move the quicker for it. Yet now he stood with nobody paying attention, shaking indignation, his rubber-ended-stick drumming quietly on the floor, and no one even turning an eye.

"You don't know what you're doing!" he shouted. Then stammered lame as his leg: "Here's Michael there—Michael, d'you hear? . . ."

But looking up at Guy she only thought, over and over again, thoughts racing at the speed of blood: "What a fool! What a blind idiot! And only this morning—in Michael's arms . . . planning, chopping things up into neat parcels,

252

dreaming all that nonsense when here's the flesh and muscle I belong to utterly, irremediably, for better or for what the hell does it matter worse, it's mine, I'm its, his, nothing's going to make me care. . . ."

Sudden wind outside and the rain-sound roared up as though a great wave had hit the street. Prescott turned startled, the sound swished still higher, the room darkened and all those others seemed to stand and sit around the lounge stiller, stonier, more lividly transfixed in the pale light than ever before.

Even Louise now heard it, and looked toward the window, and for the first time vaguely saw everybody set and staring. But now the motive coin had dropped, wherever it had come from it had set going this machinery inside her, nothing would stop it, a whole intricate confabulation of purchases and stresses had gone into motion, it rolled a momentum stronger every minute, and as she saw Michael and Molly and the Owens staring at her an overwhelming sense of triumph caught at her veins, a feeling near to cruelty—she felt suddenly powerful, merciless, careless of anyone else and this surge of power was pleasant, it was exultant and her lips formed the taste of it, no one could do anything against her, no one could stop her. . . .

Molly so crushed and hopeless in her chair, eyes wide staring appeal at her, mouth open to her as if a pain of hope had got caught there . . . Molly could simply go to—well, Molly would have to be seen later, Molly could wait, everyone could wait.

So could the old man and his wife, the old man had moved close to her and put his arm around her shoulder in protection, in bewilderment, and bewildered they watched their expectations dwindle into thin air and neither knew what they could say. . . . Well, those two could wait, too.

Michael stood there like all the rest, doing nothing, saying nothing, not even looking at her . . . he was looking down at that chicken on the table, the cold dead chicken lying in

253

oily paper on its lonely table, with a look of surprise on his face . . . he seemed ashamed to look up, but then he did, for a moment only, and he did not look at her but at Guy, and just then Guy's eyes met his and he saw in them a slow look of unholy triumph and a smile grow there—and he looked shamefully down again. . . .

But Louise did for a second then think: "Poor Michael. Poor Michael, I made a mistake, a dreadful and stupid mistake. Which can't be helped," she thought as the carelessness rose again, "which can't at all be helped. . . ."

And she broke out into a broad, happy smile as she looked from one to the other of all these people disapproving and awed.

She stood flushed and young and radiant—for all that mounting power in her she looked now no more than a young, tenderly excited girl, years had dropped from her, even her body looked more supple and free, she was like a girl danced away at her first ball, her face was happiness—and showed only that great awesome saddening truth, how heartless happiness can look.

But with no pity? With pity, rather, postponed. There was simply no time for pity now. As in that purplish watered light among the cane chairs she caught for a moment the images of Michael, of Molly, she felt momentarily a removed sympathy for them—but could do no more than that, relegating them to the future, affairs to be attended to, as parcels might be packed or contracts signed and disposed, legally, politely, with what justice could later be spared. But not now . . . later. . . .

Now she was going home—and once more for the last time a vision of England came to her, but now no dreams of summer lawns, now no more than her old flat in the mews, the well-used rooms and the gas-fire dressing gown, the drab, the wonderful image of home.

Suddenly Molly rose with a little cry, and it seemed she was going to come over, throw herself in between—but then

254

saw Louise looking at her simply, silently, slowly shaking her head, and she fell back, exhausted, heavy with injustice, much too young, and burst at last into tears.

Those were not the only tears. Madeleine stood unashamedly weeping, she had been dabbing at her eyes for all the past minute, now she shook with quiet sobbing and winced as the mascara ran, the real tears came. But they were no tears of grief. She was smiling, smiling and crying at the same time, they were the tears women shed for the passing of a bride.

And now those two together turned toward the stairs, they waved it seemed once, vaguely, and all who watched had only time to see the dark smile open across Guy's face and hear his words: "All right, I'll help you pack," before they were gone.